You only see them once.

THE GHOST RECON TEAM

Then you never see anything again.

THE BESTSELLING NOVELS OF

TOM CLANCY

THE TEETH OF THE TIGER
*A new generation—Jack Ryan, Jr.—takes over in Tom Clancy's
extraordinary, and extraordinarily prescient, novel.*

"INCREDIBLY ADDICTIVE." —*Daily Mail* (London)

RED RABBIT
*Tom Clancy returns to Jack Ryan's early days—
in an engrossing novel of global political drama . . .*

"A WILD, SATISFYING RIDE." —*New York Daily News*

THE BEAR AND THE DRAGON
A clash of world powers. President Jack Ryan's trial by fire.

"HEART-STOPPING ACTION . . . CLANCY STILL
REIGNS."
                                    —*The Washington Post*

RAINBOW SIX
*John Clark is used to doing the CIA's dirty work.
Now he's taking on the world . . .*

"ACTION-PACKED." —*The New York Times Book Review*

EXECUTIVE ORDERS
*A devastating terrorist act leaves Jack Ryan
as President of the United States . . .*

"UNDOUBTEDLY CLANCY'S BEST YET."
                              —*The Atlanta Journal-Constitution*

continued . . .

DEBT OF HONOR

*It begins with the murder of an American woman
in the backstreets of Tokyo. It ends in war . . .*

"A SHOCKER."   *—Entertainment Weekly*

THE HUNT FOR RED OCTOBER

*The smash bestseller that launched Clancy's career—
the incredible search for a Soviet defector
and the nuclear submarine he commands . . .*

"BREATHLESSLY EXCITING."   *—The Washington Post*

RED STORM RISING

*The ultimate scenario for World War III—
the final battle for global control . . .*

"THE ULTIMATE WAR GAME . . . BRILLIANT."
                                    —Newsweek

PATRIOT GAMES

*CIA analyst Jack Ryan stops an assassination—
and incurs the wrath of Irish terrorists . . .*

"A HIGH PITCH OF EXCITEMENT."
                                  —The Wall Street Journal

Tom Clancy's

GHOST RECON®

COMBAT OPS

WRITTEN BY

DAVID MICHAELS

BERKLEY BOOKS, NEW YORK

THE BERKLEY PUBLISHING GROUP
Published by the Penguin Group
Penguin Group (USA) Inc.
375 Hudson Street, New York, New York 10014, USA
Penguin Group (Canada), 90 Eglinton Avenue East, Suite 700, Toronto, Ontario M4P 2Y3, Canada
(a division of Pearson Penguin Canada Inc.)
Penguin Books Ltd., 80 Strand, London WC2R 0RL, England
Penguin Group Ireland, 25 St. Stephen's Green, Dublin 2, Ireland (a division of Penguin Books Ltd.)
Penguin Group (Australia), 250 Camberwell Road, Camberwell, Victoria 3124, Australia
(a division of Pearson Australia Group Pty. Ltd.)
Penguin Books India Pvt. Ltd., 11 Community Centre, Panchsheel Park, New Delhi—110 017, India
Penguin Group (NZ), 67 Apollo Drive, Rosedale, North Shore 0632, New Zealand
(a division of Pearson New Zealand Ltd.)
Penguin Books (South Africa) (Pty.) Ltd., 24 Sturdee Avenue, Rosebank, Johannesburg 2196,
South Africa

Penguin Books Ltd., Registered Offices: 80 Strand, London WC2R 0RL, England

This is a work of fiction. Names, characters, places, and incidents either are the product of the author's imagination or are used fictitiously, and any resemblance to actual persons, living or dead, business establishments, events, or locales is entirely coincidental. The publisher does not have any control over and does not assume any responsibility for author or third-party websites or their content.

TOM CLANCY'S GHOST RECON®: COMBAT OPS

A Berkley Book / published by arrangement with Ubisoft Entertainment S.A.

PRINTING HISTORY
Berkley premium edition / April 2011

ISBN: 978-0-425-24006-9

BERKLEY®
Berkley Books are published by The Berkley Publishing Group,
a division of Penguin Group (USA) Inc.,
375 Hudson Street, New York, New York 10014.
BERKLEY® is a registered trademark of Penguin Group (USA) Inc.
The "B" design is a trademark of Penguin Group (USA) Inc.

PRINTED IN THE UNITED STATES OF AMERICA

10 9 8 7 6 5 4 3 2 1

ACKNOWLEDGMENTS

I'd like to thank my editor, Mr. Tom Colgan, for this great opportunity.

Mr. Tom Clancy and all of the folks at Ubisoft who created the Ghost Recon game certainly deserve my gratitude, as well as the following individuals:

Mr. Sam Strachman of Longtail Studios helped me develop this story from the ground up. His contributions were great, and his willingness to take risks with the story and characters was deeply appreciated.

Mr. James Ide served as my military researcher and story expert. He reviewed every page, relying on his extensive military background to provide criticism, advice, and suggestions that greatly improved the manuscript.

Finally, Nancy, Lauren, and Kendall Telep offered their eternal patience and support. Every manuscript is a battle, and I'm fortunate to have these ladies in my platoon.

Vengeance is in my heart, death in my hand,
Blood and revenge are hammering in my head.
      —*Titus Andronicus*, Act II, sc. 3, 1. 38

The sword is ever suspended.

                           —Voltaire

PROLOGUE

"You think I'm guilty?" I ask her.

She smirks. "My opinion doesn't matter."

"It does to me."

"How do you expect me to formulate an opinion when I don't know your story?"

I sigh through a curse.

My name is Captain Scott Mitchell, United States Army. I'm a member of a Special Forces group called the Ghosts. When I'm on the job, out on a mission, I don't exist. I'd thought we operated with impunity.

But when I was ordered back home and confined to quarters, I realized everything had changed. The same organization that helped conceal my operations and erase all evidence of the people I'd killed had been forced to make an example of me. They had changed. I had changed. And we could never go back.

People don't have to talk. They can invite you to kiss them . . . or even kill them with their eyes. Talk is cheap, but I've crawled through enough rat holes to learn that for some, life is even cheaper.

I had permission. I did what I had to do. They say I had a choice, but I didn't. I have never done anything more difficult in my life.

And now they want me to pay for my sins.

I haven't slept in two days. The growing humidity here at Fort Bragg makes it harder to breathe, and when I go to the window and run a finger across the glass, it comes up sweaty. The humidity is all I have to keep me company.

My father taught me that it's easier to cut wood with the grain rather than against it, and I carried that simple metaphor into the Army. I promised myself to remain apolitical, do the missions, go with the grain, not because I was trying to cop out but because I just wanted to be a great soldier. I'd already seen what torn loyalties and jealousy could do to the warrior spirit, and I wanted to protect myself against that.

But for what? My life is now a blade caught in a heavy knot, and I'd be lying if I said I wasn't scared out of my mind. I'm fourteen again, and Dad's telling me that Mom just died, and I'm worried about how we'll get along when she did so much—when she was the person who held our family together. When I think about going to prison, I lose my breath. It's a panic attack, and all I can do is hide behind sarcasm and belligerence.

Blaisdell, who's shaking her head at me now, showed up three hours late with some bullshit excuse about a deposition running long, and I told her to have a seat at my little kitchen table so we can talk about saving my life. She gave me a look. She's a major with the JAG corps, probably about my age, thirty-six or so, with rect-angular glasses that suggest bitch rather than scholar. I hate her.

Now she lifts her chin and grimaces. "Is that you?"

"What do you mean?"

"That smell . . ."

I scratch at my beard, rake fingers through my crew cut. All right, I hadn't bathed in a couple of days, either, and I'd been growing the beard for the past month.

"You want to wait while I take a shower?"

"Look, Captain, I'm doing this as a favor to Brown's sister, but you can hire your own attorney."

I shake my head. "Before I shipped back home, Brown told me about some of the other cases you did, maybe a little similar to mine."

She sighs deeply. "Not similar. Not as many witnesses. Some reasonable doubt—the chance that maybe it was just an accident. Everything I've read in your case says this was hardly an accident."

"No, it certainly wasn't."

"And you understand that you could lose everything and spend the rest of your life in Leavenworth?"

I stare back at her, unflinching. "You want a drink? I mean as in alcohol . . ."

"No. And you shouldn't have one, either. Because if you want me to help you, I need to know everything. The narrative they gave me is their point of view. I need yours."

"You don't even know what unit I work for. They won't tell you. They just say D Company, First Battalion, Fifth Special Forces Group. You ever hear of the Ghosts?"

"No."

"I didn't think so. They want plausible deniability. Well, they got it, all right, and now I'm the fall guy."

"You're not the fall guy. From what I read, no one forced you to do anything."

I lower my voice. "I went to a briefing. They showed me a PowerPoint slide of the situation over there. It was supposed to illustrate the complexity of our mission. Somebody said the graph looked like a bowl of spaghetti, and guys were laughing. But you know what I was thinking? Nothing. I didn't care."

"Why's that?"

"They gave me a mission, and I tried to put on the blinders. I went in, and I got the job done. Usually I never give a crap about the politics. I don't feed the machine. I am the machine. But this . . . this wasn't a mission. This isn't a war. It's an illusion of understanding and control. They think they can color-code it, but they have no idea what's going on out there. You need to stand in the dirt, look around, and realize that it's just . . . I don't even know what the hell it is . . ."

She purses her lips. And now she's looking at me like I'm a stereotypical burned-out warrior with a new drinking problem and personal hygiene challenges. Screw her.

"You don't care what I think, do you?" I ask.

"I'm here to defend you."

I take a deep breath. "That sounds like an inconvenience."

"Captain, I know where this is coming from, and I've seen it before. You're angry and upset, but you'd best not forget that I'm all you've got right now."

"I'll ask you again, do you think I'm guilty?"

She dismisses my question with a wave. "Start at the beginning, and I need to record you." She reaches into her fancy leather tote bag and produces a small tablet computer with attached camera that she places on the table. The camera automatically pivots toward me.

I make a face at the lens, then rise and head toward the kitchen counter, where my bottle of cheap scotch awaits. I pour myself a glass and return to the table. She's scowling at me and checks her smartphone.

"Oh, I'm sorry if you don't have the time for this," I say, then sip my drink.

"Captain . . ."

"You got any kids?"

She rolls her eyes. "We're not here to talk about me."

"I'm just asking you a question."

"As a matter of fact, I do."

I grin slightly. "How many?"

"I have two daughters."

"You don't know how lucky you are."

"Can we get on with this now? I assume you know about attorney-client privilege? Anything you share about the mission will remain classified, compartmentalized, and confidential, of course."

I finish my scotch, exhale through the burn, then narrow my gaze. "Well, I'll tell you one thing: I am *not* a murderer."

ONE

My target's name was Mullah Mohammed Zahed, the Taliban commander in the Zhari district just outside the city of Kandahar in southern Afghanistan. His hometown, Sangsar, was located in a rural area along the Arghandab River. The Russians call that place "the heart of darkness."

Zhari and its small towns were and still are a crucial gateway region to Kandahar and also a staging area for Taliban activity. Commanders often told us that if we could take Zhari, we'd control Kandahar. I've been in the military long enough to understand the disparity between wishful thinking and the will of a dedicated and ruthless insurgency.

But again, we didn't care about the politics or the

past or even superstitious Russians. I took my eight-man team to "the 'Stan," as we call it, and invested in two days of recon using our airborne drones complemented by a local guy feeding us intel from a handful of his eight thousand neighbors. We picked up enough to justify a raid on a mud-brick compound we believed was Zahed's command post.

"Ghost Lead, this is Ramirez. Jenkins and I are in position, over."

"Roger that, buddy," I responded. "Just hold till the others check in."

I had positioned myself in the foothills, shielded by an outcropping so I could survey the maze of dust-caked structures through my Cross-Com. The combination monocle-earpiece fed me data from my teammates as well as from the drone and the satellite uplinks. The targeting computer could identify friend or foe on the battlefield, and at that moment, red outlines were appearing all over the grid like taillights in a traffic jam.

Prior to our operation, General Keating, commander of United States Special Operations Command (USSOCOM) in Tampa, Florida—the big kahuna for grunts like me—had been talking a lot about COIN, or counterinsurgency operations. Keating had expressed his concern that Special Forces in the area might've already exhausted their usefulness because the Army's new philosophy was to protect the people and provide them with security and government services rather than venturing out to hunt down and eradicate the enemy. We were to win over the hearts and minds of the locals by improving their living conditions. Once we made them our allies, we could enlist their help in gathering human intelligence on our targets. In many cases, intel from those locals made all the difference.

Nevertheless, I remember Lieutenant Colonel Gordon, our Ghost Commander, having several four-letter words to describe how effective that campaign would be. As a Special Forces combatant, he believed, like I once did, that you needed to spend most of your time teaching the people how to fight so that after we left they could defend themselves. However, if their enemies were too great or too overwhelming, then we should go in there like surgeons and cut out the cancer.

Zahed, our commanders believed, was the cancer. What they hadn't realized was how far the disease had spread.

"Ghost Lead, this is Treehorn. In position, over."

Doug Treehorn was the sniper I'd brought along, much to the chagrin of Alicia Diaz, my regular operator. Alicia had done tours in Afghanistan before, and I'd had no qualms about taking her along, despite the challenges of being female in a nation where women were treated . . . let's just say *differently*. That she had taken a fall and broken her ankle two weeks before being shipped out ruined my initial game plan.

Treehorn was good, but he was no Diaz.

The others reported in. We had the complex cordoned off, and with Less Than Lethal (LTL) rubber rounds to stun guards before we gassed them into unconsciousness, the plan was to neutralize Zahed's force, then slip soundlessly inside the compound and capture the man himself. No blood spilled. Special Forces surgery. I mean, could we make it any more politically correct? We were going in there to take out a man whose soldiers routinely blew themselves up at the local bazaars, but we were trying our best not to hurt anyone.

Well, I'd told my guys that if push came to shove, we'd go live. I'd hoped it wouldn't come to that, if only to meet the challenge. As I'd told the others before ascending the mountains, "This is not rocket science. And it ain't over till the fat man sings." Zahed was pushing three hundred pounds, according to intelligence photos and video, and we planned to make him sing all about Taliban operations in the region, including the smuggling of IEDs manufactured in Iraq and rumors about Chinese and North Korean electronic shipments into the country.

I know I'm making Zahed sound like a real scumbag, but at that time, things seemed pretty clear. But I hadn't been there long enough, and I never thought for one second that we Ghosts and the rest of our military might be causing more damage than anyone else. We were there to help.

"All right, Ghosts, let's move out."

I issued a voice command so that my computer would patch me into the Cross-Com cameras of the others, and I watched as the guards fell like puppets. *Thump.* Down. And then my men, who wore masks themselves, hit the bad guys with quick shots from a new CS gas gun we were fielding. The gun issued a silent burst into an enemy's face.

Ramirez crouched before the lock on the front gate while I rushed down from my position and joined him. It was a cool desert night. A couple of dogs barked in the distance. Laundry flapped like sails on long lines that spanned several nearby buildings. The faint scent of lamb that had been roasted on open fires was getting swallowed in the stench of the CS gas. I checked my heads-up display: two twenty A.M. local time. You always hit them in the middle of the night while they're sleeping. Again, not rocket science.

Ramirez, our expert cat burglar, picked the lock with his tool kit and lifted his thumb in victory. I shifted into a courtyard as Treehorn whispered in my earpiece: "Two tangos. One to your right, up near that far building, the other to your left."

"See them," I said, the Cross-Com flashing with more signature red outlines that zoomed in on each guard. Like most Taliban, they wore long cotton shirts draped over their trousers and held to their waists with wide sashes. The requisite beards and turbans made it harder to distinguish among them, but they all had one thing in common: They wanted to kill you.

I lifted my rifle, about to stun the guy on the right, who stood near a doorway, his head hanging as though he were drifting off.

Ramirez had the guy on the left, the taller one.

Static filled my earpiece and the images being sent via laser from the monocle into my eye vanished.

Just like that.

The lack of data felt like a heart attack. I'd grown so

used to the Cross-Com that it had become another appendage, one abruptly hacked off.

My first thought: EMP? Pulse wave? We'd lost communications, targeting, everything. And I never for one second thought the Taliban could be responsible for that.

Ramirez shifted over to me as he kept tight to a side wall beside the courtyard. "What the hell?" he asked, voice muffled by his mask.

Without warning, two shots boomed from the distance: Treehorn. He'd taken out both guards with live fire. I wanted to scream at him, but it was too late.

"We're clear!" I shouted to Ramirez. "Let's go."

I'd barely gotten the words out of my mouth when salvos of gunfire resounded all over the compound. I listened for the telltale booming of my team's rifles echoed by the popcorn crackle of the Taliban's AK-47s. Everyone had gone weapons free, live fire.

At the same time, the whir of the Cypher drone's engines resounded behind me, but then the drone banked drunkenly and dove toward the courtyard, crashing into the dirt with a heavy thud followed by the buzz of short-circuiting instruments.

The enemy was using electronic countermeasures? *They* had taken out our Cross-Coms and drone?

Impossible.

We were in rural Afghanistan, where electricity and running water were considered high-tech.

Ramirez and I ripped off our masks and switched magazines to live ammo. We reached the main door of the building, wrenched it open, and shifted inside, where, in flickering candlelight, two robed Taliban turned a corner and spotted us.

One hollered.

I dropped him with a sudden burst and Ramirez caught the second one, who was turning back.

I don't want to glamorize their deaths or emphasize our bravery and/or marksmanship. I emphasize that we had made the concerted effort to minimize casualties and initially had the advantage of our information systems. But when we lost comm and satellite, all bets were off. I'd given my men permission to make the call, given their circumstances. Treehorn was, admittedly, a bit premature, but I'm still not sure what would've happened if he'd held back fire. I'd told all of them they could go live but needed to be sure about it. I'd take the heat for their actions. The rules of engagement were as thick as a phone book and written by lawyers whose combat experience extended no further than fighting with line cutters at the local Starbucks.

Ramirez led us down a long, narrow hallway filled with dust motes and illuminated by sconces supporting thick candles. Our boots scraped along the dirt floor as we turned a corner and found a sleeping quarters with empty beds and ornate rugs splayed across the floor. I placed my hand on one mattress: still warm. On a nearby table sat a half dozen bricks of opium. No time to confiscate them now. We shifted on, out into the hall, and toward the next room.

More gunfire thundered outside, quickening my pulse.

I knew if we didn't clear the compound within the next minute or so, Zahed would be long gone. These guys always had their escape routes planned, and it wouldn't have surprised me if he'd constructed several tunnel exits, though our intel did not reveal any.

The next two rooms were more sleeping quarters, empty, and then we reached another small courtyard and rushed into the next building, where in the entrance a woman with a shawl draped over her head saw us and began crying and waving her hands. I lifted my rifle to show her we wouldn't shoot, but that sent her toward me, arms up, fingers tensing as she went for my neck.

Ramirez shoved her hard against the wall and we rushed on by, emerging into another room where at least a dozen more women were huddled in a corner, crying and yelling at us as they clutched their small children.

Lifting his voice, Ramirez, whose Pashto was a lot better than mine, told them it was okay and we were looking for Zahed. Did they know where he was?

The women frowned and shook their heads.

No, we didn't expect to find women and children in the compound. Our intel indicated Zahed had established a command center occupied by his troops.

Our investigation of the next two rooms provided more clues. They were both empty, but you could see that equipment had been there and dragged out: tables and some abandoned wires along with a gas generator that had scorch marks along its sides.

"He got tipped off," said Ramirez. "He moved the

women and children in here, thinking maybe we'd blow the place and kill them. Bad press for us."

"Yeah, yeah," I said in disgust.

We rushed outside, where we met up with two more of my guys, Smith and Nolan.

Smith, the avid hunter from North Carolina, wore his mask pushed atop his bald head and gasped as he spoke. "Cleared the building back there. Nothing. What the hell happened to our Cross-Coms?"

"I don't know. Get the others. Get to the rally point. Now!" I ordered.

They took off, and Ramirez looked to me: We had one more building on the west side to clear. I had the map of the compound committed to memory, and we'd made several guesses about this structure: food storage or maybe a weapons cache, based on what we'd seen being moved in and out of there.

The door was locked. Ramirez opted for his faster boot. In we went.

No surprise: two big empty rooms whose dirt floors showed outlines where cases had been. Probably a large weapons cache temporarily stored there and as quickly moved out.

I was reminded of an earlier operation up in Shah E-Pari, a village in the northeastern mountains. We'd been trying to disrupt the rat lines in and out of Pakistan. Insurgents were using the tribal lands in Waziristan and other places to recruit and train their members, then send them across the border on missions in Afghanistan.

A buddy of mine, Rutang, had been captured up there, but we got him out. Anyway, the Taliban terrorized members of small villages like Shah E-Pari. The men would be forced to join them or suffer the consequences. So we went up there, armed and trained the guys, and thought it was all working out. The villagers began winning battles with the Taliban and confiscating and stockpiling their weapons. Then we got the order to go in and seize those weapons, lest they fall back into the enemy's hands. Try having that conversation with the village elder: *Sorry, we taught you to protect yourselves, and you can have some guns . . . but not too many.* Ironically, what we confiscated was mostly ancient crap sold by us to the Mujahadeen during the Russian invasion. The guns we provided to help fight the Russians were now being used against us. That fact, that irony, barely garnered a reaction anymore. And by the way, that entire village fell back into the hands of the Taliban, who, the villagers said, were giving them more living assistance than either the government or our military.

All of which is to say that some if not all of the weapons Zahed was moving around had once belonged to the United States.

The second room we entered gave us pause. In fact, Ramirez looked back at me for permission to enter, as though neither of us should go on.

I took one look, closed my eyes, and gritted my teeth.

There was a Marine I knew who'd spent a long time up in the mountains laser-designating targets for the bombers. He'd described the locals as savages and tenth-century barbarians who forced their five-year-old sons into human cockfights, who clawed around all day like gorillas with AK-47s. He'd taken great exception to the media referring to the enemy as "smart," when in his opinion the enemy was cunning and crafty, but hardly smart. And when confronted directly they were, plain and simple, cowards who'd step on the necks of their fellow soldiers if that promised escape.

Although I tended to disagree with some of his generalizations because I'd spent time in both the cities and rural areas and had encountered sophisticated and simple people, I was haunted by his accusations that the Taliban had exploited their children—

And all the more so because of what lay before us in that dimly lit room.

TWO

Neither Ramirez nor I had any children, so there wasn't that moment when we projected our own kids into the situation before us.

But I'm certain that what we felt was equally shocking and painful.

"Oh my God," Ramirez said with a gasp.

Before we could take another step, footfalls echoed behind us, and a male voice came in a stage whisper, though I couldn't discern the exact words.

I turned, crouched, lifted my rifle, and came face to face with a Taliban soldier, his AK swinging into the room. My rounds drove him back into the opposite wall, where he shrank, leaving a blood trail on the wall above him. Oddly, he was still alive as he tipped onto one side and was muttering something, even as a second guy rounded the corner.

My two rounds missed him and chewed into the stone. He ducked back round the corner. I blamed my error on the shadows and not my dependence on the Cross-Com's targeting system. As I rationalized away the failure, a grenade thumped across the floor, rolled toward me, and bounced off the leg of the guy I had just killed.

Ramirez, who'd seen the grenade, too, lifted his voice, but I was already on it, seizing the metal bomb and lobbing it back up the hallway, only two seconds before it exploded. Ramirez and I were just turning our backs to the doorway when the debris cloud showered us, pieces of stone stinging our arms and legs and thumping off the Dragon Skin torso armor beneath our utilities.

We turned back for the hall.

And my breath vanished at the sound of a second metallic thump. This grenade hit the dead guy's boot and rolled once more directly into the room.

Ramirez was on it like a New York Yankees shortstop. He scooped up the grenade, whirled toward the open window, and fired it back outside. We rolled once more as the explosion resounded and the walls shifted and cracked.

I'd had enough of that and let my rifle lead me back into the hallway. I charged forward and found the remaining guy withdrawing yet a third grenade from an old leather pouch. He looked up, dropped his jaw, and shuddered as my salvo made him appear as though he'd grabbed a live wire. He fell back onto his side.

I stood over him, fighting for breath, angry that they'd kept coming at us, wondering if he'd been one of the guys who'd perpetrated the acts we imagined had gone on in that room. I returned to Ramirez, who'd gone over to the pool table. That's right, a pool table. But they hadn't been playing pool.

A girl no more than thirteen or fourteen lay nude and seemingly crucified across the table, arms and legs bound by heavy cord to the table's legs. Ramirez was checking for a carotid pulse. He glanced back at me and whispered, "She looks drugged, but she's still alive."

I tugged free my bowie knife from its calf sheath and, gritting my teeth, cursed and cut free the cords. Then I ran back and ripped the shirt off the dead guy just outside the door. Neither of us said a word until Ramirez lifted her over his shoulder in a fireman's carry, and I draped the shirt over her nude body.

I just shook my head and led the way back out.

In the courtyard, I swept the corners, remained wary of the rooftops, and reached out with all of my senses, guiding us back toward the gate without the help of the Cross-Com. Women were wailing somewhere behind one of the buildings, and the stench of gunpowder had thickened even more on the breeze.

Gunfire sounded from somewhere behind me, and the next thing I knew I was lying flat on my face. Before Ramirez could turn, the girl still draped over his shoulder, an insurgent rushed from the house.

The guy took two, maybe three more steps before thunder echoed from the mountain overlooking the town. I gaped as part of the man's head exploded and arced across the yard. The rest of him collapsed in a dust cloud.

Treehorn was earning his place on the team.

"Captain, you all right?" cried Ramirez.

I sat up. "I should've seen that guy. Damn it."

"No way. He was tucked in good." Ramirez crossed around to view my back. "He got you, but the armor took it good. Nice . . ."

"And off we go," I said with a groan as I dragged myself to my feet. I remembered the Cypher drone, darted over to it, and tucked the shattered UFO under my arm.

We hustled around the main perimeter wall, these barriers common in many of the towns and not unlike the medieval curtain walls that helped protect a castle.

It took another ten minutes before we reached the edge of the town, then made our dash up a dirt road rising up through the talus and scree and into the canyons. The gunfire had kept most of the locals inside, and what Taliban were left had fled because they never knew how many more infidels were coming.

We met up with Marcus Brown and Alex Nolan some ten minutes after that, and Ramirez handed off the girl to Nolan, who immediately dug into his medic's kit to see if he could get her to regain consciousness.

"Any sign of Zahed?" I asked Brown.

Despite being a rich kid from Chicago, he spoke and

acted like a hardcore seasoned grunt. "Nah, nothing. What the hell happened?"

I wished I could give the big guy a definitive answer. "Our boy got tipped off. And someone took out our Cross-Com and the drone. Somehow. I can't believe it was them." I handed the drone to him, and he stowed it in his backpack.

"So who did this?" he asked. "Our own people? Why?"

I just shook my head.

Brown's dark face screwed up into a deeper knot. He cursed. I seconded his curse. Ramirez joined the four-letter-word fest.

Three more operators—Matt Beasley, Bo Jenkins, and John Hume—arrived a few minutes after with three prisoners in tow, their hands bound behind their backs with zipper cuffs.

I nodded appreciatively. "Nice work, gentlemen."

"Yeah, but no big fish, sir," said Hume. "Just guppies."

"I hear that."

Treehorn ascended from his sniper's perch and joined us, fully out of breath. "Guess I blew the whistle a little too soon," he admitted.

I was about to say something, but my frustration was already working its way into my fists. I walked over, grabbed the nearest Taliban guy by the throat, and, in Pashto, asked him what had happened to Zahed.

His eyes bulged, and his foul breath came at me from between rows of broken and blackening teeth.

I shoved him back toward his buddies, then pointed at the girl. "Did you do this?" I was speaking in English, but I was so pissed I hadn't realized that. I shouted again.

One guy threw up his hands and said in Pashto, "We do not do that. I don't think Zahed does that, either. We don't know about that."

"Yeah, right," snapped Ramirez.

Nolan got the girl to come around, and she began crying. Ramirez went over and tried to calm her down; he got her name, and we learned that she was, as we'd already suspected, from Senjaray, the town on the other side of the mountains from which we operated. We had conventional radio, but even that had been fried, and Hume suspected that some kind of pulse or radio wave had been used to disrupt our electronics.

We hiked over the mountain, keeping close guard on the prisoners and taking turns carrying the girl. We eventually reached our HMMWV, which we'd hidden in a canyon. The radio onboard the Hummer still worked, so we called back to Forward Operating Base Eisenhower and had them send out another Hummer to bridge the eleven-kilometer gap. We set up a perimeter and waited.

"You know, this place makes China look good," said Jenkins, who lay on his stomach across from me, his normally hard and determined expression now long with exhaustion. "Those were the good old days. That was a straight-up mission. Pretty good intel. And good support from higher. That's all I ask."

"I don't know, Bo, I think those days are gone," I said. "No matter how good we think our intel is, we can wind up like this. And I know it's discouraging. But I'll do what I can to find out what happened."

"Thanks."

No matter how careful we'd been in leaving our FOB, no matter how secretive we'd kept the mission, all it took was one observer to radio ahead to Zahed that we were coming. We'd taken all the precautions. Or at least we'd thought we had.

And at that moment, I was beginning to wonder about our "find, fix, and finish the enemy" mantra. I still wasn't buying into the whole COIN ideology (let's help the locals and turn them into spies) because I figured they'd always turn on us no matter how many canals we built. But I wondered how we were supposed to gather actionable intelligence without help from the inside—without members of the Taliban itself turning on each other . . . because in the end, everyone knew we Americans weren't staying forever, so all parties were trying to exploit us before we left.

The second truck arrived, and we loaded everyone on board and took off for the drive across the desert. My hackles rose as I imagined the Taliban peering at us from the mountains behind. My thoughts were already leaping ahead to solve the security breach and tech issues.

Treehorn, who was at the wheel, began having a conversation with himself, offering congratulations for his fine marksmanship. After a few minutes of that, I interrupted him. "All right, good shooting. Is that what you want to hear?"

"Hell, Captain, it's something. I got the feeling this

whole op will go round and round, and we won't get off the roller coaster till higher tells us."

I considered myself an optimist, the never-say-quit guy. I'd been taught that from the beginning. Hell, I'd been a team sergeant on an operation in the Philippines and lost nearly my entire ODA unit. My best friend flipped out. But even then, I never quit. Never allowed myself to get discouraged because the setbacks weren't failures—they were battle scars that made me stronger. I had such a scar on my chest, and it used to remind me that there was a larger purpose to my life and that quitting and becoming depressed was too selfish. I'd be letting everyone down. I had to go on.

If you join the military for yourself, then you're setting yourself up for failure. Kennedy had it right: Ask what you can do for your country. I've seen many guys join "for college" or "to see the world" or "to learn a trade." Their hearts are not in it, and they never achieve what they could. Perhaps I'm too biased, but in the beginning, there was an ideal, an image of America that I kept in my head, and it reminded me of why I was there.

Kristen Fitzgerald, standing among acres of lush farmland, her strawberry-blond hair tugged by the wind. She smiles at me, even says, "This is why."

Pretty cliché, huh? Makes it sound like I do it all for a girl. But she represented that ideal. A high school sweetheart who told me she'd always wait, that she was like me, that we were not born to live ordinary lives.

My ideal was not some jingoistic military recruiting commercial or some glamorous Hollywood version of war. I didn't join because I wanted to "get some." I wanted to protect my country and help people. That made me feel good, made me feel worth something. And as the years went on, and I got promoted and was told how good I was, I decided to share what I knew. I loved teaching at the John F. Kennedy Special Warfare Center at Fort Bragg. I couldn't think of a more rewarding part of my military career.

In fact, that was where I met Captain Simon Harruck, who'd been a fellow trainer despite his youth and who was now commander of Delta Company, 1st Battalion—120 soldiers charged with providing security for Senjaray and conducting counterinsurgency operations.

I knew that when we got back, Harruck would try to cheer me up. He was indeed ten years my junior, and when I looked at him, oh, how I saw myself back in those days.

But as we both knew, the 'Stan was unforgiving, with its oppressive heat and sand that got into everything, even your soul. I threw my head back on the seat and trusted Treehorn to take us home, headlights out, guided by his night-vision goggles.

By the time we arrived at the FOB, Harruck was already standing outside the small Quonset hut that housed the company's offices, and the expression on his face was sympathetic. "Well, we got three we can talk to, right?"

I returned a sour look and marched past him, into the hut.

THREE

The three prisoners were taken to a holding room. The CIA was sending a chopper down to transfer them to FOB Chapman in Khost, where some big shot from Kabul would come in to interrogate them. FOB Chapman was the CIA outpost where seven agents were killed years ago. I knew this time the bad guys would be strip-searched, x-rayed, and then have their every orifice and cavity probed.

Didn't matter, though. I didn't think they knew much. Zahed wasn't fool enough to allow underlings to know his plans or whereabouts.

The girl was taken to our small hospital, and we could only speculate on what would happen to her after that. She was damaged goods, a disgrace and dishonor to her family, and they would, I knew, not want her back. A terrible thing, to be sure. She might be transported to one of the local orphanages and/or assisted by one of the dozens of aid groups in the country. She might even be arrested. I couldn't think about her anymore, and I'd made it a point *not* to learn her name. Her plight fueled my hatred for the Taliban *and* the local Afghans. No one cared about her. No one . . .

I sent the rest of my team back to quarters. We'd debrief in the morning. I sat around Harruck's desk, and he offered me a quick and covert shot of cheap scotch, saying we'd turn ourselves in later and receive our letters of reprimand.

Harruck was a dark-haired, blue-eyed poster boy who made you wonder why he'd joined the military. He resembled a corporate type who played golf on the weekends with clients. He was taking graduate courses online, trying to earn his master's, and he kept on retainer two or three girlfriends back home in San Diego. Because he was so articulate and so damned smart, he'd been recruited to teach at the JFK School, and when he wasn't overseas, he participated in our four-week-long unconventional warfare exercise, Robin Sage. The first time I met him, I was immediately impressed by his knowledge of our tactics, techniques, and procedures. His candor and sense of humor invited you into a conversation. Once there, you realized, *Holy crap, this guy is for real:* talented, intelligent, and handsome. If you weren't jealous and didn't hate him immediately, you wanted him on your team.

But those attributes did not make him famous around the Ghosts, no. He was, as far as I knew, the only Army officer who'd been offered his own Ghost unit and had turned down the offer.

Let me repeat that.

He'd become a Special Forces officer, had led an ODA team for a while, but when asked to join the Ghosts, he'd said no—and had even gone so far as to leave Special Forces and return to the regular Army to become a company commander.

We called it temporary insanity. Or alcoholism. Or some said cowardice: Pretty boy didn't want to get a scratch on his smooth cheek.

I'd never asked him why he'd done this. I didn't want to pry, but I was also afraid of the answer.

"I don't know how much help you want with your gear," Harruck said after we finished our drinks. "All your toys are classified, but I've got some guys that'll take a look if you want."

"That's all right. I'll have to ship a few units back and see what they say. Meanwhile, we'll have to wait till they drop in replacements."

"Any thoughts?"

"Taliban bought EMP weapons from China," I said through a dark chuckle. "It'd make sense. We're running a war on their money now. Wouldn't they do everything they can to keep us spending? It worked when we did it to the Russians."

"I hear that."

"I've still got a half dozen more drones I can send

up—if I can get some Cross-Coms. The disruption's localized, so we'll find out what they're using. I'm curious to see who they're playing with now."

"What if it's us?"

I snorted. "NSA? CIA? You think they're in bed with Zahed? Well, if that's true—"

"You sound tense."

"I'm not good with setbacks, you know that. I figured we'd capture this guy tonight and get out."

Harruck wriggled his brows. "Yeah, I mean he's a fat bastard. He can't even run."

I smiled. Barely.

"You need to relax, Scott. You're only here a few days. And the last time you were here, that didn't last long, either. You've been lucky. It's eight months for me now. Damn, eight months . . ."

"Still smiling?"

"To be honest with you—no."

I shifted to the edge of my seat. "Are you kidding me?"

"This might sound a little hokey, but you know what? I came here to build a legacy."

"A legacy?"

"Scott, you wouldn't believe the pressure they've put on me. They think this whole war can be won if we secure Kandahar."

"I hear you."

"They're calling it the center of gravity for the insurgency. That's some serious rhetoric. But I can't get the support I need. It's all halfhearted. I'm going to walk out of here having done . . . *nothing*."

"That's not true."

Harruck leaned back in his chair and pillowed his head in his hands. "I know what these people need. I know what my mission is. But I can't do it alone."

I averted my gaze. "Can I ask you something? Why did you do this to yourself?"

"What do you mean?"

I took a moment, stared at my empty glass.

"Another one?" he asked.

"No. Um, Simon, this isn't any of my business, but you could've been a Ghost."

"Aw, that's old news. Don't make me say something I'll regret."

I smiled weakly. "Me, too."

I'd had no idea that Harruck was exercising tremendous reserve in that meeting, when, in fact, he'd probably wanted to leap out of his chair and throttle me.

Forward Operating Base Eisenhower lay on the northwest side of Senjaray. It was a rather sad-looking collection of Quonset huts and small, prefabricated buildings walled in by concrete and concertina wire. The main gate rose behind a meager guardhouse manned by two sentries, with more guards strung out along the perimeter. The usual machine gun emplacements along with a minefield on the southern approach helped give the Taliban pause. The juxtaposition between the ancient mud-brick town blending organically into the landscape and our rather crude complex was striking. We were foreigners making a modern and synthetic attempt to assimilate.

Harruck knew he'd never get his job done by hiding behind the walls of the FOB, so nearly every day he went into the town to communicate with the people via TCAF interviews (we pronounced it "T-caff"), which stood for Tactical Conflict Assessment Framework. Harruck's patrols were required to ask certain questions: *What's going on here? Do you have any problems? What can we get for you?*

And he'd get the same answers over and over again: *We need a new well, we want you to rebuild and open the school. We need a police station, more canals. And can you get us some electricity?* The diesel power plant in Kandahar serviced about nine thousand families, but nothing had been provided for the towns like Senjaray.

The following week, Harruck's patrols would ask the very same questions, get the same answers, and nothing would be done because Harruck couldn't get what he needed. The reasons for that were complex, varied, and many.

Despite the cynicism creeping into his voice, I still trusted that he'd fly the flag high and struggle valiantly to complete his mission. He said that at any time the tide could turn and assets could be reallocated to him.

We Ghosts didn't have the luxury of leaving the base. In fact, higher wanted us to protect our identities by remaining in quarters when we weren't conducting night reconnaissance, so I told my boys we were ghosts *and* vampires while in country, but that didn't last very long.

I finished up a quick conversation with General Keating via my satellite phone, and he gave me the usual: "We need Zahed in custody, and we need him talking to us about his connections to the north and the opium trade. It's up to you, Mitchell."

It was always up to me, and I had a love-hate relationship with that burden.

Keating's trust in me was like a drug. Sometimes I felt like he was grooming me for his own job. I'd already turned down a promotion only because that would mean less time in the field, and I thought I was still too young to rotate to the rear. Scuttlebutt about the military restructuring was rampant, with talk of a new Joint Strike Force, and the general told me I needed to catch the wave. But I believed I could make a greater difference in the field.

I guess, even after all these years, I was still pretty naïve in that regard, probably because most of my missions had allowed me to turn the tide.

With the sun beating down on my neck with an almost heavy-metal pulse, I headed toward my quarters. Up ahead, Harruck was coming into the base, riding shotgun in a Hummer. He waved to me as the truck came under sudden and heavy gunfire.

Rounds ricocheted off the Hummer's hood and quarter panels as I dove to the dirt, and the two guys on the fifties on the north side opened up on the foothills about a quarter kilometer away. But the fire wasn't coming from there, I realized. It was from inside the FOB.

Three insurgents had somehow gotten past the wall and concertina wire and were firing from positions along the south side of one Quonset hut, which I recalled housed the mess hall.

Harruck and his men were climbing out of the Hummer when one of the insurgents shifted away from the hut and shouldered an RPG.

"Simon!" I hollered. "RPG! RPG!"

He and the two sergeants who'd been in the vehicle bolted toward me as behind them the rocket struck the Hummer and exploded, flames shooting into the sky, the boom reverberating off the huts and other buildings, whose doors were now swinging open, soldiers flooding outside.

I had my sidearm and was already squeezing off rounds at the RPG guy, but he slipped back behind the hut. At that point, reflexes took over. I was on my feet, catapulting across the yard. I rushed along the hut between the mess hall and the insurgents, reached the back, rounded the corner, and spotted all three of them—at exactly the same moment the machine gunners up in the nest did. I shot the closest guy, but only got him in the shoulder before the machine gunner shredded all three with one fluid sweep.

At that second, I remembered to breathe.

Up ahead came a faint click. Then the entire rear third of the mess hall burst apart, pieces of the hut hurtling into the sky as though lifted by the smoke and flames. The explosion knocked me onto my back, and for a few seconds there was only the muffled screams and the booming, over and over.

Something thudded onto my chest, and when I sat up, I saw it was a piece of the roof and accompanying insulation. And then it dawned on me that there'd been personnel in the mess, still coming out when the bomb had gone off. Wincing, I got up, staggered forward.

A gaping hole had been torn in the side of the mess, and at least a half dozen of Harruck's people were lying on the ground, torn to pieces by the explosion as they'd been heading toward the door. Some had no faces, the blast having shredded cheeks and foreheads, skin peeling back and leaving only bone in its wake. I began coughing, my eyes burning through the smoke, as Harruck arrived with his sergeants.

"I'll get my people out here to help!" I told him.

He nodded, gritted his teeth, and began cursing at the top of his lungs. I'd never seen him lose it like that.

The facts were clear. We Ghosts had brought this on the camp; the attack was payback for our raid the night before. Innocent soldiers had died because of what we'd done.

I felt the guilt, yes, but I never allowed it to eat at me. We had orders. We had to deal with the consequences of those orders. But seeing Harruck so cut up left me feeling much more than I wanted. Maybe that was the first sign.

My Ghosts were already outside our hut, all wearing *pakols* and *shemaghs* on their heads and wrapped around their faces to conceal their identities. I ordered them out to the perimeter to see what the hell was going on.

A roar and thundering collision out near the guard gate stole my attention. A flatbed truck had just plowed through the gatehouse and barreled onward to smash through the galvanized steel gates.

The guards there had backed off and were riddling the truck with rifle fire.

And it took Treehorn all of a second to shoulder his rifle and send two rounds into the head of that driver.

But as if on cue, the truck itself exploded in a swelling fireball that spread over the buildings and quarters beside it, setting fire to the rooftops as more flaming debris came in a hailstorm across the walkway between the huts.

We didn't realize it then, but a hundred or more Taliban had set up positions along the mountains, and once they saw the truck explode, they set free a vicious wave of fire that had all of us in the dirt and crawling for cover as our machine gunners brought their barrels around . . . and the rat-tat-tat commenced.

FOUR

Two more pickup trucks raced on past our FOB, cutting across the desert and bouncing up and onto the gravel road leading toward the town and the bazaar. Hundreds of people were milling about that area, setting up shop or making their morning purchases. If the Taliban reached that area and cut loose into the crowds . . .

I shouted for the Ghosts to follow me, and we commandeered two Hummers from the motor pool on the east side of the base. A couple of mechanics volunteered on the spot to be our drivers. We roared out past the shattered gate, me riding shotgun, the others standing in the flatbeds or leaning out the open windows, weapons at the ready. I quickly wrapped a *shemagh* around my face.

Behind us, the fires still raged, and the machine guns continued to crack and chatter.

Rounds ripped across the hood of our vehicle, and I began to smell gasoline.

"We should pull over!" shouted the mechanic.

"No, get us behind those trucks!"

"I'll try!"

About fifty meters ahead, the two pickups made a sharp left and disappeared behind a row of homes.

The mechanic floored it, and my head lurched back as we made the turn.

My imagination ran wild with images of civilians falling under our gunfire as we tried to stop these guys. I could already hear the voices of my superiors shouting about the public relations nightmare we'd created.

The second Hummer fell in behind us, and we charged down the narrow dirt street, walled in on both sides by the mud-brick dwellings and the rusting natural gas tanks plopped out front. The familiar laundry lines spanned the alleys and backyards, with clothes, as always, fluttering like flags. Our tires began kicking up enough dust to obscure the entire street in our wake, even as we pushed through the dust clouds whipped up by the Taliban trucks.

We still didn't have replacement Cross-Coms, and all I could do was call back to the other truck and tell them we weren't breaking off; we were going after these guys. And yes, the threat of civilian casualties increased dramatically the farther we drove, but I wanted to believe we could do this cleanly. I'd done it before.

Nolan, Brown, and Treehorn had already opened fire on the rear Taliban truck, knocking out a tire and sending one of the Taliban tumbling over the side with a bullet in his neck. The rear truck suddenly broke off from the first, making a hard left turn down another dirt street.

I told the guys in our rear truck to follow him while we kept up with the lead truck, whose driver steered for the bazaar ahead, the road funneling into an even more narrow passage.

Although I'd never been into the town, Harruck had told me about the bazaar. You could find handmade antique jewelry, oil lamps, Persian rugs, and tsarist-era Russian bank notes displayed next to bootlegged DVDs and knock-off Rolexes. There were also dozens of white-bearded traders selling meat and produce. Some vendors were part of an American-backed program that introduced soldiers to Afghan culture and injected American dollars into the local economy. Although locals bought, sold, and traded there, Harruck's company actually pumped more money into the place than anyone else because his soldiers purchased food to prepare on the base and souvenirs to ship back home. The Taliban knew that, too, which was why they'd come: maximum casualties and demoralization.

We nearly ran over two kids riding old bikes, and the mechanic was forced to swerve so hard that we took out the awning post of a house on our left. The awning collapsed behind us, and I cursed.

Suddenly, our Hummer coughed and died.

My guys started hollering.

"We're out of gas," shouted the driver. "It all leaked out!"

"Dismount! Let's go!" I shouted to Nolan, Brown, and Treehorn, then eyed the driver. "You stay here with the vehicle. We'll be back for you."

The four of us sprinted down the block, reaching the first set of stalls covered by crude awnings. The shopkeepers had seen the pickup fly by and had retreated to the backs of their shops.

The truck screeched to a stop at the next intersection, about fifty meters ahead, and four Taliban jumped out.

I expected them to do one of two things:

Run into the crowd and draw us into a pursuit.

Or . . . take cover behind their truck and engage us in a gunfight.

Instead, something entirely surreal happened, and all I could do was shout to my men to hold fire.

The citizens of Senjaray rushed into the street, both vendors and shoppers alike, and quickly formed a human barricade around the four men and their truck.

Two of the vendors began shouting and waving their fists at us, and from what I could discern, they were yelling for us to go home.

As we drew closer, the crowd grew, and the four Taliban were grinning smugly at us.

A man who looked liked a village elder, dressed all in army-green robes and with a black turban and matching vest, emerged from one of the shops and ambled toward us, his beard dark but coiled with gray. Most of the locals wore beat-up sandals, but his appeared brand-new.

In Pashto he said his name was Malik Kochai Kundi. "I own most of the land here. I will not allow you to hurt these men. Zahed has treated us well—much better than the governor. You will not shatter that alliance."

Brown started cursing behind me, and I shushed him, then struggled for the right words. "You heard the fighting. They attacked our base."

Kundi stroked his beard in thought. "It's my understanding that you struck first . . . last night. Now, show me your face, and I will talk to you."

I glanced over Kundi's shoulder and noted something going on among the four Taliban. The tallest one, perhaps the leader, was shifting his gaze among the others.

Kundi said something to me, but it was hard to hear him now over the rising voices of the crowd. I heard some folks telling Kundi to leave us alone, while others shouted again for us to leave.

Behind me, John Hume cursed—and I saw why.

The four Taliban turned and dashed back through the crowd, heading in four different directions.

"Take a guy!" I yelled.

We reacted swiftly, Brown, Hume, and Treehorn each going after a thug while I went for the tallest one.

I wasn't sure why they'd chosen to run. Maybe they didn't quite trust the citizenry either.

My guy rushed down a side street, leaving the bazaar

for yet another stretch of sad-looking homes. I was gaining on him when he stopped, whirled, and leveled his rifle.

Before he got off a shot I was already diving to the right side, realizing that the cover I'd sought was one of those natural gas tanks. Great.

The guy fired, but his rounds drummed along the dirt beside me. I rolled, came up, peered around the tank, saw him rushing forward between houses.

I bounded after him, sweating profusely now, my eyes itching with dust. Once I got into the alley, I caught a glimpse of him before he turned another corner. I jogged ten meters, reached the corner—and a long row of houses stretched before me.

He was gone.

But then I looked down into the dirt, tracked his boot prints, and heard a child's cry coming from one of the houses.

I jogged forward, eyeing the prints, heard the noise once more, turned and rushed toward the nearest front door, pushed it open, and burst into a small entrance area.

It all hit me at once:

The smell of sweet meat cooking . . .

A small kitchen area to my right with a worktable and some fresh flowers in a vase . . .

A woman cowering behind that table with a young girl, perhaps thirteen or fourteen, and a boy, maybe eleven or so, their eyes bulging, the girl beginning to weep. The mother pulled the children closer to her chest.

And there, at the back of a room, another man,

well-trimmed beard, turban, but with sideburns that seemed very Western. He put a finger to his lips, then pointed down the hall, where he suggested my Taliban guy had gone.

Then he held up a hand. *Wait.*

He shouted back into the hall. "All clear now. You can come out . . ."

I shifted to the left side of the room, moving toward the wall, and watched with utter surprise as this local guy who'd already volunteered to help me kept tight to the wall, gave a me a look, and then, as the Taliban fighter moved forward, my new ally tripped him.

And that was when I moved in, leaping on his back and knocking him face first onto the dirt floor. He tried to reach back for a pistol holstered at his waist, but I grabbed his wrist while my new friend grabbed the fighter's other arm. With my free hand I tugged out a pair of zipper cuffs, and we got him bound in a few seconds.

I rose, leaving the fighter still lying on the floor, and eyed the family. In a moment of weakness I lowered my *shemagh.* "I'm sorry," I said in Pashto.

"It's okay," said the man in English. "I know who this guy is and who he works for. I'm glad you've captured him."

"Where'd you learn English?"

He grinned weakly. "It's a long story. I'll help you get him up, so you can be on your way."

I pursed my lips at the wife and children. The wife shook her head in disapproval, but the girl and boy seemed fascinated by me. I shrugged and got my prisoner ready to move, confiscated his weapon, and led him outside.

When I turned back, the entire family was standing there beside the front door, watching me. I raised my *shemagh* to conceal my face and gave them a curt nod.

As I led back my prisoner, I cursed at myself for sending my boys off alone and without communications to capture those other men. We should have paired up. And we were taking an awful risk operating without comm. What the hell was I thinking? The frustration, the rage, and a bit of the guilt had clouded my judgment.

And what was worse, by the time I made it back to the bazaar and started down the main road toward the Hummer, I spotted a bonfire in the middle of the road.

But it turned out to be our Hummer.

I started running forward, forcing the prisoner to do likewise.

Another crowd had gathered to watch the infidel truck burn, and our mechanic driver was lying in the dirt with his hand on his forehead, bleeding from a terrible gash.

Kundi was there as well, and he marched up to me with several cronies drifting behind him. He spoke so rapidly in Pashto that I couldn't understand him, but he gesticulated wildly between the bazaar, the truck, and the people gathered. Then he pointed at me, narrowed his gaze, and this much I caught: "Time for you to go home."

"No," I said sarcastically. "We've come here to save you." He eyed the flaming truck, the stench of melting rubber threatening to make me gag. "Thanks for the welcome."

I pushed past him and led my prisoner over to the mechanic. "What happened?"

"They pulled me out. We can't fire till they fire at us. They didn't have any guns, then suddenly I'm lying on the ground. I don't even know who hit me . . ."

Brown, Hume, and Treehorn came charging back down the street. No luck, no prisoners.

"Sorry," Hume said. "The other three got away."

"Because they got help," said Treehorn. "They're working for Zahed, but they live here."

I snorted. "Yeah, it's good times." Then I shoved the prisoner toward Treehorn and shifted into the middle of the street. I pointed to the fallen mechanic and screamed at the top of my lungs, "WHO DID THIS?"

The locals threw their hands in the air, then dismissed me with waves and started back toward their shops. Nolan hustled over to the mechanic and hunkered down to treat him.

Kundi came forward once more. "Where is Captain Harruck?" he asked in broken English. "I want to talk to him."

"He's busy right now."

"You tell him I want to talk." Kundi turned away and started back toward the bazaar.

"So I guess we're walking," Brown said, staring grimly at the burning Hummer.

I began to lose my breath. I wanted to move all the women and children to a tent city just outside town, then call in an air strike and level the entire place and tell them we were turning it into a parking lot for a Wal-Mart Supercenter.

Then we'd go to Zahed and say, *This will happen to your village if you don't turn yourself in.* I couldn't understand how helping these people would help us win the war. I was willing to bet that even that guy who'd helped me would stab me in the back if push came to shove.

I was ready to leave, but of course the mission had just begun.

FIVE

We reached the edge of town, where in the distance two more Hummers bounced across the desert like mechanical dragons wagging long tails of dust. I squinted and saw that one truck contained the rest of my team, while the other was carrying Harruck. In about five minutes they reached us and screeched to a stop.

"Man, they were fast," said Paul Smith from the other truck. "They ditched their ride and scattered like roaches. We asked around. No one's talking. They're all too afraid to say anything. No shock there."

"All right," I said, then took a deep breath and crossed to Harruck as he hopped out of the cab. "We shot one, got one."

"What the hell, Scott? You shouldn't have followed

them into town, for God's sake! Maybe you can operate outside the ROE, but I can't. And I won't. I've spent a long time trying to work something out with them."

"With who? That guy Kundi? He's a scumbag who will burn you. Come on, Simon, you already know that. They're all opportunists, scammers, users . . ."

"Which means we have to play them just right, Scott. Just right. We need to be the ones they *think* they can trust." He glanced at my men, feeling the heat of their gazes. "Look, we'll talk about this later."

"They burned our Hummer," I said as he turned away.

He whirled back. "What?"

"They beat him up and burned our Hummer." I cocked a thumb at the mechanic, now sporting a bloody bandage on his forehead. "Nice, isn't it . . ."

"What the hell did you expect?"

I shrugged. "I don't know."

"Do me a favor, just . . . for now . . . don't try to help . . ."

Harruck's company suffered seven dead and fourteen injured. We killed about eight or nine around the base, with more dead in the mountains, but the Taliban recovered those bodies before we could confirm the kills.

Harruck's snipers were confident that at least four more had been taken down. The fires had been put out, and Harruck already had crews cleaning up the mess by the time he returned from town and nearly broke down the door of our billet. "Let's go," he snapped.

The rest of my team made faces as I followed him out and across the base, feeling like a cherry about to be trounced on by his CO, yet also resenting how upset Harruck had become. He had to take his anger out on someone, I guess. I acknowledged that he was the CO there, and though I didn't answer exclusively to him, I should respect his authority despite my far greater experience. I could easily get Keating to override him, but once I did that, our friendship would be over.

He collapsed into his chair. I took the one in front of his dusty desk. You could still smell the ash and cinders from the mess hall wafting in through the open window, and a small fan pivoting to and fro on the desk didn't help. I stared at the fan a moment, then took a deep breath and closed my eyes. "So, okay, buddy, let's have it."

When I opened my eyes, he was pouring me a drink, then one for himself.

I took the shot, downed it quickly. He did the same, swore, then said, "I need a miracle."

"I thought we were going to fight."

He shrugged. "I know where you're coming from. But I need to be honest with you—it looks like removing Zahed from power could do more harm than good."

"Simon, unless you can get my orders revised, I'm here to do one thing."

"You haven't met the district governor here, have you?"

I shook my head. "Just read about him in the briefing. He's another model citizen."

"Well, yeah, if you recall, the guy's name is Naimut

Gul. He came in here last year and promised these people the world, told them the Afghan government would
help. He didn't do anything except take their money.
He's like a Mafia kingpin, and his word means nothing.
When the people think of the government, they see
him. He's in bed with some of the warlords up north,
and it's pretty damned clear he's on the payroll for
opium production."

I snorted. "And he's the guy we're trying to support.
He's the *good* guy."

Harruck cursed through a sigh. "Look, Zahed's a
ruthless killer. His men are Huns. But the canals that
are here, the bazaar? He financed all of that, had his
people build it all. The Taliban brought in the natural
gas tanks and have been talking about getting power
lines hooked up."

"And Kundi, our big landowner, supports all of this,"
I said.

"Here's the thing. And I've been thinking about this
all day. If you take out Zahed too early—before I can
get something going here—then they'll still hate us and
align us with the government."

"They've already done that."

"Not all of them. If we can build them their school,
their police station, and dig them a new well—and we
deliver on those promises—then the timing will be perfect to remove Zahed and maybe even bring in a new
governor. I've heard talk of that, too. Start off with a
clean slate."

I sat back and tried to consider everything without

getting a migraine. "You want me to believe it's all that simple."

"I've got nothing else, Scott. I can't walk out of here as a failure."

"The legacy, huh?"

"This entire company is depending on me to help them complete the mission. We're not even close yet."

"What if your mission is bullshit?"

"It's not."

"My people seem to think that if we take out the Taliban leadership, we'll be in a better position to help these civilians—not that I agree with that, either. I mean look . . . how are you supposed to build a school with no assets and constant attacks from them?"

Harruck lowered his voice. "Maybe we can work with them."

I started laughing. "Last night I untied a girl from a pool table, and you're telling me you want to work with these people?"

"Money talks."

"Simon, if you go there, then you're no better than them. I'm telling you."

"My back's against the wall."

A knock came at the door, and the company's executive officer, Martin Shoregan, peeked inside. He was a lean black man and highly articulate, clearly being groomed to lead a company of his own. "Sir, sorry to interrupt. Dr. Anderson is here from the ARO."

Harruck bolted out of his chair. "Are you kidding me?"

"Do you want me to—"

"Send her right in!" he cried.

I glanced up at him. "Do you want me—"

"No, please stay."

The door opened, and in stepped a woman in a green-striped high-bodice dress with a swirling skirt and wide shawl draped over her head. Blond hair spilled out from the front of the shawl, and she grinned easily at us as I rose to meet her.

"Captain Harruck?" she asked, looking at me.

I shook my head.

"I'm Captain Simon Harruck." He proffered his hand. "And this is a friend."

She shook hands with Harruck, then smiled at me. "Well, hello, friend. I guess if I get your name, then you'll have to kill me?"

I shrugged. "Call me Scott. Where are you from? Australia?"

"Sydney. Very good. You?"

"I'm not here."

She liked that. "Right . . ."

Harruck told her to take my seat, and I didn't mind. She was easy on the eyes.

The two exchanged a few more pleasantries, and I learned that they'd spoken on the phone for many months. She said she was finally able to gather the resources and that the Afghanistan Relief Organization (ARO)—along with more than a dozen other relief groups—was ready to work with Army engineers on the construction of the school, police station, and solar-powered well. All of the agreements had been struck with the district governor and other elders, and they should be able to break ground within a week. Funding was finally in place.

"This is the news I've been waiting to hear for eight months now," said Harruck, his voice cracking. He glanced over at me and nodded.

I didn't hide my skepticism. "Dr. Anderson, I assume the *Doctor* is for Ph.D.?"

"That's right. My brother's the medical doctor in our family. My degree is in agricultural economics and rural sociology. Call me Cassie."

"Well, Cassie, you're a smart woman, and you understand the political situation here."

"I've been working in this country for three years now. So, yes, I'm keenly aware of what's happening. The ARO has made significant strides despite all the corruption."

"I understand, but you don't see this as a terrific waste of resources?"

"Excuse me?"

"We're going to provide all these services for the local community, but when we leave, the Taliban will move back in and destroy them, or exploit them, or hold them ransom. We should neutralize the enemy first, build a militia, then provide these people with an infrastructure only after they can protect themselves."

She looked at Harruck. "Your friend's a bit of a cynic."

"His mission has become slightly different than mine, but I think we can all work together to make this happen."

I raised my voice, if only a little. "Simon, do you think by helping these people you'll really build their trust? We'll always be foreigners."

"I need to try. At least for the children."

I took a deep breath. "I have a mission."

"I understand. But would you be willing to talk to Keating? Maybe just buy us some time?"

"That's the one thing they're telling me I don't have."

"Will you at least try?"

I shrugged, then turned to the door.

"Scott, I respect your opinion, and I'm going to need your help. Let's do this together."

I couldn't answer, and I'm glad I didn't.

"Nice to meet you . . . Scott," said Anderson.

My grin was forced, and she knew it.

I returned to quarters and sat around with the rest of my men, who were cleaning weapons. Hume and Nolan were busy dissecting the Cross-Coms for any more clues and had speculated that high-energy radio frequencies were probably to blame. I told them to keep working on it and shared with everyone what Harruck planned to do.

"He's just painting a bigger target on this town and pissing off the Taliban," said Brown. "The local government's corrupt. That's a given. So these people have come to trust the Taliban, who've kept their word. Now we're supposed to get them to trust us more by giving them more stuff, and we're supposed to think that once we've bought their trust, they'll help us capture the Taliban."

"Exactly," I said. "But what's wrong with that picture?"

Treehorn started laughing. "The Taliban ain't going to let that happen."

"Harruck actually said we might have to work with them."

"Are you serious?" asked Ramirez, who set down a magazine and turned his frown on me.

"See, Harruck knows that if we build the school and the rest of it, the Taliban will attack, so how do you get them off your back?"

"You take out their leader, disrupt their communications, and demoralize them," said Matt Beasley, who'd been very quiet the past few days. I could now hear the frustration in his tone.

"That might work, Matt, and you can bet we're going to try. But that's not Harruck's plan."

Ramirez made the money sign with his fingers.

"Oh, yeah," I said. "They'll try to cut a deal."

"Well, then, what're we supposed to do?" asked Ramirez. "Harruck's offering a handshake while we're putting guns to their heads."

"Look, he can't do that openly," I said. "Imagine the headline. Bottom line is the taxpayers need an enemy they can believe in—just as much as a hero."

"All this is making my brain explode," said Treehorn. "I need a bullet and a target. I'm easy to please. The rest of it is bullshit."

"Captain, I know Harruck's your friend," began Ramirez, "but we weren't sent here to build a school. If this is a good old-fashioned militia training op, I can deal with that, too. But we can't be tiptoeing around and still get our job done."

"I know. And there's no reason we should get caught up in all this. I want to go back out there tonight, gather more intel, and proceed on mission."

"We've got the drones but still no way to talk to them," said Hume. "Waiting on new gear. Could be a few more days."

I cursed. "Then we'll do it the old-fashioned way. Radios, binoculars, NVGs, it's not like we didn't train that way," I said.

"You going to tell Harruck?" asked Treehorn.

"No choice. We still need company support. He wanted me to call Keating and delay our mission. I don't know about you guys, but I'd rather get the job done and get the hell out of here as soon as possible."

"So just lie to him," said Treehorn.

I thought about that.

And I wondered if maybe I was just being a selfish bastard, but my guys felt the same way, so I lied and told Harruck no go. Our mission remained unchanged. We needed to find and capture Zahed.

"Don't you understand?" he asked me, raising his voice when I returned to his office later in the day. "This is eight months' worth of work finally coming together, and you want to screw it up just to nail that fat bastard who'll be replaced by his second in command! If we don't reach some kind of an agreement, nothing will happen."

"They didn't send me here to debate the politics, Simon. They sent me to get a guy, and you can't blame me for doing that. I understand your mission here. All I'm asking is that you understand mine. If I can capture Zahed and they get him to talk, he could turn the tide for us."

"Okay, yeah, I get it now. I understand how you're going to incite them and create an even more volatile situation, as evidenced by today's attack. And at the same time that I'm trying to earn the locals' trust, you're pissing them off by hunting down one fool who in the grand scheme of things means nothing. He's a local yokel. You're making him sound like Bin Laden."

I balled my hands into fists. "You're assuming that I can't demoralize them, that I can't get the whole leadership party, that no matter what I do it's going to be status quo over there."

"That's right, because that's the way it's been here. If we're going to change anything, it has to be big and swift, and we need to do it together—if we leave them out, we're doomed to fail."

I couldn't face him any more and looked to the door.

"Scott—"

I took a deep breath. "I understand now why you didn't become a Ghost."

"Don't be this way."

"Sorry, I'm not like you, Simon. I'm a soldier."

"Wow, what the hell was that?"

I faced him and spoke slowly . . . for effect. "What I see here is us building another welfare state, socialism at its finest, but remember what Margaret Thatcher said: 'Socialism only works until you run out of other people's money.' I'm not ready to negotiate with these bastards."

"Captain," he snapped. "I'll be contacting the general. I'll take this all the way up. There's just too much at stake here. Nothing personal."

"That's fine. You won't like the answer you get. We're doing a recon tonight. I'll need company support. I'll expect you to provide it. Check the registry, Captain."

SIX

Without our Cross-Coms, satellite uplinks and downlinks, and targeting computers, we were, for all intents and purposes, traditional old-school combatants relying on our scopes and skills. We did, however, have one nice toy well suited for Afghanistan: the XM-25, a laser-designated grenade launcher with smart rounds that did not require a link to our Cross-Coms. Matt Beasley had traded in his rifle for the XM-25, saying he predicted that he'd finally get a chance to field-test the weapon for himself. His prediction would come true, all right . . .

I couldn't deny the fact that long-range recon from the mountains would gain us only a small portion of the big picture. We needed HUMINT—human intelligence—

which could be gathered only by boots on the ground . . . spies walking among the enemy.

The guy I'd captured back in town was worthless. He wouldn't talk, make a deal, nothing. Harruck handed him off to the CIA and wished him good riddance.

So at that point it was both necessary and logical that I try to recruit the only local guy I knew who was seemingly on my side.

I won't say I fully trusted him—because I never did. But I figured the least I could do was ask. Maybe for the right price he'd be willing to walk into the valley of the shadow of death and bring me back Zahed's location. The Ghosts gave me an allowance for such cases, and I planned on spending it. I had nothing to lose except the taxpayers' money, and I worked for the government—so that was par for the course.

Ramirez and I got a lift into town, and dressed like locals with the *shemaghs* covering our heads and faces, we had the driver let us off about a block from the house. Ramirez would keep in radio contact with our driver.

I wouldn't have remembered the house if I didn't spot the young girl standing near the front door. She took one look at me, gaped, then ran back into the house, slamming the door after her. Ramirez looked at me, and we shifted forward. I didn't have to knock. The guy who'd helped me capture the Taliban thug emerged. I lowered my *shemagh*, and he didn't look happy to see me. "Hello again."

"Hello."

I proffered my hand. "My name is Scott. And this is Joe."

He sighed and begrudgingly took the hand. "I am Babrak Shilmani." He shook hands with Ramirez as well.

"Do you have a moment to talk?"

He glanced around the street, then lifted his chin and gestured that we go into his house.

The table I'd seen earlier was gone, replaced by large colorful cushions spread across newly unfurled carpets. I'd learned during my first tour in the country that Afghans ate on the floor and that the cushions were called *toshak* and that the thin mat in the center was a *disterkahn*.

"We didn't mean to interrupt your dinner," I said.

"Please sit. You are our guests." He spoke rapidly in Pashto, calling out to the rest of his family down the hall.

I knew that hospitality was very important in the Afghan code of honor. They routinely prepared the best possible food for their guests, even if the rest of the family did without.

As his family entered from the hall, heads lowered shyly, Shilmani raised a palm. "This is my wife, Panra; my daughter, Hila; and my son, Hewad."

They returned nervous grins, and then the mother and daughter hustled off, while the boy came to us and offered to take our *shemaghs* and showed us where to sit on the floor. Then he ran off and returned with a special bowl and jug called a *haftawa-wa-lagan*.

"You don't have to feed us," I told Shilmani, realizing that the boy had brought the bowl to help us wash our hands and prepare for the meal.

"I insist."

I glanced over at Ramirez. "Only use your right hand. Remember?"

"Gotcha, boss."

"You've been here before," said Shilmani. "I mean Afghanistan."

I nodded. "I love the tea."

"Excellent."

"Will you tell me now how you learned English?"

He sighed. "I used to work for your military as a translator, but it got too dangerous, so I gave it up."

Ramirez gave me a look. Perhaps we were wasting our time and had received the *no* already . . .

"They taught you?"

"Yes, a special school. I was young and somewhat foolish. And I volunteered. But when Hila was born, I decided to leave."

"They threatened you?"

"You mean the Taliban?"

I nodded.

"Of course. If you help the Americans, you suffer the consequences."

"You're taking a pretty big risk right now," I pointed out.

"Not really. Besides, I owe you."

"For what? You helped me capture that man."

"And you helped me get him out of my house. I was afraid for my wife and daughter. In most cases it is forbidden for a woman to be in the presence of a man who is not related to her—but I am more liberal than that."

"Glad to hear it."

As if on cue, the wife and daughter entered and provided all of us with tea. I took a long pull on my cup and relished the flavor, which somehow tasted like pistachios.

"So, Scott, what do you do for the Army?"

"I take care of problems."

"But you cannot do it alone. You want my help."

"I don't trust you. I don't trust anyone here. But my job would be easier, and fewer innocent people would get hurt, if I could get some help."

"What do you need?"

"Not what. Who."

Shilmani took a deep breath and stroked his thin beard. "You've come for Zahed."

I smiled. "Why not?"

"Because that's impossible."

"Nothing's impossible," said Ramirez.

"He has too many friends, even American friends, and too many connections. He has too many assets for you to ever get close. They always know when you're coming. And they're always prepared. They have eyes on your base every hour of every day. You cannot leave without them knowing about it."

"So they know I'm here."

"Yes, they do."

"And I've already put you in danger?"

"No, because I work for Mirab Mir Burki, who is the master of water distribution here in Zhari."

"I don't understand."

"Burki knows you Americans want to dig a new well. He wants that well, and he's already negotiated with Zahed over rights to the water and the profits. We're just waiting for you to build it. Any contact I have with Americans is part of our water negotiations—so as you might say, I have a good cover."

"What is it you want?"

"What all men want. Money. Safety for my family. A better life." Shilmani finished his tea, then topped off our cups and refilled his own.

"You want to see Zahed captured?"

"He's not a good influence here—despite what others may say. He does not break promises, but when he gives you something, the price is always very steep."

"Kundi seems to like him."

"That old man is a fool, and Zahed would put a knife in his back. There is no loyalty there."

"Would you go over to Sangsar and work for us?"

Shilmani's gaze turned incredulous. "No. Of course not."

"But you said you wanted money. I can work out an arrangement that would be very good for you—and your family."

"I am no good to my family if I'm dead."

"We can protect you."

"You're not a good liar, Scott."

We finished the tea, and Shilmani's wife and daughter served rice and an onion-based *quorma* or stew, along with chutneys, pickles, and naan—an unleavened bread baked in a clay oven. The food was delicious, and the wife continued urging us to eat more.

Afterward, while his family retreated to the back of the house, Shilmani wiped his mouth, then stared hard at me. "You have to remember something, Scott. After all of you are gone, we are left to pick up the pieces. We're just trying to do the best we can for ourselves."

I stood. "I know that. Thanks for the meal. If you want to give me some information about Zahed, I'll pay for it. If you change your mind about going to Sangsar, then just tell one of the soldiers on patrol that you want to speak to me. I'll get the word."

"Okay. And one more thing. Walk in my shoes for a moment. I cannot trust the Taliban. I cannot trust my village elder or my boss. I cannot trust the district governor. And I cannot trust you, the foreigner."

"You know something? I think I'm already there," I told him.

Ramirez pursed his lips and gestured that we leave. I called back to the family, said our good-byes, then ambled out into the street, as Ramirez got on the radio and hailed the Hummer driver.

"What do you think?" he asked as we started around the corner. "Waste of time?"

"I don't think so. He doesn't like Zahed."

"Yeah, seems like there's more to it."

"And maybe we can use that to our advantage."

Around eleven P.M. local time I got a satellite phone call from Lieutenant Colonel Gordon back at Fort Bragg. He'd just arrived in the office and was telling me that his morning coffee tasted bitter because I had yet to capture Zahed.

Then, after he finished issuing a string of epithets regarding the call he'd just had with General Keating, he cleared his throat and said to me point-blank, "Is Captain Harruck going to be a problem?"

"I don't know. To be honest with you, Colonel, I think higher's just throwing stuff at the wall to see what sticks, and we're all just part of the plan."

"Well, you listen to me, Mitchell, and you listen to me good. We both know this COIN mission is complete and utter nonsense. It's politicians running the war. You don't secure the population and let the enemy run wild. We ain't playing defense here! And we can't have that. As far as I'm concerned, it is *not* a good day to be a Taliban leader in the Zhari district. Do you read me?"

"Loud and clear, sir."

"New Cross-Coms are en route. Meanwhile, you do what you need to do. Next week at this time I'd like to be powwowing with the fat man."

"Roger that, sir."

"And Mitchell?"

"Yes, sir?"

"Is something wrong?"

"No, sir. I'm fine. Talk to you soon."

I'd thought he'd heard me cracking under the pressure, but later on I realized that my heart was just darkening, and the old man could sense that from a half a world away.

At about three A.M. local time, in the wee hours, we left the base in a Hummer driven by Treehorn. Harruck made no attempts to stop us. I'd assumed he'd been told by Keating that he should not interfere with my mission.

Instead of driving out into the desert, toward the mountains, we headed off to the town, so that the Taliban now watching us from ridgelines and the desert would assume we were just another village patrol.

Once in town, we went to the bazaar area, where several vendors had their old beater pickup trucks parked out behind their homes/stalls.

We split into two teams and entered the homes behind the stalls, accosting the shop owners and demanding their keys at gunpoint.

The old merchants saw only a band of masked wraiths with deep, angry voices.

Within five minutes we had two pickup trucks on the road, and the old men who could blow the alarm were gagged and tied. They might guess we were Americans, but we spoke only in Pashto and were dressed like the Taliban themselves.

I sent Jenkins back with the Hummer, and though he was bummed to remain in the rear, I told him I needed a good pair of eyes on the base . . . just in case.

We drove out to the main bridge over the Arghandab River, dropped off Brown and Smith, then crossed the bridge, heading along the mountain road that wound its way up and back down into the valley where Sangsar lay in the cool moonlight. The town reminded me of the little villages my grandfather would build for his train sets. He had a two-car garage filled with locomotives and cars and towns and enough accessories to earn him a spot on the local news. When he passed, my father sold it all on eBay and made a lot of money.

The Taliban sentries watching us through their binoculars probably assumed we were opium smugglers or carrying out some other such transport mission for Zahed. In fact, we were not stopped and reached the top of the mountain, where the dirt road broadened enough for us to pull over, park the vehicles, and move in closer on foot.

We'd taken such great care to slip into Sangsar during our first raid attempt that I'd felt certain no Taliban had seen us, but according to Shilmani, they had. Interesting that Zahed did not tip off his guards at the compound and allowed them to be ambushed. That was decidedly clever of him.

However, this time our plan was more bold. Be seen. Be mistaken. And be deadly.

Hume had rigged up a temporary remote for the Cypher drone, and though there was no screen from which we could view the drone's data, he could fly it like a remote-controlled UFO, keeping a visual on it with his night-vision goggles.

We were bass fishing for Taliban, and the drone was our red rubber worm.

Within five minutes we'd taken up perches along the heavy rocks jutting from the mountainside and had, yet again, an unobstructed and encompassing view of the valley and all of Sangsar.

The drone whirred away, and I lay there on my belly, just watching it and thinking about Harruck and Shilmani and that old man Kundi and remembering that every one of us had his own agenda, every one of us was stubborn, and every one of us would fight till the end.

"Sir," whispered Treehorn, who was at my left shoulder. "Movement in the rocks behind us, six o'clock."

SEVEN

When I was a kid, D.C.'s *Sgt. Rock* and Marvel's *The 'Nam* were among my favorite comics. I didn't realize it then, but what drew me to those stories was the simplicity of the plots. The good guys and bad guys were clearly defined, and you understood every character's desire and related with that desire. Kill bad guys. Save everyone. Win the war. For America! Be proud! Come home and get a medal, be worshipped as a hero, live happily ever after. As a kid, you're looking for admiration and acceptance, and being a superhero soldier always sounded pretty damned good to me.

However, that would never happen if I stayed in Ohio. There weren't too many opportunities for me growing up in Youngstown. Sure, I could've gone to work in the

General Motors assembly plant in Lordstown like my father had, but I doubt I would've matched his thirty years. Boredom or the tanking economy would've finished me. My brother Nicolas got out himself and became an engineering professor down in Florida, while Tommy owned and operated Mitchell's Auto Body and Repair in Youngstown. He loved cars and had inherited that passion from our father. He'd had no desire to ever leave home and had tried to persuade me to stay and run the shop with him. Because Dad was an avid woodworker, Tommy even tried to persuade me to open a custom furniture shop and work with Dad, but that didn't sound very glamorous to an eighteen-year-old. Jennifer, the baby of our family, married a wealthy software designer, and she lived with him and their daughter in Northern California.

So I'd gone off to see the world and serve my country. Because that sounded so hokey, I told everyone I was joining the Army to pay for my college education—which Dad resented because it made us sound poor.

I can't lie, though. During my service I've seen the good, the bad, and the ugly—and it's easy to become disenchanted. When I'd joined, I was just as naïve as the next guy, but for many years I clung to my beliefs and positive attitude, and I let my passion become infectious.

But I think after 9/11, when the GWOT (global war on terrorism) got into full swing, my veneer grew a bit worn. It didn't happen overnight, but every mission seemed to sap me just a little more. I grew older, my body became more worn, and my spirit seemed harder to kindle.

When I raised my right hand and they swore me in, I never thought I'd have to wrap my head around no-win situations in which everyone I dealt with was a liar, in which my own institution was undermining my ability to get the job done, and in which my own friends had drawn lines in the sand based on philosophical differences.

Before my mother had died from cancer, she'd held my hand and told me to make the best of my life.

I figured she was rolling over in her grave when they started calling me a murderer . . .

Treehorn had a good ear and better eyes, and I glanced back to where he'd spotted the movement along the mountainside. My night-vision goggles revealed two Taliban fighters peering out from behind a pair of rocks, but before I could get on the radio and issue an order, Beasley appeared from behind a few rocks and slipped down toward the Taliban thugs. As they turned back, he took one out with his Nightwing black tungsten blade while Nolan, who dropped down at Beasley's side, broke the neck of the other fighter.

Beasley called me and said, "Looks like only two up here, boss. Clear now."

I called up Ramirez, who was packing our portable, ultrawide-band radar unit that could detect ground movement up to several hundred meters away. I'd considered leaving the device behind in case we got zapped again, but now I was glad we had it. I hadn't expected sentries this far up into the mountains. Within a minute Ramirez would be scanning the outskirts of the town.

Off to the northeast, along a section of wall that was beginning to crumble, a pair of jingle trucks were parked abreast. The trucks were colorfully painted and adorned with pieces of rugs, festooned with chimes, and fitted with all sorts of other dangling jewels that created quite a racket as they traveled down the potholed roads between villages. These trucks had become famous and then infamous among American soldiers. They were typically used by locals to transport goods, but in more recent years they had become instruments to smuggle drugs and weapons across the borders with Iran and Pakistan. Thugs would hide weapons within stacks of firewood or piles of rugs, and young infantrymen would have to search the loads while wizened old men glared on, palms raised as they were held at gunpoint. I must've seen a hundred roadside incidents of search and seizure during my time in country.

That Zahed had several of these trucks in the village was unsurprising. That there was a man posted in the back of one truck and pointing his rifle up at us gave me pause.

Treehorn already had him spotted with his scope, and he'd attached the gun's big silencer, so he could do the job in relative quiet.

I told him to wait while I scanned for more targets.

"Ghost Lead, this is Ramirez," came the voice in my headset.

"What do you got?"

"Just the one guy in the jingle truck so far. The

compound we hit looks empty. Picking up movement from all the farm animals in the pens. Nothing else, over."

"Roger that. Hume, talk to me about the drone."

"Nothing. Just flying around. If they're here, they're not taking the bait. Not yet, anyway."

"All right, just keep flying over the town. Maybe get in close to the mosque."

"I see it. I'll get near the dome and towers."

"Ghost Lead, this is Treehorn, I have my target."

"I know you do. Hang tight for now. Still want to see if they take the bait, over."

"Roger that. Say the word."

I continued scanning the village, which stretched out for about a quarter kilometer, swelling to the south with dozens more brick homes that had open windows and rickety wooden ladders leading up to storage areas on the roofs. Most windows were dark, with only a faint flickering here and there from either candles or perhaps kerosene or gas lanterns. I imagined that somewhere down there, sprawled across a bed whose legs were buckling under his girth, was the fat man who wielded all the power in this region.

"Still no takers on the drone," reported Hume.

I listened to the wind. Glanced around once more. Scanned. Saw the shooter still sitting there in the truck. Time to move in.

"Treehorn, clear to fire," I said.

"Clear to fire, roger that, stand by . . ."

I held my breath, anticipated the faint click and pop, no louder than the sound of a BB gun, and watched through the binoculars as the gunman in the jingle truck slumped.

"Good hit, target down," reported Treehorn.

"Ghost Team, this is Ghost Lead. Advance to the wall. Hume, get that drone in deeper, and feel 'em out. Two teams. Alpha right, Bravo left. Move out!"

I'd be lying if I didn't admit I was an adrenaline junkie and that this part of the job quickened my pulse and was entirely addictive. You stayed up nights thinking about moments like this. And there was no better ego-stroking in the world than to play God, to decide who lives and who dies. There was nothing better than the hunting of men, Ernest Hemingway had once said, and the old man was right.

But I always stressed to my people that they had to live with their decisions, a simple fact that would become terribly ironic for me.

"Ghost Lead, this is Ramirez. Radar's picking up something big behind us."

"Ghost Lead, this is Brown. Paul and I are all set here, but FYI, two Blackhawks inbound, your position, over."

Even as he finished his report, the telltale whomping began to echo off the mountains, like an arena full of people clapping off the beat, and abruptly the two helicopters appeared, both switching on searchlights that panned across the desert floor like pearlescent lasers.

"Ghost Team, take cover now!" I cried, dodging across the sand toward the jingle trucks.

Ramirez, Jenkins, and Hume rushed up behind me,

while Nolan, Beasley, and Treehorn darted for a large section of fallen wall, the crumbling bricks forming a U-shaped bunker to shield them.

"Hume, bring back the drone," I added. Then I switched channels to the command net. "Liberty Base, this is Ghost Lead, over."

"Go ahead, Ghost Lead," came the radio operator back at FOB Eisenhower.

"I want to talk to Liberty Six right now!" I could already see myself grabbing Harruck by the throat.

"I'm sorry, Ghost Lead, but Liberty Six is unavailable right now."

I cursed and added, "I don't care! Get him on the line!"

Meanwhile, Ramirez, who like all of us had received Air Force combat controller training, gave me the hand signal that he'd made contact with one of the chopper pilots, as both helicopters wheeled overhead, waking up the entire village. I listened to him speak with that guy while I waited.

"Repeat, we are the friendly team on the ground. What is your mission, over?"

I leaned in closer to hear his radio. "Ground team, we were ordered to pick you up at these coordinates, over."

Ramirez's eyes bulged.

"Tell him to evac immediately," I said. "We do not need the goddamned pickup."

Ramirez opened his mouth as a flurry of gunfire cut across the jingle truck, and even more fire was directed

up at the two Blackhawks, rounds sparking off the fuse-
lages.

With a gasp, I realized there had to be twenty, maybe
thirty combatants laying down fire now.

I knew the choppers' door gunners wouldn't return
fire. Close Air Support had become as rare as indoor
plumbing in Afghanistan because of both friendly fire
and civilian casualty incidents, so those pilots would just
bug out. Which they did.

Leaving us to contend with the hornet's nest *they* had
stirred up.

"What do you think happened?" Ramirez cried over
the booms and pops of AK-47s.

"Harruck figured out a way to abort our mission," I
said through my teeth. "He'll call it a miscommunication, and he'll remind me that I needed company support. But those birds had to come all the way from
Kandahar—what a waste!"

"Well, he didn't screw up our entire mission," said
Ramirez, then he flashed a reassuring grin. "Not yet!"

A breath-robbing whistle came from the right, and I
couldn't get the letters out of my mouth fast enough:
"RPG!"

The rocket-propelled grenade lit up the night as it
streaked across the wall and exploded at the foot of the
concrete bricks near the rest of my team.

As the debris flew and the smoke and flames slowly
dissipated, I led my group along the wall and back
toward the brick pile, where we linked up with the

others, who were stunned but all right. Nolan had found a hole in the wall, and we all passed through, reaching the first row of houses and rushing back toward them, where to our right the wall continued onward until it terminated in a big wooden gate. "We'll get out that way," I hollered, pointing.

We reached the first house, sprinted to the next, and then had to cross a much wider road, on the side of which stood a donkey cart with the donkey still attached but pulling at his straps. The moment I peered around the corner, a salvo ripped into the wall just above my head. I stole another quick glance and saw a guy ducking back inside his house, using his open window and the thick brick walls as cover. We could fire all day at those walls, but our conventional rounds wouldn't penetrate.

Another glance showed a second gunman in the window next door. Two for one. Double your pleasure. Wonderful. We were pinned down.

I turned back to the group and gave Beasley a hand signal: *We can't get across. Got two. You're up.*

Over the years I've come to appreciate advances in weapons technology for two reasons: One, as a member of an elite gun club called the Ghosts, I couldn't help but be fascinated by the instruments that kept me alive, and two, like everyone else in the Army, I enjoyed things that went BOOM!

The XM-25 launcher that Beasley was about to present to the enemy made one hell of a twenty-five-thousand-dollar boom, which was the CPU or cost per unit.

"Hey, wait, before he fires, maybe we can call Harruck and ask for mortar support," said Ramirez, making a very bad joke.

I snorted and gave Beasley the all clear.

The team sergeant lifted the launcher, which was much thicker than a conventional rifle and came equipped with a pyramid-shaped scope.

With smooth, graceful movement, Beasley laser-designated his target, used the scope to set range, and then without ceremony fired.

Each twenty-five-millimeter round packed two warheads that were more powerful than the conventional forty-millimeter grenade launchers. Next came the moment when gun freaks like me got our jollies: The round didn't have to burrow through the wall and kill the guy on the other side, no. The round passed through the open window and detonated in midair, sending a cloud of fragmentation inside that would shred anyone, most particularly Taliban fighters attempting to play Whac-A-Mole with Ghost units.

The moment his first round detonated, Beasley turned his attention to window number two, got his laser on target, set his distance for detonation, and boom, by the time the echo struck the back wall, we were already en route toward the wooden gate, even as that donkey broke his straps and clattered past us.

"This one's a keeper," Beasley told me, patting the XM-25 like a puppy.

Before Ramirez could try the lock, Jenkins put his size thirteen boot to the wooden gate panel and smashed it open. We rushed through and ran to the right, working back along the wall while Treehorn lingered behind, throwing smoke grenades into the street to create a little chaos and diversion.

The choppers were still whomping somewhere over the mountains, out of range now, as we charged toward the foothills, only drawing fire once we reached the first ravine. There, we dove for cover, rolled and came back up, on our bellies, ready to return fire—

But I told everyone to hold. Wait. Keep low. And watch. Treehorn's smoke grenades kept hissing and casting thick clouds over the village.

Many of the Taliban were running from the front gate, and two went over to the jingle trucks and fired them up.

"They're going to chase us in those?" Ramirez asked.

"Looks like it," I said. "Let's fall back. Up the mountain, back to the pickup trucks."

We broke from cover and ran, working our way along the mountainside and keeping as many of the jagged outcroppings between us and the village as possible. I wish I could say it was a highly planned and skillful withdrawal performed by some of the most elite soldiers in the world.

But all I can really say is . . . we got the hell out of there.

Up near the mountaintop road, we climbed breathlessly into the pickup trucks as down below, headlights shone across the dirt road. My binoculars showed the pair of jingle trucks and two more pickups with fifty-caliber guns mounted on their flatbeds. I breathed a curse.

Since Harruck had already sabotaged my mission, I decided not to throw any more gasoline on the fire. We wouldn't engage those guys unless absolutely necessary.

Treehorn took us down the mountain road at a breakneck pace, and I was more frightened by his driving than by the Taliban on our tails. The pickup literally came up on two wheels as we cut around a narrow cliff side turn, and that drew swearing from everyone as the road seemed to give way in at least two spots.

"This thing's got some power," Treehorn said evenly.

We came down the last few slopes and turned onto the dirt road leading up to the bridge. With our headlights out, Smith and Brown were watching us with their NVGs and gave us a flash signal. We found them at the foot of the bridge, and Brown climbed in the back of our truck.

"Good to go, Captain," he said. "Just give me the word."

"Soon as we cross," I told him.

"You don't want to wait and take them out, too?" he asked, cocking a thumb over his shoulder.

"Nah, it's okay. This'll be enough."

A double thud worked its way up into the seats, and we left the bridge and crossed back onto the sand.

"All right," I cried back to Brown. "Blow that son of a bitch!"

He worked his remote, and the C-4 that he and Smith had expertly planted along the bridge's pylons detonated in a rapid sequence of thunderclaps that shook both the ground and the pickups themselves. Magnesium-bright flashes came from beneath all that concrete, and just as the smoke clouds began to rise, the center section of the bridge simply broke off and belly flopped into the ink-black water, sending waves rushing toward both shorelines.

The drivers of the jingle trucks must have seen the explosions and bridge collapse, but the guy in the lead truck braked too hard, and the truck behind him plowed into his rear bumper, sending him over the edge where the concrete had sheared off. He did a swan dive toward the river, while the second guy attempted to turn away, but he rolled onto his side and slid off the edge. Three, two, boom, he hit the water.

Behind them, the two pickups with machine gunners came to brake-squealing halts and paused at the edge so that the drivers and gunners could stare down in awe at the sinking trucks—

As we raced off toward Senjaray in the distance.

EIGHT

While I was blowing up bridges and trying to hunt down my target, the president of Afghanistan was in the United States, making speeches about how his government and the United States needed to build bridges in order to unite his people. He argued that not all Taliban were linked to terrorist groups like al Qaeda and that many Taliban wanted to lay down their arms and reach reconciliation with the national government.

That may have been true. But I wanted to know how you sorted out the friendly Taliban from the ones wiring themselves with explosives, even as the Afghan president allied himself with his neighbors: Iran and Pakistan, nations that served as training grounds and safe havens for those wanting to destroy the United States.

Everyone had answers that involved false assumptions, sweeping generalizations, and a skewed understanding of the complexities, contradictions, and culture of Afghanistan.

But that was all politics, right? None of my business. I just needed to capture a Taliban commander. One of the first things I learned after joining the military was to focus on my mission and leave the debates to the fat boys back home. I talked to my colleagues, and it was the same old story: Officers who got too caught up in the politics of their missions were, in most cases, not as successful as those who did not. Success was judged on whether the mission goals had been achieved and at what cost.

Lest we be accused of theft instead of borrowing, we dropped off the pickup trucks at the edge of town and were met by a driver and Hummer for the ride back to the FOB.

En route, I made a satellite phone call to Lieutenant Colonel Gordon, who suggested I speak directly with General Keating. I tried to restrain myself from exploding as I described the situation to the general. He told me Harruck had contacted him already. "Sir, the bottom line is, I want the guy's head on a platter."

"You guys were very well liked and made a great team during that Robin Sage."

"Yes, sir. But I don't think the captain is playing on our team anymore."

"I know you feel that way, but you need to understand something. First, I can't stop you from lopping off his head. If you put it in writing, I'll have to forward the charge."

"I'll have it to you right away."

"Slow down, son. Our situation is complicated, and Captain Harruck's mission further complicates matters. But that can and should work to our advantage."

"Excuse me, sir?"

"Mitchell, we can use his mission as a distraction to keep everyone busy while you hunt down our boy. The COIN mission is our screen. Harruck's attempts to win over the locals will keep the Taliban busy."

"Sir, how about the same plan, only we let the XO take over. Lose Harruck."

The general sighed deeply. "Better the devil we know than the devil we don't, Mitchell."

"Sir, you've got to be kidding me."

"Son, this has already become a huge task management problem. We don't need to make it more difficult. Go talk to Harruck. Work it out. I know you can."

I could barely answer. "Yes, sir."

"I'm counting on you, Mitchell."

I ended the call before cursing.

Harruck was waiting for me outside his office when the Hummer pulled up. "You were wrong about Keating," he said to me abruptly.

"Oh, yeah?"

"He's not a soldier. He's a politician, just like the rest of them."

"Just like you."

He shook his head. "Come inside."

I raised an index finger, deciding I was going to make this bastard suffer a little more for what he'd done. "At this point, I advise you to speak very carefully, because you've just committed a court-martial offense, and even worse, an immoral and ethical offense. You've not only disobeyed an order from a superior, you've broken the code of honor by endangering me and my Ghosts."

"Scott, this is the part where I say I don't know what you're talking about."

"Look, buddy, I won't even ask what kind of proof you have or how you tried to orchestrate this thing to get yourself off. Point is, without authorization you called in those birds to abort my mission. And you know, if word of this gets out, it'll spread like wildfire. No one will trust you."

"I got two merchants who said people tied them up and stole their trucks. I got chopper pilots telling me you blew the bridge over the river. Hell, we heard the thing go up. And now you're playing angel? Jesus Christ, Scott . . . you can't walk in here and take over. I told you I got eight months in here! EIGHT GODDAMNED MONTHS!"

As he raised his voice, I grew more calm and para-phrased regulations, which I knew would spike his pulse. "By law, you were required to carry out the last order given to you by your superior officer and only afterward were you to question that order by going up the chain of command to my superiors. I'm sure neither Gordon nor Keating gave you the okay to abort my mission."

"Don't stand there and think you can burn me, Scott. I've got a lot on you, too. I'm talking lots of stuff in the closet, friendly-fire crap that was covered up . . . you know exactly what I'm talking about."

Actually, I didn't because there were too many close calls, too many missions where collateral damage needed to be addressed by my superiors, who, for the most part, kept me and my team out of the loop. Whatever he thought he had was probably bullshit . . . but then again, you never knew . . .

He turned and headed into his office. I followed. He crossed around his desk but remained standing. I kept near the door and didn't take a chair, either.

After a deep breath, I said, "Simon, I'm trying to decide if I should have you removed from command."

"That's not your decision."

"Once I light the fuse, there's no putting it out."

"Yeah, you like blowing things up. So why the bridge?"

"Changing the subject?"

"Do you realize what you've done?"

"Yeah, made it harder for them. They've been using the bridge *we built* to come over here and attack us. Now if they want to come, they get to go swimming."

"That bridge was symbolic of our presence here."

"Like the school and the police station and the well you want to drill?"

"Yeah. What's wrong with that?"

"Man, I would've never seen this coming." I closed my eyes and took another deep breath. "We can agree to disagree, but you cannot interfere with my mission."

"You know your mission is worthless. And it might mean we have to sacrifice everything—even now when things are finally going to happen."

"They gave me a target."

"And you think you can act with impunity?"

I tensed. "I can and will act with impunity."

"So now you're God."

My hands turned into fists. "Why are you doing this? We're on the same side. Zahed is a thug."

He rubbed the corners of his eyes. "You think I'm a bleeding-heart liberal now?"

"They sent you here to secure the town and help the people, and they're calling that counterinsurgency. It's a goddamned joke. They sent me here to capture or kill the bad guy. To them, it's all very simple."

"I just want to help these people, give their kids a school, let 'em have a police station, and let them have more drinking water so they're not constantly screwed over by the Taliban, who're selling it to them at outrageous prices. What's wrong with that? We're talking about basic human rights."

I hardened my gaze. "At what cost? My life? The lives of my team?"

He couldn't meet my gaze.

"Simon, you're not here to create a legacy. Just get

the job done. Secure the town. Assist in building the infrastructure."

"They're already talking about pulling me out. Giving me four months—if I'm lucky."

"Well, you got the ball rolling now."

He swore under his breath. "Maybe. So what's next?"

"Well, I can't trust you, but I still need this company's support to get my job done. Does the XO know what happened?"

"Shoregan's on my side. He'll do whatever I say."

"Don't trust him. He wants your command, and I could give it to him right now."

"Scott, I don't want to take this any further."

"Yeah, because you got caught." I snorted. "I don't care what you got on me. Bring it."

"Just slow down, and think about what you're doing . . . one minute you sound like you'll let me off, the next you're blowing the whistle."

He was right. I was torn. I could still go against Keating's wishes, burn Harruck, and back the old man into a corner; however, if I did that, Keating could easily ruin me.

I glanced over to the wall, where Harruck had proudly displayed pictures of his various tours. One on the left caught my eye: our Robin Sage training. I stood there with our class, with Simon at my side, his arm draped over my shoulder.

So right there I reasoned that now I could better control and even manipulate him. The guilt persuaded me to give him a chance.

At the same time, I couldn't help but see him as a mindless cog in the wheel of socialism. Sure, we'd build the locals an infrastructure, but they'd screw us over and probably forget about us after we left. Nevertheless, Harruck billed himself as a humanitarian—one who'd been willing to sacrifice us for his "larger cause." You had to love that irony.

"Here's the plan," I began. "You get word out to the village elders that the Taliban blew up the bridge and tried to frame some of the local merchants. That way we save face with Kundi and the rest of those idiots in the town."

"I don't think they'll go for it."

"Doesn't matter. All we need is doubt. Just make them think *everyone* is lying. Now, with the bridge out, you'll have a little more freedom to begin construction, because the Taliban will use the shallowest part of the river to cross, and they'll have to move through the east side and approach through the valley and our choke point, so you guys can better defend against them now. I'll help your men set up some overwatch positions and some gun emplacements."

"So you knew that blowing that bridge would actually help my construction project?"

"Yeah, I did."

"Then why didn't you tell me?"

"I don't know, Simon. You pissed me off the last time we talked, all right?"

He flumped into his chair. "I still can't have you going into Sangsar and raising hell. And now that you've blown the bridge, they'll attack us again."

"Let them. They have to fight on our terms now. Zahed's army will get smaller and demoralized, and then we'll swoop in."

"I can't see this ending well, Scott."

"It's hard to see right now." I found myself quoting Keating and hating myself for that. "Our situation is complicated." I started for the door.

"So we have an agreement?"

I turned back. "What?"

"We call the chopper pickup a miscommunication, and from here on out, I won't interfere with your mission."

"You're damned right you won't."

"But can you do me a favor?"

I almost chuckled, and there was no hiding my sarcasm. "Sure, we're still bestest buddies."

"Try contacting Zahed."

"Excuse me?"

"Try to make direct contact with him. Maybe we can call a truce. If we can get him talking, maybe your mission can change."

"He's a terrorist."

"That hasn't been proven."

"I plucked a little girl out of there—and she told me he's a scumbag terrorist. That's definitive."

In truth, she hadn't uttered a word about Zahed himself, but her eyes had told me enough.

Harruck went on with his speculation. "Maybe he doesn't have full control of his men. He's a politician, too. He wouldn't condone that."

"So it's okay that I talk to the leader of an insurgency

who rapes children in the name of saving these other children over here."

"Scott, we can debate this all night."

"No, we can't. And we won't. The fat man will be captured or killed before I leave. And if he's not, then I'll be the one leaving in a body bag."

I hurried out into the cooler air as two Hummers came rolling by. Harruck had put the entire base on alert, and all the engines and shouting made me wince. I couldn't wait to collapse into my rack. Maybe I'd wake up back in North Carolina. I could tell Auntie Em that I'd had a terrible dream about a sandstorm that had carried me away to a land where camels had wings and no one told the truth.

NINE

The next morning while I was in the mess hall, I ran into Dr. Anderson, the woman from ARO, who'd been given temporary quarters on the base to begin coordinating with the engineers for the construction projects.

She remembered my name. I called her Dr. Anderson. I didn't want to get too chummy with her.

"Eating alone?" she asked.

My team had already chowed down, allowing me to sleep in. They'd understood the night I'd had.

"Yes, I am."

"Want some company?" she asked.

I glimpsed her blond hair, now flowing easily over her shoulders. No veil required here. She was probably in her late twenties, early thirties. Just stunning. An oasis. "Oh, I wouldn't be good company right now."

"Don't underestimate yourself," she said, following me to my table and sitting across from me.

"Aggressive," I muttered.

"I eat my dead."

"Not bad—"

"For a bleeding-heart liberal, right?"

"I didn't say that."

She smiled. "Your expression did."

"I told you, I'm not good company."

"I don't need your permission."

"Then why'd you ask? What is this?"

"This is me taking on a challenge."

"Oh, yeah, what's that?"

"I don't know what it is you do here, but I guess you have some pull with Captain Harruck, and he's a great guy, doing everything he can to help these people. So I'm wondering why you don't support him."

"So the challenge is to get me talking so you can find out who your enemies might be on the base?"

"That's how we recon. Same as you, actually. Keep your enemies close, too."

"I'm not your enemy. Just a skeptic."

She took a bite of her toast, sipped her black coffee. "And why is that?"

"I could tell you . . ."

"But then you'd have to . . ."

"No, not kill you . . . just start an argument, and it's

not worth it. I'm just here to get a job done, and when I'm finished, I go on to the next problem."

"Me, too." She stared out the window at the dust blowing across the road. "This place . . . it has a way of draining all your energy. Some days I just feel like sleeping."

"Yeah, I know what you mean."

"So you think I'm wasting my time, don't you? You think we're all just spinning our wheels."

I didn't look up, just ate my toast and found great interest in the black pool of my coffee.

"Scott, maybe in the end we can do more good by showing kindness," she added.

"We're a fighting force, trained for battle, not police work. These people need a police force and a better army to protect them, and then people like you can come and offer aid. We're doing it all for them right now, and when we pull out, you watch . . . it'll all crumble."

The guys decided that they hated Harruck. I couldn't blame them. I shared what Keating had told me. They snorted, cursed, wished we had beer.

At the same time, they were getting cabin fever, so I told them we'd bend orders and don regular Army uniforms and pose as grunts to assist with arranging and constructing defensive positions along the choke point near the river.

"We just finished telling you how much we hate Harruck," said Brown. "Now you want us to help him?"

I smiled. "That's right. Don't you love this place?"

They threw up their hands.

I put Ramirez in charge and sent my boys out there to help a few sergeants, who were glad to have more hands on shovels in the one-hundred-plus-degree heat.

Meanwhile, I paid a long overdue visit to our friendly neighborhood CIA agent, a guy who called himself "Bronco." I wasn't keen on working with those bastards, but I figured the least I could do was feel him out. I'd thought his agency wanted Zahed as much as I did, so we had a common goal.

Bronco didn't live on the base but paid rent for a one-room shack on the west side of the village. He'd been working the district for the past two years and had, according to Harruck, earned the respect of Kundi and the rest of the elders.

I found him sitting outside his shack, reading a book and smoking a filterless cigarette. His gray beard, sun-weathered skin, and turban made it hard to discern him as an American. I'd taken a private with me for security and had donned regular Army gear myself.

Bronco took a long pull on his cigarette, flicked it away, then exhaled loudly and spoke in Pashto. "Good morning, gentlemen. What do you want?"

I answered in English. "My name's Scott. I was hoping we could go inside and talk in private."

"You're not the asshole who blew up our bridge, are you?"

"I can neither confirm nor deny any information you

have regarding bridges in this region," I answered curtly, then gave him my lucky fuck-you smile.

He rolled his eyes. "Come on in, Joe."

"Scott."

"No, Joe."

We went in, and I wasn't sure how a human being could live like that. One meager bed, small washbasin, a table, and two chairs. No power, no running water. He did have natural gas to cook, but that was about it. A laptop with satellite link sat improbably on the table, and he told me had a dozen solar-powered batteries to keep the thing running—his lifeline to home. He plopped into a chair.

"I'm surprised they didn't attach me to your mission," he said suddenly.

"And what mission would that be?"

"Cut the crap. You're an SF guy come here to take out Zahed. He knew you were coming. We knew you were coming. No one wants you here. No one needs you here. So what the hell are you doing here?"

I started laughing and looked around. "I keep asking myself the same question."

"Go home, Joe."

"Aren't you here with the same agenda?"

He just stared at me. Squinted, really, deep lines creasing his face. "I can neither confirm nor deny any information I have regarding the whereabouts or intended capture of Zahed."

"All right. You're me. What do you do?"

"Are you deaf? Go home, Joe."

"You don't think removing Zahed will have any effect on what's happening here?"

"Yeah, actually I do. This place will tank even more."

"You don't think capturing him will gain us valuable information regarding the Taliban's activities in this region?"

"Nope. We got predators flying around, watching every move they make. We don't need one fat man to spill his guts."

"So you're JAFO."

His was old enough and experienced enough to know the term: Just Another Fucking Observer.

"What's happening here is a little too complex for the average military mind to grasp. I'm sure you saw the PowerPoint they made. That's why I'm here. We're not JAFOs. We're specialists. You guys are just overpaid assassins. And you're what? Oh for two on night raids now? I mean, that's amateur crap. Really."

"I was hoping we could share some intel, so that the next time something happens, it'll be the last."

"Of course you were."

"I need to know whether or not your agency will pose any interference with my mission."

He threw his head back and cackled at that.

I just stood there.

Finally, his smile evaporated. "Joe, my agency interferes with everything. That's what we do."

I envisioned myself crossing to the table, grabbing the bastard by the neck, shoving him against the wall, and saying, *If you get in my way, you'll be on my target list.*

"No help from you, then."

He shrugged. "Have you met the provincial governor?"

I shook my head.

"You should. The people here want him dead more than Zahed. You want to be a hero, kill him."

"Are you nuts?"

"Look at me, Joe. I could be sitting in a hotel room in Laughlin, going downstairs every night to gamble my ass off, drink my ass off, and have sex with a different hooker every night. But no, I'm here. Of course, I'm nuts."

"You doing this for America?"

He gave me a sarcastic salute and said, "Apple pie, baby."

"If I told you that I wanted to talk to Zahed, would you be able to get word back to him?"

"That might depend on what you want to discuss." Bronco withdrew another cigarette from his breast pocket and was about to light it up when I answered:

"I want to discuss the terms of his surrender."

He dropped his Zippo and looked up. "Dude, you are a comedian. I'm so glad you came."

"Do you know anything about EMP disruption being used by the Taliban?"

"You're talking *Star Trek* to me. What?"

"Weapons that disrupt electronic devices. Have you seen or heard anything about Zahed's people using weapons like that?"

He lit his cigarette and took a long drag. "Go home, Joe."

I grinned crookedly. "I was kinda hoping we could be friends."

He hoisted a brow. "Well, I do enjoy your humor and sarcasm, but to be honest, you're pretty much screwed here . . ."

I caught up with Shilmani out near the town's old well, which would soon run dry. He was loading water jugs onto a flatbed, and the old man behind the wheel of the idling pickup got out when he spotted me.

Mirab Mir Burki wore cream-colored robes with a long white sash draped over his shoulders. His turban sat very low on his head and drooped at the same angles as his eyes. Bushy gray brows furrowed as he cut off my approach. "If you're going to ask all the same questions, then don't bother," he snapped in Pashto.

"I'm not here to interview you," I said in English.

He looked to Shilmani, who set down his jug and translated quickly.

"What do you want?" asked Burki.

"They're going to build you a new well," I said.

Burki answered quickly in broken English. "They talk and talk. But no well."

"They will dig it soon."

"You are Captain Harruck's friend?"

I gave a slow if somewhat tentative nod, then said,

"I'm very worried about what will happen to the new well, though. We must protect it from the Taliban."

Shilmani translated, and Burki suddenly threw up his hands and climbed back in the car.

I looked at Shilmani. "What did I say?"

Shilmani took a deep breath. "He doesn't want you to protect the well from the Taliban, remember?"

"Yeah," I groaned. "Now I do. I'm in a difficult situation right now. If I can just remove Zahed, then maybe your boss can negotiate for water rights with the next guy."

"He's very upset about the bridge. We have to drive fifteen kilometers to cross at the next one."

"Why do you need to cross?"

"To make our deliveries in Sangsar."

"To the Taliban."

He glanced away. "Scott, I did not contact any of your men. Why are you here?"

"I need you to help me find Zahed."

"It's too dangerous for me right now—especially with the bridge destroyed."

Burki started hollering for Shilmani to finish up. I raised a palm. "It's okay. For now. When you're ready."

His eyes grew glassy before he looked away and finished loading his last jug.

My boots dragged through the sand as I crossed back to the Hummer.

I thought about that little girl who'd been raped and kept pinning that on Zahed so he could remain the "bad guy" in my head. But then I heard Harruck saying that maybe she'd been raped without Zahed's knowledge. Maybe he wasn't linked to a lot of the crime going on. Maybe he would, in the end, do much more for the people than the government could.

After biting my lips and swearing once more, I hopped into the Hummer, and the private took the wheel. "Where to now, sir?"

"They got a bar around here?"

He laughed. "Uh, no, sir."

I smelled something. Gasoline. Burning. I looked at the private. "Get out!"

TEN

I opened the door and looked back to spot a burning rag stuffed into our open fuel tank. Both the private and I ran from the truck just as, in the next second, the tank ruptured under a muffled explosion and flames began rushing up the sides. There was no heaving of the HMMWV off the ground, no cinema-like burst of flames, but black smoke and a thick stench spread quickly as I drew my sidearm and scanned the row of houses behind us.

There he was. A kid, maybe eighteen. Running.

"Come on!" I shouted to the private.

Off to my left, Shilmani and Burki were already on their way off, but the truck stopped. Shilmani bailed out and started after us.

The private, whose name I'd already forgotten, and I

charged down the street after the wiry guy, who sprinted like a triathlete. We reached the next intersection, glanced around at all the laundry spanning the alleyways, and the kid was gone.

"I'm sorry, sir," said the private.

"Yeah. Call it in."

As the private got on his radio, I walked back toward Shilmani, who threw his hands in the air and yelled, "It won't be a big attack now. It'll be this. Every day. Day after day. Until they wear you down."

"I get it," I answered. "But I'm pretty tough. We're tough. They don't torch one Hummer and expect me to go home. No way, pal."

"This is not the war you expected. This will never be the war you expected." He spun on his heel and jogged back toward Burki and the truck, now sagging under the weight of water jugs.

We left the alley and returned to the small crowd watching our truck burn. That was two Hummers I'd lost since coming to Senjaray. I was cursed.

The private told me at least three other patrols had also been attacked in a coordinated effort by Taliban residing inside the village. Shilmani was, of course, right. We'd be harassed and terrorized, even as we tried to help.

I was in my quarters, reviewing all the data Army intelligence had gathered from the aforementioned Predator drones, when Harruck arrived. He stood in the doorway with the XO at his shoulder.

"Next time you head into town, I'll need you with a more heavily armed escort," he said tersely.

"Next time I'll ride my bike. Then again, they might try to blow that up, too."

"Well, there it is, Scott. Before you got here, my patrols were attacked two, maybe three times at the most. Now it's begun."

"You know, I actually considered what you said—putting the word out to Zahed. But I can't even find a way to do that."

"You can't stop trying."

"I want to meet with Kundi and the provincial governor—what the hell's his name again?"

"You mean the district governor. Naimut Gul," he said. "And they call the meeting a *shura*. And there's no reason for you to meet with either of them. I'm taking care of all that, and within the next week I'll have a document signed by all twelve elders."

"You going to get Zahed to sign it, too?"

He just glared at me. "I assume you spoke to Bronco?"

"You think I wouldn't?"

Harruck grinned weakly. "He's no help. I've already tried. His buddies in Kandahar handle our prisoners, and that's about the extent of it. I think they're working on something with the opium trade that goes way over Zahed's head."

"Have you tried tailing him?"

"Who? Bronco? I don't have the resources."

"I do. Maybe I'm not your biggest problem here, Simon. Maybe he is . . ."

"The agency's got its own agenda, no doubt. I even heard a rumor about the NSA having field agents out here, but I think my mission is too damned simple to be on their radar."

"You never know . . ."

I spent about a week laying low and examining imagery from the drones, trying to pick out Zahed among the thousands of people living in his village. Twice, I'd thought I'd seen him in the bazaar, but I couldn't be sure. A half dozen Army intelligence analysts back home were doing the same thing, but I always thought a guy behind a desk somewhere in Virginia might not notice the same things as a grunt in the sand.

My Ghosts continued to pose as regular Army and help with defenses along the defile leading down into Senjaray. Harruck's patrols were harassed by gunfire a few more times, but no one was hurt, and the attackers, after firing a few rounds, fled before they could be caught. I contended that teenagers sympathetic to the Taliban were to blame.

Anderson, along with the Army Corps of Engineers and a half dozen other aid groups, began moving in building materials and breaking ground for the school and the police station, which would be constructed directly north of the defile so that locals could best defend them from attack.

Our replacement Cross-Coms arrived, but I was hesitant to have the guys use them until we pinpointed the source of the disruption.

I assigned Ramirez and Beasley to maintain surveillance on Bronco, who'd been spending a lot of time with landowner Kundi, water man Burki, and a few more of the elders from Senjaray and the other towns in the district.

Bronco hadn't gone over to Sangsar, as I suspected he would. Ramirez told me that the engineers had assessed the damage we'd caused to the bridge and estimated it would take four to six months to complete repairs. We wouldn't be in country long enough to see that happen, I assured him.

One night I took a four-man team into the mountains to run some long-range surveillance via Cypher drone and make another attempt to lure out the Taliban and their disruption devices. Nolan flew the drone in low enough for them to have heard and seen it, but there was no response.

"Ghost Lead, this is Jenkins. Suggest we move in past the wall, over."

The guys were trying to goad me into a close recon of the village, but they always did that. They'd grown restless and longed for the sound of gunfire. They didn't need good intel or just cause—just a clear night and full magazines. I was supposed to think responsibly.

"Negative. Hold position."

"You're not listening to Harruck, are you?" Ramirez whispered to me from his position at my elbow.

"No reason to swat the hornets yet," I said.

"I don't know, boss. Something's gotta give."

I glanced over at him; he was right.

The next morning, Marcus Brown woke me from a sound sleep. There was trouble out in the old poppy field where the Army engineers had proposed to drill the next well.

Kundi was there, causing a big ruckus, as were Harruck, Anderson, and a half dozen other engineers and construction supervisors.

Brown and I drove out there, and Harruck pulled me aside and told me I "wasn't involved."

"That's fine. So I'll just watch. And listen," I told him, my tone making it clear that I wasn't going anywhere.

"So what's the bottom line?" one of the Army engineers asked Kundi.

"That's it," said Kundi, who was waving his hand over the broad area within which the drilling would occur. About fifty yards to the south lay the base of the foothills—a mottled brown moonscape of pockmarks and stones rising up toward orange-colored peaks. "You cannot put the well here. Over there, on the other side of the field, yes."

"But we'll have to drill a lot deeper over there," said the engineer.

Kundi shook his head.

"Why not? Is this some kind of sacred ground?"

Kundi frowned and looked over to Burki, who in turn cast a quizzical glance at Shilmani, whom they'd obviously brought along to translate. He did, and Kundi nodded vigorously. "Yes, yes. God is here!"

I turned to Brown. "You know what God wants? He wants ground-penetrating radar and metal detectors all over this area."

Brown nodded. "Hallelujah."

A couple of days later, Harruck caught up with me in the mess hall and wanted an explanation for my request to have a team go out into the field with radar units and metal detectors. I'd had to put in those requests through regular Army channels, Gordon had told me, so Harruck's interference came as little surprise.

"Kundi's hiding something out there," I said.

"So what if he is?" Harruck asked. "If we instigate him, the agreement goes south."

"We need to have a look."

"We're telling him we don't trust him if we got guys sweeping the ground out there."

"Tell him I lost my watch."

"Don't be an ass, Scott. Who knows why he doesn't want a well over there? Maybe he plans to grow cannabis there, plant cherry trees, who knows? So we move the well to the other side of the field. No big deal. Drill a little deeper. If he's got a bone buried—or an opium stash—out there, I don't want to know about it. Not right now, anyway."

"So you'll look the other way on that, too."

"I'm just taking my time. So should you . . ."

"That a threat? Because we both know where this will go."

"Scott, this whole damned country is full of thugs and gangsters. You'll run out of fingers to point. So let's move on."

Harruck took his tray to another table to join the rest of his officers. Anderson was at a nearby table, and she came over to me and said, "Have you seen the site yet? We're breaking ground for the school."

I shook my head.

"You look finished here. Why don't you come out and take a look?"

I shrugged and followed her outside. She had a civilian car, a Pathfinder, and she drove me over to the construction site, where at least fifty workers were placing broad wooden footers in the ground. Several concrete trucks were parked behind us, and piles of rebar and pallets of concrete blocks were stacked in long rows.

"All these guys that you hired . . . they're from the village?"

"Some from this one . . . some from the others . . . but we've had a little problem, which is really why I brought you out here . . ."

"You weren't trying to soften me up? Turn me into a humanitarian or something?"

"No. I need you to be a killer."

"Excuse me?"

"Oh, I figure you're intel or spec ops or something . . ."

"I'm just an adviser."

"Right . . ."

"How many classrooms in this building?"

"Six. It's going to be beautiful when we're done. And the police station will be right out there. See the stakes?"

I shielded my eyes from the glare and noted the wooden stakes that outlined the L-shaped building.

"Yeah, we're going to build it, and they'll come and blow it back up."

"You mean Zahed?"

I shrugged.

"Maybe not. I think Zahed is forcing the workers to give some of their pay to the Taliban. And I think when the school and the police station open, he'll try to control the police. He'll close down the school, too, but not right away—if he thinks he can make a buck."

"What makes you think he's blackmailing the workers?"

"At the end of the week when they're paid, three men come around, and they form a line. I've seen them giving some of their money to those guys."

"You pay them in afghanis?"

"It's the only way."

"Tell you what? The next time that happens, come find me. I'll have a talk with them."

"Thanks."

"Why didn't you bring this to Captain Harruck?"

"I did. He told me that it wasn't any of my business what the workers did with their money."

"Maybe it isn't."

"I just . . . I don't like it. Feels like we're in bed with the Taliban."

I grinned crookedly and told her I needed to get back.

Three things happened at once when I reached my quarters:

Nolan was telling me I had an urgent call from Lieutenant Colonel Gordon . . .

Bronco had come onto the base and was screaming at me to have my two bulldogs chained up and to stop following him . . .

And a young captain I'd trained myself at Robin Sage, Fred Warris, was standing at my door, waiting to speak to me.

In fact, he was in the same training class that Harruck and I had taught, which I initially thought was a coincidence. I'd heard that Warris had gone on to become a Ghost leader, so his presence outside my billet was suspicious . . . and strange.

I lifted a palm as all three men vied for my attention, but Nolan shouted:

"Sir, like I said . . . it's urgent. Something about your father back home."

ELEVEN

Nolan told me the call had come from the comm center, so I ran across the base, leaving the shouters behind. I reached the center and discovered that Gordon was on a webcam and seated at his desk back at Fort Bragg. He wanted to talk to me "face to face."

I shuddered as I sat before the monitor and tried to catch my breath. "Sir . . ."

His voice echoed off the steel walls of the Quonset hut. "Scott, I'm afraid I've got some bad news about your dad. He's in the hospital, intensive care. He's had a heart attack."

"Who called you?"

"We got word from your sister."

"Wait a second . . ." I cocked my thumb over my

shoulder. "Warris is back at my . . . how long ago did this happen?"

"I'm not sure. Last night? Yesterday afternoon, she didn't say."

"And so you've sent Warris to relieve me?"

"Actually, I didn't. I sent him to serve as a liaison officer between you and Harruck."

"A what?"

"Well, we wanted to limit your contact with Captain Harruck. The general's deeply concerned about the situation there. The idea was that all communications with Captain Harruck would go through Captain Warris. But now I'd understand if you want to take an emergency leave and go home."

A vein began throbbing in my temple. "Sir, I'd like to talk to my sister before I make that decision."

"I understand. And I'm sorry about your dad."

"Sir, I'm sorry about Captain Warris being here. He's too valuable to be a liaison officer."

"Mincing words with the old man?" Gordon smiled. "I know you think this is bullshit, but I gotta do something to defuse what's going on out there. Harruck's pounding hard, so we'll let Warris act as the go-between."

"I don't need a go-between."

"Apparently, you do."

I glanced around, groping for a response, anything, but then I just sighed in disgust. "Yes, sir."

"Why don't you take the leave right now, Scott?"

"Because . . ."

He sat there, waiting for me to finish.

"Because I still want to believe that my mission means something, that capturing the target will make a difference, and that the United States Army hasn't sold its soul to the devil. *Sir.*"

He averted his gaze. "If there's anything I can do on my end to help, just let me know—and I'm not just talking about the mission."

I couldn't hide the disgust in my voice. "All right, sir. I'll be sending some coordinates about a field. I want some satellite imagery on it."

"No problem. Scott, I got your back."

"I know that, sir."

That was a lie to make me feel better. It wasn't his fault, really. As everyone had said—the situation was complicated.

I remained in the comm center and finally got in touch with my sister, who told me Dad was stable, but the heart attack was a bad one and now they thought he had pneumonia. He'd slipped into a coma and was on a ventilator.

"I haven't even seen him yet," Jenn said. "Gerry and I will be flying in from Napa tomorrow. Did you try to call Nick or Tommy?"

"Not yet."

"They should know more. How're you doing? You don't sound too good."

"Just having one of those days."

"Where are you now? Classified?"

"Not really. I'm back in Afghanistan."

"Again?"

"It's the war that keeps on giving."

"Will we ever finish there?"

I snorted. "Maybe next week."

"Why don't you retire, Scott? You've done enough. Do like Tommy. Work with your hands. You love the woodworking just like Dad. And you're good at it, too. Get into the furniture business or something. Gerry says niche markets like that are the future for American manufacturing."

"Tell Gerry thanks for the business analysis. And retirement sounds pretty good about now. Anyway, I'll try calling you tomorrow night. Let me know how Dad's doing. Okay?"

"Okay, Scott. I love you."

"Love you, too.

I sat there, closed my eyes, and remembered sitting next to my father while he read Hardy Boys books to me. Frank and Joe Hardy, teenaged detectives, could solve any mystery, though finding one Mullah Mohammed Zahed was beyond the scope of even their keen eyes and deductive lines of reasoning.

Suddenly, I shivered as I thought of Dad lying in the coffin he had built for himself in our woodworking shop behind the house. He'd been so proud of that box, and the rest of us had thought it so creepy and morbid of him, but then again, it was fitting for him to design and build his "last vehicle," since he'd spent most of his life in the auto plant.

After calming myself, I stood and thanked the sergeant who'd helped me, then left the center.

I was numb. The reality of it all wouldn't hit me till later.

Warris and Bronco were still waiting for me at my quarters. I apologized to Warris and asked him to wait inside my billet while I spoke to Bronco.

"Mind if I listen in?" asked the young captain.

Here we go, I thought. "Yeah, I do." I pursed my lips and looked fire at "the kid."

"Hey, Captain Warris," called Ramirez from the doorway. "Come on, and I'll introduce you to the rest of the guys."

Warris took a deep breath and scratched the peach fuzz on his chin. "All right . . ."

I waited until he was out of earshot, then took a step forward. "See this? Get used to this. This is me in your face."

Bronco frowned. "I didn't figure you for a cowboy."

"I'm not."

"And I figured you've been here before."

"I have."

"Then maybe you have an idea of what you're dealing with here . . . or maybe you don't. Like I said, just lock up your dogs, and you and I will be just fine."

"Okay."

I stepped back from him, took a deep breath.

His eyes narrowed, deep lines spanning his face. "Just like that?"

"Where are you from?"

"I'm a Texas boy. You?"

"Ohio. So you're the cowboy."

"And you're the farmer. I think what you need to do is listen to the CO here. He's got it together. He understands the delicate balance of power."

"Unfortunately, that's not my mission."

Bronco checked his watch. "You got a minute. I've got some friends I want you to meet . . ."

"Who are they?"

"Men who will provide, shall we say, enlightenment."

"Oh, I've got that up to here."

"Trust me, Joe. This will be worth your time."

I thought about it. "I'm not coming alone."

He looked wounded. "You don't trust me. It's not like I work for the CIA or anything. Look, we're just going into the village. You'll be fine. My car's right over there."

"This is important to you?"

"Very."

"You think it'll get me out of your face?"

"I don't know. We'll see."

Maybe I was feeling suicidal, but I told Ramirez to entertain Captain Warris until I returned. I drove off with Bronco to a part of the village I hadn't visited before, where the brick houses were more circular and clustered in a labyrinth to form curving alleys that opened into courtyards full of fruit trees and grapevines. In the distance lay great fields of wheat, sorghum, and poppy, and off to my right was a mine-sweeping team along with their dogs working the field where Kundi said it was okay to drill the well. At least Harruck hadn't been a total fool about that. And for all intents and purposes, he could have those minesweepers check the area where Kundi had refused to drill . . . but he wouldn't . . .

Bronco parked along a more narrow section of the road, then led me onward into the dust-laden shadows of the warren.

Several old men with long beards were trailed by children holding a donkey by its reins. The animal was carrying huge stacks of grass to feed cattle penned up in the south. Farther down the street, I spotted one of Harruck's patrols questioning a young boy of ten or twelve wearing a dirty robe. The soldiers looked like high-tech aliens against the ancient terrain.

We reached a narrow wooden door built into a wall adjoining two homes and were met by a young man who immediately recognized Bronco and let us in. He spoke rapidly in Pashto to the boy, who ran ahead of us.

The courtyard we entered had more grapevines and several fountains along a mosaic tile floor; it was, perhaps, the most ornately decorated section of the village I'd encountered. To our left lay a long walkway that terminated in a side door through which the boy ran. We started slowly after him, and I detected a sweet, smoky smell emanating from ahead.

I was dressed like a regular soldier and still packing my

sidearm. I reached for the weapon as we started through the door, and Bronco gave me a look: *You won't need that.*

"Force of habit," I lied.

Light filtered in from a windowless hole in the wall as we came into a wide living area of crimson-colored rugs, matching draperies, and shelving built into the walls to hold dozens of pieces of pottery, along with silver trays and decanters. Dust and smoke filtered through that single light beam, and my gaze lowered to the three men sitting cross-legged, one of whom was taking a long pull on a water pipe balanced between them. The men were brown prunes and rail-thin. Their teacups were empty. Slowly, one by one, they raised their heads, nodded, and greeted Bronco, who sat opposite them and motioned that I do likewise. He introduced me to the man seated in the middle, Hamid, his beard entirely white, his nose very broad. I could barely see his eyes behind narrow slits.

He spoke in Pashto, his voice low and burred by age. "Bronco tells me they sent you here to capture Zahed."

I glowered at Bronco. "No."

"Don't lie to them," he snapped.

"Yes," said Hamid. "The rope of a lie is short—and you will hang yourself with it."

"Who are you?" I asked him in Pashto.

"I was once the leader of this village until my son took over."

I nodded slowly. "Kundi is your son, and your son negotiates with the Taliban."

"Of course. I fought with Zahed's father many years

ago. We are both Mujahadeen. The guns we used were given to us by you Americans."

"Zahed's men attack the village, attack our base, and rape children."

"There is no excuse for that."

"Then the people here should join us."

"We already have."

"No, I need your son to cut off all ties with the Taliban. There's a rumor that the workers building the school and police station have to give their money to Zahed."

"I'm sure that is true, but Zahed is a good man." Hamid nodded to drive the point home.

"Do you know if he is working with al Qaeda?"

"He is not. He is *not* a terrorist."

"Hamid, forgive me, but I don't understand why your people support him. He's a military dictator."

"He comes from a long line of great men. The people in his village are very happy, safe, and secure. All we want is the same. We did not ask you to come here. We do not want you here. We would be happier if you went home."

"But look at what we're doing for you . . ."

The old man pursed his lips and sighed. "That is not help. That is a political game. I had this very same conversation with a Russian commander many years ago. And he thought just like you . . ."

A muffled shout from outside wafted in from the window. "Hasten to prayer."

Bronco looked at me, and we quickly excused ourselves and headed out while they began their prayers.

Back in the courtyard, the old agent turned to me and said, "Do you see the nut you're trying to crack? These guys are all family, brothers in arms, old Soviet fighters. They bled together. You think they'll go against Zahed? Not in a million years."

"Then what're you doing here?"

"My job."

"Which is . . ."

"Which is making sure you dumb-ass Joes don't fuck this all up."

"What's *this*? Having villages controlled by the Taliban? Little girls raped?"

"What if I told you Zahed works for us?"

"I'd say you're full of it."

"Money talks, right?"

"He's not a terrorist."

"Why should I believe you?"

"Because if you do, you have a better chance of staying alive."

"So now you want to help me stay alive? I thought you wanted me to go home."

"Going home will keep you alive."

"Sorry, buddy, can't help you there."

"Well, then, Captain Mitchell, I guess we should head back to my car."

I froze. "How do you know my name?"

"Captain Scott Mitchell. Ghost Leader. The elite unit that"—he made quote marks with his fingers—"doesn't exist. Top secret. Well, we're the goddamned CIA, and no one keeps secrets from us."

I had to smirk. I'd tried to dig up intel on him and come up empty.

His tone softened, if only a little. "Years ago, you rescued a couple of buddies of mine in Waziristan. Saenz and Vick. They weren't too thrilled about the rescue itself, but you saved their lives—which is why I figure I can return the favor. If you stick around long enough, they'll put a target on your head."

"I've been wearing one of those for a lot of years."

"Look, you must be a smart guy. Go call your boss. Tell him this mission is a dead end. Literally. Get out while you still can."

"Whoa, I'm scared."

"Turn around and look up."

I did. There was a Taliban fighter with an AK-47 standing on the roof, his weapon aimed at my head. And no, he was not hastening to prayer.

"See what I mean? They're giving you a chance to bail, and they're doing that as a favor to me. But if you decide to stay and attempt to carry out your mission, then I won't be able to help you. I want to be very clear about that."

"How can you do this with a clear conscience?"

"Do what?"

"Betray your country."

"Are you serious? Come on . . ." He spun on his sandal and shuffled off.

I glanced back at the Taliban fighter, whose eyes widened above his *shemagh*.

TWELVE

I kept quiet during the ride back to the base, and as I got out of the car near the main gate, Bronco started to say something, but I cut him off. "I appreciate what you're trying to do."

"Then do the right thing. This ain't worth it. And if you think you can beat them with all your fancy gadgets and gizmos, think again, right?"

"Are you helping Zahed?"

"Me?"

"I'm asking you a direct question. Yes? Or no?"

"No."

"Why do I find that hard to believe?"

"Listen to me, Joe. Don't let your ego get in the way here. They gave you a mission, but they don't understand.

They didn't give you orders to upset the balance here."

"Balance?"

"Yeah. You might think this doesn't work, but to these people, it ain't half bad."

I smirked, slammed the door, and walked on toward the gate. The mine-sweeping team was just coming in as well, and I asked a lieutenant at the Hummer's wheel how they'd made out.

The skinny redhead wiped a bead of sweat from his brow and answered, "Looked clear to us."

"Hey, can you do me a favor and sweep the original zone?"

"You mean where we were supposed to drill?"

"Yeah."

"I'm sorry, sir, but I haven't received orders or authorization to do that."

"Yeah, but it wouldn't take long, right? Thirty minutes? I mean you're all loaded up already."

He grinned slyly. "You think those bastards are hiding something out there, don't you?"

"I know they are."

"I'm surprised Captain Harruck didn't ask us to sweep it."

"That hottie Anderson is keeping him real busy now," I said.

"Oh, yeah, she's hot."

"Australian accent. What an ass on her, too."

I was talking his talk. He wriggled his brows. "Tell you what, we'll give it a quick look. I'm sure the CO would make us check it out eventually." He threw his truck in reverse, backed out, and started away from the gate.

Damn, I thought. I didn't think he'd go for it. Now I was committed to the plan.

I watched them leave, then hurried back to our billet, where inside, the guys were doing the usual: reading, playing computer games on their iPods, cleaning weapons, and/or creating battle profiles for our Cross-Coms, something Nolan truly enjoyed. We always killed more time than enemy insurgents. So it was in the Army. Hurry up and wait.

Ramirez and Warris were seated at the small conference table near the door, and Ramirez gave me a sour look as I entered. "What's up?"

"Sir, just had a nice, long talk with Captain Warris. Seems he's in charge now."

"Say again?"

"That's not exactly true," said Warris.

I quickly said, "Gordon told me you're our new—"

"Liaison officer?" Warris finished. "Yeah, well, that was the initial thought. They say they won't relieve you of command, Mitchell, but I've been told that anything and everything you do must be screened through me first, and at that point I'll bring it up with Harruck. I'm sorry. I know how this is. But they were emphatic."

"Outside," I snapped.

"Excuse me?"

"I said, *out . . . side . . .* do you read me?"

"Whoa. You'd better check the registry."

"Not now, *son*."

I opened the door and waited for the punk I had trained, the punk who thought he was replacing me, to head outside, where we could talk away from my boys.

So I'd just learned that my father was in a coma, that my chances of capturing my target were next to nil, and that some kid with barely two combat tours under his belt was going to "oversee" my operation. I guess I'm trying to rationalize or justify what I did next.

Sure, my hand itched with the desire to reach for my pistol and put it to Warris's head—just to teach the cocky bastard a lesson. And my other hand shook with the desire to strangle him until he was blue and his eyes rolled back in his head.

Wasn't it just yesterday that I was standing there with Warris as his evaluator during the training exercise we'd just completed?

I'd been playing the role of a tribal chief and he'd misjudged my character and how I might behave in the heat of battle. Sure, I threw him a few surprises, but he should have been ready for them, and he was not.

Indeed, he'd screwed up big-time and I'd chewed him out, but he'd been humble and had never questioned my authority. I hadn't known his true feelings about that experience and the aftermath . . . until now.

"Mitchell, don't think you can throw your weight around like you did back at the school. Those days are over," he began. "You were the wise old man back there, but over here, it's a whole different ball of wax. Old school doesn't work anymore. We might be Ghosts, but we still have to learn, adapt, and overcome."

I smiled. "So you're an asshole, too?"

His eyes widened. "I could write you up for that."

My grin darkened. "Listen, kid, if you think I'm going to ask your permission for anything I do here—"

The explosion came from the other side of the wall, and I knew in the next breath who was involved: the mine-sweeping team. Had they found a mine? Were they under attack?

My imagination raced through fragmented images of blood-filled sand fountaining into the air and human appendages tumbling end over end . . .

I pointed a finger at Warris, about to say something, then just sprinted away toward the rear wall, where a ladder would take me up to the machine gun nest. From there I'd have a clear view of the field.

The report of automatic weapons echoed the first boom immediately, and it sounded like an all-out gun battle by the time I mounted the ladder.

By the time I neared the gunner's nest, the two guys there were already firing, one on the fifty, the other on his rifle. Two trucks had driven out to the field to join the minesweepers' Hummer, and about twenty Taliban thugs had jumped out and were firing from behind their vehicles.

Still more guys were firing from the foothills, at least six more strung out along a broad reef of stone, muzzles flashing.

There were only five guys out there, huddled around their Hummer and being surrounded by four times as many Taliban.

An RPG whooshed from behind one of the Taliban trucks and struck the Hummer, exploding inside the cab and sending the fireball skyward.

"Get off that gun," I screamed to the kid manning the fifty. I shoved him out of the way and began directing fire myself, first on one Taliban truck, then on the other. My bead drove the Taliban away toward a ditch behind their trucks, tracers gleaming, big rounds thumping hard into steel, glass, plastic, and sending sparks and then gasoline pouring onto the sand.

Within another two heartbeats, both trucks caught fire, and the Taliban now ran toward the foothills. Between me and the guy on his rifle, we cut down five guys making their break.

Someone was shouting my name, and when I glanced below, I saw Ramirez in a Hummer with the rest of the team, including Warris, whose expression seemed neutral. I came back down the ladder and hopped in the flatbed. Ramirez floored it, and we rushed past the open main gate and hightailed it toward the field, along with two other Hummers carrying a pair of rifle squads.

We took sporadic small-arms fire from the hills for a minute, but the rifle squads returned fire and suppressed those guys. We parked behind the burning trucks for cover, then charged out and raced toward the mine-sweeping team.

Six guys were there, every one of them on the ground. I rushed over to the lieutenant I'd spoken to at the gate. He'd been shot in the neck and the arm and was bleeding badly. "Nolan!" I screamed.

The medic rushed over while guys from the rifle squads went to assist the other fallen sweepers.

"It's right next to our truck." The lieutenant gasped. "Right there."

"GET BACK! GET BACK!" Ramirez screamed.

I turned my head.

And it all unfolded in a weird slow motion that people describe during traumatic events. Sometimes they say they felt "outside themselves," as though swimming in an ether while watching the event from far, far away.

Ramirez pointed to the ground, where an insurgent had just rolled over. He'd been shot up badly but was wearing a vest of explosives with a detonator clutched in his right hand.

He'd been waiting for us to get close.

I've always wondered what would've happened if Warris had been within the blast radius. How might the rest of the story have played out?

But Warris was back near our truck, calling it all in, probably talking to Harruck, when I turned and lunged away, toward him, along with the rest of our group.

I hit the ground near the Hummer's right front tire, crawled once on my elbows, and the deafening burst sounded behind me, followed a half second later by blasting sand and shrapnel pinging all over the truck.

Ears ringing, pulse racing, drool spilling out of my mouth, I rolled, then pushed up on my hands and knees as the fire and smoke mushroomed above us.

Guys were screaming, but no noise came from their mouths. I took a few seconds to search out each of my men, and I found them all except for Beasley, who was lying near one of the other Hummers. I rose and staggered over to him.

He was missing a leg, an arm . . . the side of his face. I turned away and gagged.

A few of the others gathered around me, and Nolan and Brown dropped to their knees.

Two more pickup trucks were racing across the desert now, heading toward us from the village. I shielded my eyes from the glare and saw Kundi in the passenger seat of one vehicle and the water man, Burki, at the wheel.

My arms and legs were stinging because I'd taken some minor hits, but I was still too shocked to even look for the wounds. With the fires raging all around us, I shifted around the trucks to where I spotted a shovel stuck in the sand. The lieutenant had found something all right, and one of his guys had begun digging.

I knew that once Kundi arrived—and no doubt Harruck would, too—it'd all be over, so whatever the villagers or the Taliban had buried out there needed to be uncovered—immediately.

I'd just lost a guy, and I'd be damned if it was for nothing. I seized the shovel and began digging like a maniac, sand arcing through the air, while Ramirez came over to me, wanted to know what I was doing.

"Grab the other shovel! Dig now! Dig!"

"Matt's gone! He's dead!"

"I know. Dig!" I cursed at him, kept digging, going down another two feet when my shovel hit something. I dropped to my hands and knees, dug around with my hands, found wood. Maybe a hatch. "Got something! Help me out!"

My gaze was torn between clearing away more dirt and the approaching vehicles.

And now came the heavily armed and armored Hummer carrying Harruck himself, streaking across the sand.

I found the edge of the hatch, a rope pull, and tugged on it. Nothing. Just a creak. Still too much sand holding it down.

Ramirez leaned over and began clearing sand with his hands, and within thirty seconds we began to pull free the wood. It finally gave and we came up with it: a rectangular piece of plywood about three feet by four.

As dirt poured down into the hole, sunlight revealed a wooden ladder and a chamber at least two meters deep. I stole one more look at the pickup trucks and Harruck's ride, then descended the ladder. I turned around and in the shadows saw that the chamber extended another two or three meters to my left and was filled with cardboard boxes and crates.

No, it wasn't some Afghan wine cellar, that was for sure, and what I'd uncovered was both significant and alarming. A creak from the ladder drew my gaze, and Harruck reached the bottom, turned, and let his gaze drift past me.

Another man I didn't recognize reached the bottom of the ladder. He was middle-aged, had a thick mustache, and wore a green uniform with red insignia on the shoulders: AFGHAN NATIONAL POLICE.

"It's all American," I said, my voice cracking. "Probably

a hundred rifles or more. Thousands of rounds of ammo. Grenades, gas masks . . . all stuff that was meant for the national army and the police."

"I agree," said the man in uniform. He looked at me. "I am Shafiq, the new police chief here in Senjaray."

Harruck spun around, his eyes now glassy, his cheeks turning red. "Mitchell, get your people back to the base. We'll take over from here. I'll work this out with Captain Warris."

"Yes, sir."

He blinked hard, coughed, then looked at me, as though to say, *No argument?*

But then, as I ascended the ladder, he threw a verbal punch that I could not ignore: "I'll find out why the minesweepers were here, Mitchell."

"Look around. Kundi's been letting the Taliban store weapons. They figured we wouldn't look here, right out in the open—unless of course we wanted to drill a well. And that's why the old man got so bent out of shape. He was protecting his little cache here."

"He is right," said Shafiq.

I gave Harruck a final look and climbed out, where I shouted for my men to rally back on our Hummer. Nolan had already removed a body bag from the truck, and he and Ramirez had just finished zipping up Beasley. They carried his body to the flatbed and eased it onboard.

The fires were still whipping in the breeze behind us, the scene now like an anthill that had been disturbed. Kundi was out near the hole, throwing his hands in the air, along with Burki, as Warris, Harruck, and the new police chief faced them.

Warris turned away from the group and looked at me, and for just a moment, I thought he longed to be in my boots, not having to deal with any of the crap.

But then, suddenly, he waved me over.

I looked over my shoulder, then back to him. *Me?*

He nodded.

Harruck turned around and cried, "Mitchell? We need you over here right now!"

I liked how he called me Mitchell around everyone else.

"You wanna just take off?" Ramirez asked me. "Screw them all. Screw all these assholes."

"No. You guys take Beasley back. Then get to the hospital and get everybody else checked out. If these idiots want to talk to me, then they'd better strap in and get ready for the ride . . ."

I took a deep breath, winced over a shooting pain in my leg, and marched toward them.

THIRTEEN

I wanted to beat down at least three of the four men in front of me. I already saw them lying unconscious and bloody.

You have to give me some credit for my honesty.

The new police chief hadn't earned my hatred yet.

Kundi and Burki were shouting at Harruck, pointing to the ground, and then gesturing back up to the foothills.

Shilmani was there and came over to me. "The guns belong to Kundi. He says he bought them from the Taliban."

"Do you believe that?"

"It doesn't matter what I believe. What matters is that you can't take them away, but I know you will."

I raised my chin to Harruck. "Well, he'll have to confiscate them, and no one's going to be happy about that."

"He speaks English?" Harruck called out to me.

"Yes, he does. His name's Shilmani. He works for Burki."

"Then come over here and help me translate," said Harruck. "They're talking way too fast for me."

"Do you really need me here?" I asked Harruck.

"Yeah, I do," he said.

Behind us, the rifle squads had finished up with their extinguishers, and the pickup trucks and Hummer were still smoldering. I'd grown far too used to the stench of burning rubber.

While Harruck went back over to Kundi and the water man, with a tense Shilmani forced to go along, I pulled Warris aside. "Now, where were we? Oh, yeah, I was telling you that if you think I'm going to filter my plans through you, you're dreaming. Okay?"

"Looks like you've got some good plans here, too. Pissed off the locals. Got a whole sweeper team killed, one of your own guys killed." He gasped. "All right, that was too far. Sorry . . ."

"Wow, when did you grow a pair?"

He puffed air. "The situation has changed. They brought me in here to clean up an old man's mess. I'm hating it. I resent you for putting me in this situation. And every time I set eyes on you it's an instant replay of that ass-chewing you gave me back at Robin Sage. I still hear about it to this day."

I balled my hand into a fist and drew it back.

He sensed it coming. "Do it. Do us both a favor."

"Mitchell?" cried Harruck.

He kept calling me by name in front of everyone, but who was I to argue at that point? They were going to dump it all on me anyway. I staggered over there like a drunk and didn't realize I was favoring one leg until another pain needled up the hip and into my spine.

"Why were the minesweepers out here?"

I played dumb. "Uh, you told me you were going to find out."

"They had specific orders to sweep the other part of the field."

"Wish I could help you."

"No, you don't."

I stood there, my gaze traveling a thousand miles away.

"Scott?"

I finally looked at him. "What?"

"I want an answer."

"I don't know why the sweepers were here. And I guess you can't ask them. Maybe they got lost. Or maybe they wanted to check out this side of the field, too. Who knows . . ."

"You sent them here, didn't you?"

"Guys, let's get this under control," said Warris.

Harruck looked at him, cursed, then told him to shut the hell up.

Warris recoiled, stunned.

"I need to be with my men," I said, my tone growing even more sarcastic.

"And I need an answer," snapped Harruck.

"All right, let's cut to the chase, then," I said. "I got a four-star behind me and my mission. And I was perfectly within my mission's envelope when I ordered the field searched. I was defending my perimeter and protecting my men. The problem here is mission conflict. All three of us are doing exactly what we should be doing—which is why we've got a problem."

"Why didn't you notify me of what you did?" Harruck asked.

"I would have . . . eventually."

He gave a slight snort. "Well, I got the entire United States Army supporting my mission, Scott. And it *will* take precedence."

Kundi drifted over to me and raised his finger. "You went with Bronco. You talked to my father. You know the right thing to do now. These weapons belong to us. Don't let anyone take them."

"What's he talking about?" Harruck asked.

"I don't know. They smoke a lot of opium here. They forget things."

"This isn't over, Scott. It's just begun."

I winced in pain. The leg again. "I hear you."

"I'll get with you later," said Harruck.

"So will I," Warris added.

I made a face. "I'll be at the hospital if you need me."

I took a detour before getting treated. I went back to the comm center and called Gordon. I updated him and asked for anything he could dig up about Bronco and any connection the spook might have to Zahed and the technology industry. "I think he has something to do with the EMP knocking out our Cross-Coms—if it's EMP at all."

"I'll see what I can do."

"Thanks, and oh, yeah, Warris tells me he's in command."

Gordon's expression turned guilty. "Not exactly."

"Good, then I'm *exactly* in command. Does that make sense to you, sir? Two officers, one in command, the other not exactly in command?"

"Mitchell, we knew how difficult this job could become. That's why we picked you for it. And you're the last guy on earth I thought would be bothered by the politics. Everyone's a bad guy there."

"Even me?"

He nearly smiled. "Even you."

"And you still believe that Zahed is the target and I need to capture or kill him?"

"Absolutely. Without any doubt."

"And what will that change?"

"Say again?"

He'd heard me. He couldn't believe I was asking. I sharpened my tone. "Sir, I asked what will capturing or killing Zahed change?"

"Yours is not to question why but to do or die, soldier."

"Well, if we get him, then that's one less terrorist here, right? Oh, I forgot, we don't have confirmation that he's actually a terrorist."

"He's scum. You said so yourself."

"I did. But frankly, sir, there are too many people attempting to undermine my mission. I'm losing confidence in my ability to complete it and I'm concerned about our contribution to the overall effort here."

"What the hell is that?" he cried. "The Ghosts fear no one! Don't throw that crap at me. You will complete your mission—but if you're telling me right now you want out, I'll relieve you on the spot and give it to Warris."

"He's a yes man for Harruck, so you won't get jack if you give it to him. He's not playing for us anymore, sir. Somebody got to him."

"Are you serious?"

"As a heart attack, sir. And now I'm supposed to go through him before making a move. I'm letting you know right now that I can't do that."

"I understand. Unless your OPORDER changes, you stay on target, all right?"

"Yes, sir."

"Any more news about your dad?"

I told him about my conversation with my sister. We were waiting to hear more.

Most of my guys picked up minor wounds, as I did, and the doctor was able to remove the pieces of shrapnel from my legs and stitch me up. He'd asked about the scar on my chest, as I suspected he would.

All I said was that I'd been serving in the Philippines and been stabbed with a very interesting sword shaped like a Chinese character. The weapon was now resting comfortably in a glass case at an old friend's house.

After all these years, the scar still itched. And I could still see Fang Zhi's eyes as he'd thrust the blade into me. I was just a kid back then. And the missions seemed crystal clear. Ironically, Fang Zhi had questioned his own commanders' orders and become torn over his duty versus the lives of the men in his charge. Though I don't regret killing him, I better understood his position after spending time in Afghanistan.

Back in our billet, most of the guys were sitting on their bunks, staring blankly or rubbing the corners of their eyes and trying not to lose it. We'd been a closely knit team for the past two years. We'd lost a family member.

"We need to get out there tonight and get some," said Ramirez, just after I entered. "They need to pay for killing Matt."

The response was natural, rudimentary, entirely human, and I felt the same—despite its sounding like a knee-jerk reaction of less experienced soldiers.

Hume, Nolan, and Brown began nodding. Treehorn joined them. Jenkins, the biggest, most intimidating guy on the team, started crying. Smith, who was near him, offered a few words of encouragement.

Master Sergeant Matt Beasley had hailed from Detroit, had tooled around the 'hood in a Harley Sportster, and was a latchkey kid who'd made a name for himself in the Army. I don't expect my words to do him justice, and you'll never know him the way we did, but you need to understand how important he was to us.

In recent months Ramirez had become more of my right-hand man, but Beasley had been the first guy to help out, had treated me with respect and had welcomed me into his fold. NCOs could make or break you, and much of my success was due to his experience and guidance. We always had Alpha and Bravo teams, with Charlie team being our "one-man" sniper operation, and Beasley always led Bravo for me. I never once doubted his abilities and knew that if I was ever injured or incapacitated, my guys were in his more-than-capable hands.

I could tell myself that if I hadn't sent the minesweepers out there, then Matt would still be alive. But I wouldn't have made that decision. I would have sent them no matter the risk. Of course, I'd seen a lot of guys die in combat—and a lot of guys die just getting blown up while they were on their way to the latrine. Sometimes I took the blame and just buried it. But I'd been working with Matt for a long time, and though I couldn't help but feel the guilt, I could already hear him telling me not to worry about it. *Sorry, Matt, that's easier said than done.*

The guys, no doubt, wanted payback. So did I. And not just against the Taliban.

Before I could speak, a big Chinook rumbled overhead, shaking the hut with its twin rotors.

"That was fast," said Ramirez, his gaze shooting up to the ceiling.

"Well, that might not be our bird," I said. He was

referring to our having Beasley's body shipped back to Kandahar.

He nodded. "So, are we game on for tonight?"

I raised a palm. "Take it easy. I've got no actionable intel."

"They've been poking around, trying to feel out our new defenses in the defile," said Treehorn. "There are some foothills in the back with a couple of tunnel entrances—or at least they looked like entrances from where I was at."

The door swung open, and in walked Captain Warris.

No one spoke.

"Guys, I'm deeply sorry about the death of Master Sergeant Beasley. I just wanted you to know that. I wanted you to know that I'm a Ghost, too. I'm on this team. Not anyone else's . . ."

Ramirez raised his hand. "Sir, can we talk off the record?"

Warris showed his palm. "Let me stop you there. I already know where this is going."

I glanced sidelong at him. "So do I." There was no mistaking the threat in my tone.

"What's going on here, people, is a philosophical difference between commanders that's playing out in the ditches, and we got stuck with the raw deal. I need to be in the loop on everything because I'm supposed to smooth things over between us and the CO. I don't blame your captain for being upset over what's transpired here, but for now, we just make the best of it until higher gets its head out of its ass."

Oh, he was a clever bastard, all right, I thought. He'd let me have it, then had softened his tone to try to win over the hearts and minds of my guys. He had no idea who he was dealing with . . .

"That's right, everyone," I said, widening my gaze on them. "And as I just told you, we have no actionable intelligence at this time, so we'll continue in our holding pattern. Meanwhile, I'll be in close touch with the colonel to see if they can get us something."

"Very well," said Warris.

We all stood there. You could cut the awkwardness with a bowie knife.

"Uh, yeah, one other thing," I said. "I always bunk with my team, and this billet is full. I'm sure Harruck has room with the other officers."

He snorted. "Right. I'll work that out. And one more thing. Captain Harruck has decided to turn over that weapons cache to the local police chief. Kundi has agreed. They'll use those weapons to begin arming a new police force."

"Interesting," I said. "And where are they recruiting this new police force?"

"From the local villages," Warris answered.

"Which includes Sangsar," I pointed out. "Zahed's hometown."

"I think it's a good compromise, rather than simply confiscating the weapons."

"Before these COIN ops, this wouldn't have happened," I said. "The weapons would be gone. No chance of them falling back into the enemy's hands."

He sighed. "It is what it is." And with that, he hurried out, the door slamming after him.

Not three seconds after he was gone, Treehorn looked at me and said, "All right, Captain. Let's plan this out. Time to rock 'n' roll. And that fool there? He ain't invited to this party."

FOURTEEN

That night after dinner I agonized over an e-mail to Matt Beasley's parents. I would send the message once the Army notified them of his death. He'd never married and was an only child, but he stayed in close contact with his mom and dad, who still lived in Detroit. I'd written letters like that before, but this one was particularly hard because of the admiration and respect I'd had for the man and because of the growing futility—and anger—I felt about the mission.

He died for something. I must've told myself that a million times. He died while protecting his comrades. I was citing him for a Silver Star for distinguished gallantry in action against an enemy. That had to be enough. But it wasn't. My bitterness only made me feel more guilty.

I wanted to get drunk. I knew Harruck had some booze, but I wouldn't go to him now. I even entertained the idea of paying Bronco a visit to see if he had anything stashed.

The boys were going over our gear with a fine-toothed comb. We were heading out for the big show. Guns would boom. Grenades would burst apart. Blood would spill.

That first chopper that'd come in had brought medical supplies and was not scheduled to pick up Beasley's body. A second Chinook finally landed at sundown, and the transfer went off with a very brief prayer service. Warris was there. He never met my gaze.

Now, while we prepared to saddle up, Brown came over as I was packing magazines. "Maybe this isn't such a good idea, sir."

"Second thoughts?"

"Not about the mission or being short one man. It's just . . . we were talking while you were on the computer. No one wants to see you take any more heat."

"Don't worry about it. That's part of my job description. They create officers so they know who to hang when the mission goes down the toilet. I live in the fire. We all do. If Zahed's got some tunnels he's using to move troops forward so they can attack our defenses, then it's our job to find them and destroy them. It's a no-brainer. We're not just out here to get payback for Matt."

"I know. And I don't want to piss you off, but you keep saying this could all be pretty straightforward, and they keep telling us it ain't that simple."

I hardened my gaze. "Maybe we just have to open

our eyes a little more and stop convincing ourselves that this is so complex. What if it's not? What if these people are just playing us all for fools? Turning us against each other, so they can get what they want? Maybe . . . it's as simple as that."

He shrugged.

Yes, I was trying to convince myself more than him. He didn't buy it, and really, neither did I. But we needed to trick ourselves into thinking it was good guys versus bad guys, especially in the hours before we committed. If we started thinking about the millions of dominoes we might kick over with every move, we'd become paralyzed.

I slapped a hand on his shoulder. "Thanks for having my back. You always do."

He gave a slight nod. "What's the plan to get off the base?"

I beamed at him. "We're Ghosts. I think we can come up with something."

"Yeah, we'll figure it out."

At about two A.M. we piled into a Hummer and drove straight for the main gate. I had no clever plan. I just told the sentries we were relieving a security detail at the construction site. I showed him the fake credentials that identified us as regular Army personnel. We weren't on the guy's list. I argued. At the sound of my first four-letter word, we got ushered through. It wasn't as glamorous as sneaking off the base, but it did work.

Or at least I'd thought it had.

After we left, the son-of-a-bitch guard called the XO, who in turn woke up Harruck.

We left the truck and driver at the edge of the construction site and talked to the rifle squad posted there. I told them we were on a classified operation but if they heard gunfire and explosions, they were welcome to join us. The sergeant in charge grinned and said, "Is it bring your own beer?"

"Hell, no. We supply everything."

He smiled. "I like the way you guys roll."

We hustled off into the desert, the sand billowing into our eyes, the sky a deep blue-black sweeping out over a moonless night.

The foothills lay directly ahead, cast in deep silhouette, and I strained to see the tunnel entrances that Treehorn so fervently believed were there.

At the base of the first hill, with our boots digging deeply into the soft, dry earth, Ramirez called for a sudden halt, and then we dropped to our bellies, tucking in tightly along a meandering depression. Someone was approaching.

Actually two figures.

I whispered into my boom mike to activate my Cross-Com. The hills lit up a phosphorescent green as the HUD appeared and the unit made contact with our satellite. Within the next two seconds my entire team was identified by green diamonds and blood types via their Green Force Tracker chips.

So, too, were the two men approaching, and I gave a

deep sigh as I read the names. Warris had come along with a private, probably his driver.

"Ghost Team, this is Ghost Lead. Friendlies approaching. Hold fire."

"Roger that," said Ramirez. "But are you sure about that?"

I grimaced over the remark, but yeah, I understood how he felt.

Warris, unbeknownst to me, was wearing a Cross-Com and had linked to our channel. He'd been clever enough to research the access codes. He'd heard Ramirez's remark and suddenly said, "Ghost Team, this is Captain Warris. I'm coming up. And if I were you, I'd be sure about holding fire."

Ramirez shifted over to me, covered his boom mike, and issued a curse.

I saw his curse and raised him two.

Warris, crouched over, slipped up to the depression and dropped down beside us, with his private doing likewise.

"Ghost Team, this is Ghost Lead. Turn off your Cross-Coms and huddle up."

They immediately complied. I didn't want anything recorded at this point.

"How you doing, Scott?" my former trainee began, as though he were about to offer me a beer. I sensed, though, that he was speaking through clenched teeth.

"What's up, Fred?"

"Harruck sent me out here to relieve you of command and bring the team home."

I pretended I didn't hear him. "Maybe we shouldn't've slipped off the base, but you know what? I'm just too lazy and just don't care anymore. We're heading up to find, fix, and destroy the enemy. We've got enough actionable intel to justify this raid. If we let 'em keep moving in and doing overwatch of our construction site, they'll set up their offensive, and all of Harruck's work will go to hell. So you need to go back now and tell him that. Tell him we're out here to save his ass."

"You can tell him yourself. We'll contact him right now."

"I don't have time for this—"

"Captain, I'm here to relieve you of command."

"Okay, but can you give me about an hour?"

Warris's voice came in a stage whisper, but he would've shouted if he could: "This is serious shit, asshole! I'm relieving you of command!"

"I'm sorry, sir," said Ramirez, butting in and ignoring my glare. "But we don't recognize your authority here, nor will we obey your orders."

"You think you speak for the rest of them?" Warris asked.

Ramirez looked at the others. "Oh, yes, sir. I know I do. We won't follow you. Trust me."

I shook my head. "Freddy, the problem is you're trying to play by the book with people that don't exist."

He looked lost for a second, then said, "I'm not going anywhere."

"That's fine. You can wait for us."

"No, I'm coming on this mission."

"Negative. I need you to return to the FOB, and bring your driver along."

"Excuse me? I'm here to relieve you."

"I am *not* relieved."

"You've got no authority to refuse me." He glanced around at my team. "Captain Mitchell has been relieved of command and will be returning to the base with my driver."

"Guys, just ignore him. I'm in command. Prepare to move out."

"Scott—"

Now *I* was talking through my teeth. "You listen to me, and you listen good. Each one of my guys has got two rifles. One's their favorite toy. The other's an AK confiscated from the Taliban. Do you understand what I'm saying?"

"That I could accidentally get shot? You gotta be kidding me. You don't threaten me with that. We're on the same team, and you just need to suck it up. I'm in. You're out."

He told the private to hold his position and wait for us.

Ramirez whispered to me, "The hell with it. Let him come. We can babysit. He could get hurt . . ."

I lay there, panting. If I abandoned the mission, I'd still go home to be hung. So the hell with it. We were going.

Biting back a curse, I got to my feet. "Guys, you will ignore any and all commands from Captain Warris. Moving up. Let's roll."

I looked at Warris. "What're you going to do now, Freddy? Phone a friend?"

"No, I'm still coming along. I'll document all this insubordination, and by the time I'm done, you *and this entire team* will go down."

Then he told me to fuck myself and broke off with Jenkins, Hume, and Brown, our Bravo team. I took Ramirez, Nolan, Smith, and Treehorn. I put Treehorn on point. Bravo shifted off to the north side. I told them to activate their Cross-Coms and to watch what they said—we were being recorded.

Ramirez looked back at me, as if to say: *Oh my God, what's happening now . . .*

I just steeled my gaze and got back on the horn. "Brown, this is Ghost Lead, over."

"Here, Ghost Lead," he said, as I patched into his Cross-Com's camera and watched them scurrying along the foothill, climbing higher along a lip of gravel and dirt.

"Stay in touch."

"Roger that."

Warris didn't know it, but Brown was in command of that team. He would be reporting to me, and I knew that Hume and Smith would fall in line.

Ramirez hadn't lied. The military might have been full of backstabbers and ass-kissers, but my men were fiercely loyal—every last one of them. They would do anything for me. I mean *anything.*

I kept close to Treehorn as we ascended, hunched over, our computers scanning the mountainside for enemies.

Clear so far. We climbed for another fifteen minutes, making good progress, when Treehorn called for a halt, and I zoomed in with my camera to see the ragged depression in the mountain, like a bruise against the stone.

"Cave entrance, right there," reported Treehorn.

"We got one, too," said Brown.

"I'll report that," cried Warris. "We've got a tunnel entrance. Can't get a good read on it, but I'm guessing it runs deep. Could connect to your entrance, over."

"Roger that. If we get in too deep, we might lose contact with the satellite."

"Understood. Recording. Let's do it."

I hadn't mentioned anything to Warris about our Cross-Coms' being knocked out during our first night raid, but I'd assumed he'd read it in my report. I wondered if being inside the tunnel would protect the gear from whatever the Taliban was using against us.

The answer would come shortly.

As in the second we entered the caves.

It all went dead. Again. Everything. High-tech gear reduced to crap.

We'd taken along some old MBITR radios, standard-issue stuff as backup, and strangely enough they still worked. Maybe they had thicker casings and were better shielded from EMP waves or other countermeasures.

We had penlights taped to our rifles. Even as I turned mine on, the first wave of gunfire stitched across the mountain. They were coming at us from outside, from above the entrance.

"Move, move, move!" I screamed, driving the group into the tunnel.

Treehorn rushed forward. He hadn't taken along his sniper's rifle; instead he had a terrifically loud shotgun, and when it boomed, sending pellets into the face of the Taliban guy rushing toward us, I dropped to one knee and crouched tight to the dusty rock wall at my shoulder.

"Ghost Lead, this is Brown! We are taking fire inside and out, over!"

"Roger that," I said. "Move in. Flush them out!"

"He's right," said Warris. "Let's move in!"

Like I needed his confirmation.

The tunnel was barely two meters high, about three meters wide, but it grew more narrow as we stepped over the guy Treehorn had shot.

Pops and booms echoed from somewhere deep in the tunnel, telling me that yes, Bravo team's tunnel was, in fact, connected to ours.

"Look at this," said Ramirez, crouching down beside the dead guy. In the dirt lay an odd-looking rifle with a funnel-like barrel.

"I know what that is," said Nolan. "HERF gun for sure. Like EMP. High-energy radio frequency. Just what I thought. Works better in close quarters. They must've been very close when they zapped us the first time."

"But look at this thing. Seems homemade," said Ramirez, lifting the gun up to his penlight.

"They didn't make 'em up here, or even in the town," I said. "Somebody's supplying them—somebody who knows they'd need them. Like the CIA. Pack up that gun. Let's go!"

Ramirez shoved the gun in his backpack, and we began to work our way along a curve that dropped sharply. I had to hang on to the wall to prevent sliding forward for a few meters.

Ramirez was pulling up the rear now, keeping his rifle pointed back while shuffling to keep up with us, the thin beams of our penlights playing like lasers over the walls.

Treehorn remained up front, ready to blast the hell out of anyone who tried to confront us. He stole a quick glance back at me, and I'd never seen his eyes as wide. The sergeant was wired to the moment, and I had every confidence in him.

"Mitchell, this is Warris. We dropped two tangos. Picked up a gun of some sort. EMP, over."

"Same here," I answered. "Keep moving in, but call out if you see our lights."

"Roger that."

I noticed how Warris wouldn't refer to me as "Ghost Lead." What a fool . . . I wondered why he hadn't called Harruck to "tell on me" yet. Then I thought, he's just a kid and wants a little action, that's why he's delaying the call. What a bigger fool!

And then, before he could say contemplate anything else, Ramirez opened fire behind us. We hit the dirt, and I whirled back, along with Nolan, to add our fire and drive back a pair of fighters who vanished behind the curve.

"Keep moving!" I ordered.

"They're still back there," warned Ramirez.

"That's why you keep watching," I said.

The air grew dank as we descended even farther. Trash appeared along the walls—discarded wrappers, even some bottles of soda, along with MREs, which had obviously been stolen from U.S. and coalition forces.

"Looks like an intersection coming up," said Treehorn. "Two tunnels."

"Warris, do you see us?"

"Not yet."

"Do you see an intersection?"

"Yeah, we do."

"All right, we're coming at you. Hold fire."

I think we got another ten meters, maybe fifteen before it all went to hell.

The two guys dogging us from behind attacked again, and Nolan and Ramirez were on their bellies, cutting loose with salvos that ricocheted off the back walls. I dove forward, just behind Treehorn, who in turn spotted two guys rounding a corner from the intersection.

Before they could open fire, he blasted them with his first shot, just as Warris and Brown were coming up behind them.

Warris clutched his leg, having caught some of the buckshot, then looked to his right and saw something. I lost him for a second in the shadows as his gun rattled and then Brown appeared for a second in my light and was as quickly lost.

But then his shout came loudly up the tunnel: "Grenade!"

The Taliban were suicidal fools to drop a grenade

inside the tunnel, and as Brown dove back from where he came, the blinding flash made me blink and drop my head. I gasped as the explosion tore through the tunnel ahead, my ears ringing loudly, the shattering rock and streaming sand barely discernible as debris pelted us and Ramirez and Hume kept firing to the rear.

I lifted my head, my face already covered in dust, the beam of the penlight thick with more dust as the ground reverberated a second time . . . and then Brown once more hollered, "Cave-in! Get back! Cave-in!"

FIFTEEN

I'd read some accounts of Marines and other Special Forces operators who'd dropped into Afghanistan just after 9/11. They'd discussed how difficult it was to flush the enemy out of the labyrinth of caves and tunnels that lay along the border with Pakistan. One Special Forces operator from the storied group known as "Triple Nickel" had described the tunnels as "great intestines of stone" that were, in fact, "part of the innards of some ancient warrior who'd died millennia ago."

That was damned poetic. I would describe them as damp, dark holes that made perfect burial grounds, like the catacombs of Europe. They smelled and foretold of death and were the setting of many of my nightmares.

Ramirez ceased fire, reached out, grabbed something, threw it. I realized those fools behind us had tossed in another grenade. I didn't know where Ramirez got his reflexes, but I wasn't complaining.

"Get down!" I screamed, but my order was lost in the second explosion, this one much louder, the debris striking more fiercely as up ahead, a flurry of gunfire also vied for my attention. Smith, Brown, and Hume were advancing toward the intersecting tunnel where the explosion had occurred, and they were engaging more troops.

The air grew thicker as the ceiling collapsed and heavy rocks and earth poured in from above. Ramirez rose and began running back as pieces of the ceiling the size of truck tires came down and split apart across the floor. The stench of the explosives and the choking dust had me coughing, along with the others, and my eyes burned as I turned forward and called, "Brown? Brown?"

I couldn't hear myself screaming through the echo of the explosion. I finally staggered to my feet, and, dragging a gloved hand along the wall for balance, I moved forward to find Brown, Hume, and Smith about four meters down the intersecting tunnel to my right. A wall of rocks and sand blocked the entire path, and the guys were covering their faces and letting their penlights play over the obstruction.

"Where the hell's Warris?" I asked, swinging around.

Brown shook his head.

"What?" I cried, growing even more tense. "Is he dead?"

"I don't know. He was on the other side when the grenade went off."

I got on the radio, tried to call him, nothing. "Wait," called Smith, pressing his ear against the rock while Ramirez and Nolan approached to cover us.

"I hear something," Smith added. "Sounds like him! He's calling for help."

"Are you sure?" I asked.

"Yeah, I'm sure."

"All right, start digging," I said.

"We'll cover the back tunnel," said Ramirez, waving Nolan after him.

"Do it," I said.

"Bad night," said Brown, grabbing the first large rock he could find and groaning as he lifted and threw it aside. "Very bad night."

"We'll be here for hours," said Smith. "And they're probably massing for us outside."

"We'll need backup," Brown said.

"You guys are right," I said. "Go back down there, tell that private we need a digging team out here and two rifle squads. Then get right back."

As they were about to leave, Ramirez and Nolan opened fire on the tunnel ahead, and I remembered only then that all other exits had been blocked by the cave-ins. There was only one way out.

Brown realized it as well and said, "Guess, we ain't going anywhere . . . yet!"

"All right, everybody, mask up!" I said. I didn't like

it, especially within the confines of the tunnel, but the Taliban guys were ready for us, so we had no choice. I fished out a couple of CS gas canisters and let them fly down the tunnel.

We waited as the gas hissed into a thick fog, and then we rushed forward, enveloped in the smoke, Brown and Smith covering our rear, Treehorn and Ramirez up front.

"How deep does this go?" I said aloud, though no one could hear me. We ventured on at least another hundred meters, then turned to our left and saw an opening and the faint stars beyond.

Treehorn and Ramirez moved up front and signaled to me that they'd check it out.

I gave them a thumbs-up and kept back with the others. They reached the opening, a narrow leaf-shaped break in the stone, and shifted warily forward. Both men vanished for a second, then Ramirez ducked back inside and waved us on.

We emerged on the mountainside facing Sangsar, and all the booming from inside the mountain had not gone unnoticed. Lights burned from the houses nearest the wall, and two pickup trucks loaded with Taliban were already bouncing across the desert, en route to us. I ripped off my mask, as did the others, and then said, "There's got to be another entrance. Warris must be looking for it, too."

I whirled around, faced the ridgeline, got my bearings, and waved the rest of the team up, toward a cluster of outcroppings that looked promising.

We got there in a hurry—because several Taliban had already reached the ridge just below us and had opened fire. With dirt popping at our knees and making us grimace, we reached a broad wall of stone and ducked behind it. I waved my team on, one after another, and we all huddled behind the rock.

"We got a problem," said Ramirez. "Even if we find the other entrance, we already know it's a dead end. And if we all go in there, they could pin us down, drop in some grenades, and that ruins my plans to marry a supermodel."

"Mine, too," said Smith with a wink.

"All right, Joey, me and you go up and look for the entrance," I told Ramirez. "The rest of you set up here along the rocks. See if you can hold them for a just a couple of minutes."

I rushed forward with Ramirez on my heels. We ascended through a steep passage that reminded me of a vacation I'd taken to go hiking in Sedona, Arizona. Ramirez spotted the tunnel exit before I saw it, and we both came across the top of the next outcropping and headed toward a narrow seam in the rock. We got within ten meters when a Taliban fighter appeared.

Again, Ramirez put his lightning-fast reflexes to work and gunned down the guy before I could blink. We rushed forward now, coming around him, and came up on both sides of the entrance. I looked at him, raised three fingers. On three, two, one—

We rolled away from the wall and rushed inside, him

dropping to one knee to shoot low, me on my feet, standing tall to strike high.

And there, standing before us, like a lost puppy, was Warris's private, the kid who'd driven him up to the mountain. He clutched his pistol and just looked at us, trembling. He had to be just eighteen, and thinking about buying his first shaving kit . . .

"Dude, what the hell are you doing here?" asked Ramirez.

He lowered his weapon. "I heard the shooting. I came up to help."

"You had orders to stay there," I said.

"Didn't seem like anybody was obeying orders."

I snickered. "What's your name?"

"It's right here on my uniform."

I ripped off the Velcro-attached name patch and read the word: Hendrickson, then shoved the patch back at him. "All right, junior, you just got promoted to Special Forces. Did you see Captain Warris on your way in here?"

"No, sir."

I cursed. "But this tunnel cuts through the mountain?"

"It does, sir."

"Any bad guys in there?"

He almost laughed. "Not when I came through, sir."

"All right." I was about to turn back to Ramirez when a series of explosions rocked the mountain, and just a few seconds later the rest of the team came sprinting up toward the entrance.

A breathless Nolan reported, "RPGs. They're moving

in fast. We need to move now! Got twenty or thirty coming up. It's going to get hairy, boss."

"Gotcha. Everybody? This is Private Hendrickson. He's in charge. Where do we go to get out of here, Private?"

The kid looked around and nearly passed out from the weight I'd just dumped on his shoulders. After blinking hard he finally said, "Follow me."

We dropped in behind him, as the shouts of the Taliban rose behind us. Ramirez set two more CS canisters just outside the entrance to delay them, while Brown and Smith hung back to plant a small amount of C-4 on a remote detonator, which they confirmed still worked.

Once they rejoined us about fifty meters down the tunnel, they detonated the charges. Twin thunderclaps shook the walls around us, and I imagined a cave-in that would help in our escape.

We came around another long curve and reached an intersecting tunnel. "You go down there?" I asked Ghost Leader Hendrickson.

"No, sir."

"Ramirez?" I called. "The rest of you hold here."

We hustled down the intersecting tunnel, which grew so narrow at one point that we had to turn sideways just to pass through. Then it opened back up and filtered into a broad chamber. To our left was a pile of rocks and dirt—the cave-in where Warris had been. We were on the other side now. No sign of him. My light played over the floor. Nothing. No evidence.

"Well, he ain't here," groaned Ramirez.

I tried calling Warris on the radio again. No answer.

Consequently, I stood there, wiping dirt off my nose and cheeks. "How am I going to explain this shit?"

"When we get out, we need to get on the same page," Ramirez said. "And we need to buy the kid."

"What're you talking about?"

"He overheard everything. He's a problem."

"Whoa, Joey."

"Scott, Harruck wants to burn you. Warris is MIA. This is way out of control."

"I know. Let's just get out of here, then we'll talk to the kid."

"All right, but what happens if he decides to burn us, too?"

"We're not going to do anything to him. Don't even imply that, all right?"

"If you say so . . ."

We returned to the intersection, where Treehorn told me he'd heard voices from the tunnel behind us. The C-4 had not sealed up the tunnel, damn it. The Taliban were climbing over the debris and coming.

"Get some more ready," I told him. "We'll blow the exit."

The group charged forward, with the kid leading the way. He burst through the exit and quickly turned left, coming along a very steep ridge, where he almost lost his balance and tumbled down the mountainside. For a dark moment, I wished he had.

Treehorn and Brown planted the charges. We rushed along the ridge and ducked behind a jagged section of rock that shielded us up to our shoulders.

"Just wait for the first guy because you know the rest are right behind him," I said.

Too late. Three guys came bursting out of the entrance, and while Ramirez and Nolan took them out, Brown triggered the explosives. A chute of rock-filled smoke lifted as the deep boom resounded, the vibration working its way into my boots.

"Aw, hell," said Smith, pointing up at the ridge lines high above the cave.

At least twenty or more fighters had already cleared the summit and were coming down. They obviously knew a shortcut to get up there, and as they ascended they opened fire on us, the incoming dropping like hail and forcing us tight against the rocks.

About fifteen meters to my left were Ramirez and the kid, huddled against the rock. And I'll never forget how it all looked—

The silhouettes of my two men as Ramirez popped up from behind cover and cut loose with two salvos from his own AK-47 . . .

The lightning-bug flashes of muzzles drawing a jagged line across the mountain . . .

And the next moment, as I blinked and looked again at Ramirez, who pulled back from the rock, fired up at the Taliban again, then turned his rifle on Private Hendrickson.

My mouth opened.

I thought for a second that Ramirez had seen me. Everyone else was engaging the enemy now, complete chaos all around us, with only me, the conscience of our team, shouldering the stone and watching as Ramirez pulled the trigger and put three rounds in the private's back, dropping him instantly.

He immediately huddled to the rock and screamed, "He's hit! Hendrickson is down! Nolan! I need a medic! Medic right now!"

I dodged over to Ramirez's position and rolled the kid onto his side. He didn't move. I checked for a carotid pulse. No, he was dead.

"I'm sorry. I tried to cover him."

I was beginning to lose my breath.

My men were fiercely loyal, all right.

Agonizingly loyal.

Another spate of incoming drove both of us to the rock, and Ramirez faced me with a blank stare.

SIXTEEN

I thought I knew everything about Master Sergeant Joe Ramirez. His parents had emigrated from Mexico and had held fast to the old ways. They'd raised him in North Hollywood, California, and had kept him on the straight and narrow path. He was a devout Catholic, an altar boy, a Boy Scout.

In his teenaged years he'd become a computer hacker and had almost gotten busted for identity theft, but he'd been taken under the wing of a detective who'd persuaded him to join the Army. His older brother Enrique had enlisted, and I'd met him—nice guy, quiet demeanor, and a good soldier, as reported by many of his superiors. Ramirez followed in his footsteps.

It wasn't long before he was tapped for Special Forces,

and he now had more experience in Afghanistan than any of us. Two tours as an Army Ranger plus some shorter ops. Old man Gordon had handpicked the kid himself to become a member of the Ghosts, and Ramirez had done a great job when I'd taken him to Waziristan and, later on, into China. He was one of the most levelheaded guys I'd ever served with and the last person on earth I'd thought capable of murder. He was the epitome of an outstanding soldier.

And he'd become my good friend.

"Joey." I gasped.

"I'll get him out of here," he said. "Just have them cover me. I can see the Hummer down there!"

Before I could do anything, he scooped up Hendrickson's body and started shakily down the mountain. Nolan came running up and cried, "Wait!" He was already sloughing off his medic's pack.

"Too late," I said. Then I raised my voice. "Everybody, fall back! Fall back! Let's go!"

We started a serpentine descent, following the ridge lines and those areas where the outcroppings provided some slight cover from the Taliban behind us.

Treehorn and Brown covered our withdrawal, retreating only when they spotted a guy shouldering an RPG. They vacated their position only seconds before the rocket struck, heaving fiery flashes and pulverized rock.

At the foot of the hills we were met with a curious sight: About a half dozen Afghan National Army troops had driven up in a truck, and beside them was Bronco. He waved me over and cried, "Let's go, Joe!"

"What the hell are you doing here?"

"We're the cavalry. We'll cover you."

"How'd you know we were out here?"

He rolled his eyes, then climbed back into the truck as the Army troops dropped to the ditches and began firing on the advancing Taliban.

"Why are you doing this?" I asked.

"I like it when people owe me," he said.

The rest of my guys came darting over and, using Bronco's truck for cover, returned a few more salvos before breaking off to make one last run for the Hummer.

Two more vehicles pulled up, a big Bradley and another Hummer, and rifle squads bolted out: the security team from the construction site.

I talked to the sergeant there, handed over the fight, and jogged back to the Hummer. The earlier wounds in my leg began throbbing again.

Harruck confronted me before I could climb out of the Hummer.

I barely heard what he was barking about. I just spoke over him: "Warris was cut off from us during a cave-in and he's missing. He might've been captured by the Taliban."

"Say again?"

I did. His jaw fell open, then: "Well, isn't that goddamned convenient for you!"

"My mission is to capture Zahed. I can and will do that without interference. Our mission tonight was completely within my rights."

"I sent him up there to relieve you of command."

"I know. But we got attacked." Not exactly a lie. Not the full truth, either. "His driver was also killed on the way out of there."

"And what did you gain?"

I looked back to the Hummer, and Nolan got out, carrying one of the HERF guns.

"This is how they've been knocking out our Cross-Coms. Also, I'll be sending you a rough map of the tunnel complex they've got up there. We need a team to blow it up, otherwise they'll plan their offensive against your school and police station."

He studied the HERF gun, then faced me. "Are you really trying to help me?"

"Simon, I understand where you're coming from. I don't have to like it. With the all crap going down in Helmand, I bet Gordon can't spare another guy to come out to relieve me. If they got Warris, you need to let me work on that, work on taking out Zahed."

"And we're back to square one, with you stirring up the nest and me crying foul."

"I don't know what to tell you. I'll be filing my report. You can read it. You can suggest I'm relieved of command all you want. But I'll fight you all the way. Keating knows I get results. Hard to argue with that."

I turned around and walked back toward the truck before he could reply.

At the comm center, Colonel Gordon told me that they'd received a good signal from Warris's GFTC. Every Ghost operator had a Green Force Tracker Chip embedded beneath his arm. The GFTCs were part of the Identification, Friend or Foe (IFF) system so we knew who was who on the battlefield. Warris was being moved, but the colonel said that Warris's chip suddenly went dead. Either they'd taken him to a deep cave where the signal was blocked, or they'd cut the chip out of his arm and found a way to deactivate it. If they knew about our Cross-Coms, they might've known about our chips . . .

Back in our billet, I collapsed onto my rack and just lay there a moment, staring at the curved metal ceiling. The guys were removing gear, groaning about aches and pains, and recounting moments from the battle. I glanced over at Ramirez, who was sitting on his bunk, shirtless, with his face buried in his palms.

We both knew the talk was coming.

But all I wanted to do at that moment was sleep. So I draped an arm over my eyes and found myself back in the tunnels, as Warris confronted me with a band of Taliban at his shoulders.

"See, Scott, you never know who's working for who. I work for the Taliban. And so does Harruck. In fact, the whole Army's in bed with them, everyone except you. You're the only idiot who didn't get the memo."

I wrote my report in the morning, hating myself with every word I typed. I lied about the time of the attack and about me resisting Warris's attempts to take my command.

But more important, I lied about Private Thomas Hendrickson's death. He'd been shot point-blank in the back, but no one would question that. An AK-47 had been used, and seasoned Special Forces operators were vowing that the kid had been in the wrong place at the wrong time. Hendrickson was a private, a cherry, with barely any experience. That he'd gotten killed would hardly raise a brow. I couldn't help but do some morbid research on the kid. And what I'd learned just broke my heart.

After a few conversations with the others, I felt certain that no one else had seen Ramirez shoot the kid.

At breakfast, Ramirez avoided me like the plague, and then, afterward, I asked him to join me on a ride up to see the construction site.

Oh, he knew it was coming.

"Maybe we should talk about this elephant in the desert," he said.

I couldn't help but snort. "The elephant? You mean the one being ridden by a murderer?"

He slammed the door on the Hummer, and I drove. We left the main gate and headed about halfway down the desert road, and then I pulled off to the side, and we just sat there in the growing heat. I was reminded of the times when my dad was mad at me and would take me out for a drive and a talk. In fact, it dawned on me only then that I was doing the same thing . . .

After breakfast, I'd put in a call to my sister and brothers and was still waiting to hear back on Dad's condition. I could only pray for an improvement.

"Scott, before you say anything, can I talk?" Ramirez's voice was already cracking.

"Go ahead."

"As soon as you started having problems with Harruck, he came to me and Matt, set up a conference call between us and the battalion commander. Basically, they were trying to recruit us as spies and allies. They were trying to convince us that our mission was going to do more harm than good here."

I chuckled darkly. "I'm not surprised."

"You know what we told them to do with that offer . . ."

"Good."

"But still, they put a lot pressure on us. I don't think Matt ever caved in, but I know they're gunning for you and gunning hard. Not sure if you've made an enemy upstairs or what, but I started thinking that maybe this whole mission to get Zahed is just a way for them to get rid of you."

"Whoa, now you're getting paranoid."

"Scott, I don't think I could do this without you. If you're gone, I'd just drop out of the Ghosts. I would. I wouldn't trust anyone else."

"That's crazy. But Joey, listen. None of this is justifying what you did—and do you really understand what you did?"

He lowered his head. And my God, he began to cry.

Special Forces operators never say quit. And we certainly do our best NOT to cry.

"He was going to burn us," he said. "I could tell. I just snapped. And I did it."

"Did you know anything about him? About how his dad fought in the first Gulf War, about how he'd come from a long line of military guys? Did you know he had a girlfriend who's pregnant?"

Ramirez shook his head, turning away from me to sink his head deeper into his hands.

"You know, being in Special Forces is one thing. But we were chosen to be in the Ghosts because we don't just talk about the tenets of being a great soldier, we live by them. We live by the creed. And I quote, 'I will not fail those with whom I serve. I will not bring shame upon myself or the forces.'"

I guess hearing myself say those words was a little too much to bear. I screamed at the top of my lungs, "JESUS CHRIST, JOEY! JESUS CHRIST! WHAT THE HELL DID YOU DO?"

"I don't know! I don't know! Please don't turn me in. I got nothing else. You know that. This is my entire life. Scott, please . . ."

"I lied in my report. Do you realize the position you've put me in? I need to call Gordon and tell him you killed that kid to protect me."

He backhanded tears from his eyes, then looked at me, trying to catch his breath. "Why do you need to do that?"

"Because I swore an oath. Because you swore an oath."

"If you go to them, they'll make me talk. They'll make me tell everything. You refused to be relieved. That'll come out. And we'll both be burned."

"I know."

"Then what the hell, Scott?"

"Joey, I just can't believe any of this . . ."

"How about I make it easier for you to stay quiet. You can blame it all on me. I'm telling you right now, that if you turn me in, you'll be hanging from the rope next to me. I'll make sure of that, not because I want revenge, but because you're too damned good of a leader for the Ghosts to lose. Don't you get it, Scott? I killed a guy for you! You can't just throw your life away now! I killed a guy!"

"I don't know what I'm going to do. I really don't. I thought I had enough going on already. I didn't expect this. Not from you, Joey. Not from you."

"I'm sorry."

"Tell that to the kid's family."

SEVENTEEN

We returned to the road and reached the construction site about ten minutes later. A tent village had been erected behind the half-built school, and there I noted about twenty or thirty children seated in neat rows on blankets and listening as two teachers took turns reading to them. The kids were surprisingly attentive, still wiping their noses and scratching themselves, but their gazes were fixed on the storytellers. Many of them had no shoes or simply thick socks. The boys wore short hair and the girls had scarves draped over their heads. Chalkboards stood on easels, and several small tables held other props like balls, water pitchers, and clay pots. Plastic crates brimmed with dusty, weather-beaten books.

In truth I'd gone to the site in part because I thought I

might run into Anderson again. I needed a pretty face to help temper all the ugliness around me. She was watching a group of laborers erect the walls of the school on the broad concrete foundation. Just behind her stood the sandbagged machine gun nests my team had helped build.

"I'm glad you're getting a chance to see them," said Anderson, turning toward me and gesturing to the tent full of children.

"I assume they'll have desks, once they move inside . . ."

"Yes, they will. These kids need a sense of dignity. And we'll give that to them. We've made a great deal here. We train the teachers and provide the educational materials if the community provides us with those teachers. And we're trying to recruit more girls to the classes, at least thirty percent for us to receive full funding from some of my sources."

"The Taliban doesn't want girls educated," I said.

"It doesn't matter what they want. It's what the people want. And if the Taliban know what's good for them, they'll follow the example of some of the other villages up north. This works. I've seen it."

"It works until we leave. And hey, you haven't called me about these guys turning over their paychecks to the Taliban."

"I know. I think they know I'm watching them, and they've become more discreet. But it's going on, I know it."

"All part of the great legacy we're building here."

She hoisted a brow and looked me dead in the eye. "When Harruck told me about trying to build a legacy, do you know what I told him?"

"That he's dreaming?" I guessed.

"No, that it's obvious: This school is the legacy. But we need to protect it. We need to train the police and whatever National Army troops we can get here."

"We've already done what we can," I said, gesturing to the sandbagged nests and the observation posts beyond. I lifted the binoculars hanging around my neck and panned the horizon, coming to a stop on a cluster of Taliban fighters, at least ten of them, perched on the mountainside, watching us. Our machine gunners were watching them, too.

"No, that's not enough. We need more police, more Afghan Army troops. We need a garrison here. We need police to patrol the town."

"Talk to Harruck."

"I already did. I'm talking to you."

"Why do you think that'll make a difference? You don't even know who I am . . ."

She smiled as if she did. She couldn't. Unless, there was much more to her than met the eye.

"I know who *he* is," she said, gesturing toward an old white sedan that was rumbling toward us, its hood caked in dust, its windshield wipers still working to clear away more dust. Bronco was behind the wheel. She continued: "I know you guys talk."

"I'm not at liberty to discuss this any further."

"I'm just telling you, please . . . help us." She gave me a curt nod, and Ramirez and I stepped away as Bronco parked near the school tent and climbed out.

"You're not looking for me, are you?" I asked.

"I figured you'd be looking for me. Buy me flowers. Something for saving your ass," he said.

I wished I could tell him my ass was far from saved.

"What're you doing out here?" I asked.

"Saw you. Figured I'd let you know about your buddy."

"What're you talking about?"

"They captured one of your men. I heard about it. I talked to a few of my contacts in Sangsar. They've got him. I'm sure you'll hear from them soon."

I glanced over at Ramirez, who just shook his head and sighed.

Though I hate to admit it now, when Bronco said he had news concerning "our buddy," I'd hoped that Warris had been killed. That's a terrible thing to wish on the man, but that was how I felt.

And I just knew, beyond a shadow of a doubt, that Keating would want me to rescue Warris, the very man who would burn me at the stake when we got back.

"All right, thanks for the info," I told Bronco. "Always nice doing business with the friendly neighborhood spook. And now, what is it you want from us, because I know you want something."

He smiled—an unfortunate grin that revealed his aversion to modern dentistry. "I want HERF guns. You came back with two of them, didn't you?"

"Classified," I said.

"I need one."

"Too late. Already turned them over to Army intel."

He looked away. "Damn it."

"So that's why you're here?"

"Among other things. We've got some Chinese agents in Sangsar. They're supplying the HERF guns."

"You got proof?"

"I got it. But hard evidence is always better. It allows me to more definitively make a move. It allows me to have my three-letter agency call your agency and get the job done right."

I nodded. "Assholes or allies. Hard to tell the difference sometimes . . ."

"That it is."

"How come you're willing to play nice all of a sudden?"

"Because now it benefits me. What else you need to know?"

"Just where my guy is and where I can find Zahed . . ."

"I'll get back to you on those . . ." He winked and hobbled back toward his car. Only then did I notice his limp and the deep scar running across his ankle. What I didn't notice, though, were all the lies he'd just told me. He could've won an Oscar for that performance.

I dropped off Ramirez back at the base, then headed over to Harruck's office. I was about to open the door to enter the Quonset hut when I noticed a car parked outside and an old man, a local from Senjaray I figured, unloading luggage from the trunk. I opened the door, stepped inside, and just as the door was closing behind me—

A thundering explosion rattled the walls followed by the pinging of debris.

Ahead was Harruck, seated at his desk, talking to a dignified-looking man with gray beard and expensive-looking Afghan clothes. I assumed he was a government official of some sort, and I was correct.

As Harruck and the other man shouted behind me, I took a deep breath, then slipped back outside.

The car had exploded, the man removing the luggage lying in pieces across the dirt, the flames still pouring up from the shattered windows. I raised an arm against the intense heat as Harruck's security people were screaming and rushing to get fire extinguishers.

Harruck came out behind me and screamed orders to his people, while the older man hollered in Pashto, then covered his eyes and began speaking so rapidly that I barely understood a word.

We watched as Harruck's teams began putting out the fire, and the black smoke sent signals to the Taliban in the mountains and everyone in Senjaray—indeed, something had happened on the American base.

Harruck ushered the old man back into his office, and I entered behind them. The old man collapsed into his chair and tried to catch his breath. His eyes brimmed with tears.

Harruck glowered at me and said, "Well, Scott, this is obviously not the time for you and I to talk."

"I understand." In Pashto, I said to the old man, "I'm very sorry about this."

He answered in English. "They must've rigged my car on a timer. And I guess it went off too late. They are amateurs, the men who are trying to kill me."

"Who are they?" I asked.

"The same people you are trying to help."

I looked at Harruck, who rolled his eyes. "Scott, this is Naimut Gul, the district governor."

"Sir, I wish we could have met under different circumstances."

"My driver was a very good man. Highly trusted." He shuddered and rubbed the corners of his eyes.

"Governor, if you'll just give me a moment to speak with him?" Harruck asked.

Gul nodded. "And now, Captain, I think you fully understand what I'm talking about."

"Yes, sir, I do."

Harruck motioned me back outside, where we walked around to the pathway between huts. The officers' barracks lay to our right, and one of the guys had designed a little putting green in the middle of the desert, an oasis of sorts that Harruck pointed to and said, "See that? Crazy right here in the desert, right? Well, that's what I got right now, with that fool inside my office."

"What're you talking about?"

"Everybody in the district hates the guy. He's former Taliban, and he's been extorting these people for years. He's a crime lord with ties to the opium trade, but he's still in tight with the government, and higher now tells me it's my job to protect him. He's moving his office onto our base. And you know what? Everybody wants this guy dead: the Taliban, the people here, even some guys in the government because they know what a scumbag he is."

"So you're not having a good day. Join the club."

"Scott, I might need your help here."

I almost laughed. "What?"

"If this guy sets up shop here, we'll be painting an even bigger target on our backs."

"But you got orders to protect him—just like I got orders to capture or kill Zahed. By the way, I ran into Bronco. His contacts confirm that the Taliban have Warris. I'll be taking that up to higher in a few minutes."

"That's what I thought. And now I'm thinking about a trade—not one that higher ever knows about."

"What?"

Harruck lowered his voice even more. "The Taliban would love to get their hands on Gul. What if we trade him for Warris? We just make it look like the governor got kidnapped."

"Are you serious?"

Harruck spun around, cursed, then whirled back. "I don't know what I am anymore, Scott. I really don't. What the hell am I supposed to do with this guy?"

"Just do your job."

"No one makes that easy—especially you. I read your report."

"Then you know if we can't get air support, I'll be organizing my team to head back into the mountains and blow up that tunnel complex. We need to destroy that in order to better protect the school."

"Are we really on the same page?"

"I don't even know if our pages are in the same book, but those tunnels need to go. And if you got a problem with that, you'd better let me know right now."

"That man sitting in my office is my bigger problem. Blow up the tunnels, Scott. Screw it. Blow 'em all up . . ."

I stood outside the communications hut, just watching Harruck's guys deal with the burning car and begin cleaning up the mess. That the captain's people had not done a bomb search of the car before it had passed through the main gate was odd. I walked over to the gate and questioned the guys, who told me they had orders from Harruck to waive the search and not delay the governor's arrival—a mistake made by the young captain. That car should've been left on our perimeter, and the governor should've been transferred into a Hummer and transported to Harruck's office. Oh, but that was so inconvenient. I'm sure security would tighten now that Harruck had his 20/20 hindsight.

After leaving the gate, I found it harder to drag myself back to the comm hut. I couldn't get the images of Ramirez killing the kid out of my mind. And I kept shuddering as the shots rang out and the kid fell back.

I kept seeing that blank stare on Ramirez's face.

And I kept wondering what I looked like. What expression had he seen on my face? I couldn't remember how I'd reacted.

And then I began playing over his rationale, hearing him tell me again and again that he'd killed for me and that he'd saved our careers. The more I thought about that, the more the paranoia filled my chest cavity like blood. I knew Ramirez was worried sick about me taking what he'd done to higher. Yes, I'd lied in my report. But that still didn't mean I wouldn't bring it up, fall on my own sword with him, and end both of our careers because it was the morally correct thing to do. My own sense of guilt would fuel his paranoia.

And because that doubt had to be in his head, I wondered if maybe, just maybe, I might be a target. I was the only witness to what he'd done, and if I "died in combat" the same way the kid had, then no one would be the wiser.

After all, he'd told me he had nothing else in his life.

In the middle of the desert, in one-hundred-degree-plus heat, an intense chill ran up my spine. What if Joey did find some way to off me? No one would know.

I couldn't bear that thought.

EIGHTEEN

It took another thirty minutes to finally get Gordon on the line, and we switched to a video call, which was a little grainy, with some boxy dropouts, but I still could note the old colonel's deep concern.

"You know I'm caught in the middle here, Scott. I didn't want to send Warris. Keating's taking a lot of heat, and he's got no choice but to pass the buck. You know how this works. I'm getting ready to tell them all where to go."

"Me, too. Well, there's no media here, so unless Zahed and his people get on Al Jazeera, we'll be okay. I don't know about his contacts in that department, but suffice it to say we haven't got much time."

"No, we don't."

"Obviously, you want me to rescue Warris."

"Not exactly."

I sighed deeply. That phrase was becoming a knife in my back. Then again, maybe they were writing off the young captain? No way. They couldn't be. "Sir?"

"We might be able to use Warris's capture to justify a big offensive in the area. It's what that place really needs anyway. Some big units moving through and sweeping out the cockroaches. It's too damned corrupt to send you guys in there to take out one man. The guy's laying low, and if he does move, they've got him disguised. We even thought they might've moved him in a body bag from one part of the village to another. I've got nothing actionable to hand you at this point."

"So you're giving up on my mission?"

"No, you've still got time to do what you can. It'll take another two weeks for the logistics to be worked out. They'll need to pull some people out of Helmand. But once that happens, Zahed won't know what hit him. However, the Ghosts can save face by pulling Zahed out of there before the hammer drops."

"So you want me to get Zahed and rescue Warris, but you want me to take my time on the rescue op."

"Obviously this call is not being recorded and the transmission is fully encrypted," he said with a wink. "Otherwise, I wouldn't confirm that. But hell yes, son, you need to begin some negotiations, but buy us the time on our end."

"What if they torture him? What if he spills his guts to those bastards?"

"We'll have to take the hit, because higher believes that securing Kandahar and the outlying areas—"

"You don't need to finish," I told him while sighing in disgust.

I leaned back from the cubicle and glanced around the comm center. I was wearing headphones and the screen had glare protection, so no one could peer over my shoulders.

And at that moment, I stopped calling him "sir." I'd known Buzz Gordon for a very long time, and that was the most tense few moments I've ever had with a CO. "Buzz, I need your advice on something."

"Glad I'm still good for something."

"I, uh, I can't tell you everything."

"Scott, it's me."

"I know, I know." I took a deep breath and spoke slowly. "I've got a problem with Ramirez. I want you to know that if something happens to me, you'll need to confine and question him. That's all I'm saying."

"Whoa, what the hell are you talking about?"

"I'm just saying I got a problem."

"Scott, what's going on out there?"

"If it comes down to it, I just want you to question Ramirez, all right?"

"I'm shocked. He's one of the top five operators we have, and you're telling me you think he's going to frag you?"

"I don't know."

"Why would he want to do that, Scott?"

"Like I said, I'm not in a position to tell you everything."

"You don't need to protect me."

"I know. I'm trying to save my own ass here."

"So let me give you the company line here: You're the on-scene commander, and I expect and trust you to resolve the situation in a professional and expeditious manner. You have been and will continue to be put in situations where you have two competing obligations."

"I understand."

"And now as a friend and fellow soldier, I'll tell you this: If Ramirez is a problem—in the way that you suggest—then, for the good of the Ghosts, for the good of all operators, you need to address that problem."

"In any way I can?"

"That's right."

"Would you consider that an order?"

"You know I can't."

I sighed and closed my eyes. "Yeah . . ."

"Scott, I wasn't aware it's gotten that bad."

I couldn't meet his gaze. "Well, Harruck's baby-sitting the governor on our base, the spook is working on something that involves the Chinese smuggling in HERF guns, and the local police and Army are nonexistent. So yeah, it's pretty bad."

Gordon shook his head. "Two weeks, Scott. Get Zahed. If you wind up rescuing Warris early, then do it if you have to, but if you can sit on your hands, then do that, too."

"All right."

I couldn't help but rejoice over his order to delay rescuing Warris. And I couldn't believe the irony of that, either. Warris's capture was giving them an excuse to

break out the big guns and finally put some steel on terrorist targets. Maybe they were realizing that COIN
operations needed some teeth behind them.

Then again, I wondered how effective even a major
offensive might be. Word would get back to Zahed that
forces were moving toward Sangsar, and he would just
skip town until the fireworks were over. Then he'd come
back and set up shop once more. Just a vicious circle. We
had to get him before he left. They needed to cordon off
that entire village.

When I left the comm center, I got word from the
main gate that someone had come to see me: Shilmani. I
went out there and had a seat on the tailgate of his water
truck. "What are you doing here?"

"I want to help you."

"Really?"

"Yes. Do you trust me?"

I shouldn't have hesitated. But I did. "Okay, I trust
you."

"Then change your clothes. Burki wants to see you.
I'll wait here for you."

"We always travel in pairs. I'll need to bring another
soldier."

He didn't flinch. "Okay."

When I walked into our billet, several of the guys came
over to me, and Brown said, "We think Ramirez is sick.
He's been throwing up since you guys got back. Nolan's
taking him to the hospital."

"Oh, okay, good. Treehorn?"

The big guy looked up at me from his bunk. "Yeah, boss?"

"Get dressed like an Afghan. We're going for a little ride."

"You got it."

I headed to the back of the billet, where Nolan was handing a canteen to Ramirez. "Come on, bro. You need to go over there."

Ramirez, who was wearing only his skivvies now, shook his head.

"Hey, Joey, you okay?" I asked, my tone more of a challenge than an expression of concern.

He could barely face me. "Perfect."

"Then why are you throwing up? You didn't look sick a little while ago . . ."

He snorted. "You see that crap they're serving in the mess hall? I guess it takes a while to seep into your guts."

"Well, I hope you feel better. Soon." I walked back to my bunk and began changing. Before I was finished, Nolan and Ramirez pushed past me and headed outside.

Brown lifted his head from his bunk. "Hey, Captain? Everything okay? I'm getting some bad vibes from you and Joey."

"We're cool. I'm just worried about him."

"We're worried about you."

I drew back my head. "Me?"

"Yeah. You got a lot of pressure. We lost Matt. Warris is out there. We get new orders yet?"

I gave a short nod. "I'll brief you guys when we get back."

Shilmani drove Treehorn and me to one of two shacks positioned along more foothills on the far west side of the town. The shacks rose improbably from the dirt and pockmarked hills, and they looked as though they'd been there for centuries. Long rows of water jugs were stacked on a rickety framework, and two more pickup trucks were parked behind them.

Two men with AK-47s sat on the roof of one shack, and the rickety ladder they'd used to ascend to their perch leaned against one wall, casting a long shadow.

They eyed our group with deep suspicion, and I was glad to move into the cooler shadows of the first shack, where the water man sat on a thick carpet and sipped tea, along with a much younger man, who suddenly shot to his feet as we entered.

Shilmani gestured that we take seats on the crimson-colored *toshak*.

"We'll have some tea first," said Burki.

"Thank you," I said, settling down on the cushion and making sure the soles of my feet were not showing. I muttered for Treehorn to do likewise and to remove his sunglasses.

Shilmani poured us cups of tea, which we quickly accepted.

The young man stood in the corner, just watching us.

His beard was short, his eyes fiery. If he had a weapon, I'd say he wanted to use it on us, but thus far he appeared unarmed.

"How is the new well coming? I haven't had time to go out there."

Burki's English wasn't very good. Shilmani translated, and Burki said, "Oh, good, good, good. A lot of water!"

"He sounds happy," I said to Shilmani.

"He is. Even with the Taliban cutting into our profits, we'll still have a very good year. The solar-powered pump is a brilliant idea."

"Not mine," I said.

"But great nonetheless."

"How are your wife and children?" I asked.

"Very well," he answered. "Perhaps some time you could join us again for dinner. My children have a lot of questions about America."

"I'll try to answer them."

Shilmani grinned, then leered up at the young man in the corner.

"Who is he?"

"Just the bodyguard."

"He wants to kill me," I said.

"Me, too," Shilmani said with a smile. "I hate him."

Burki leaned forward and gave me a long appraising stare. "I want you to kill Zahed," he said slowly.

I drew back my head and looked at Shilmani, who simply nodded.

"What's going on now?" I asked.

Shilmani spoke quickly, "We had a deal with Zahed for the water coming out of the new well, but he has chosen to break that deal and increase his demands. So we have chosen to kill him—and we will hire you to do the job."

"Okay," I said matter-of-factly.

Treehorn looked at me: *Are you nuts?*

I winked at him. Then faced Burki and made the money sign. "How much will you pay me?"

He looked at Shilmani and spoke rapidly, and I could only ferret out every third word.

"He says we'll pay you with information rather than money."

"Tell him I said that's very clever and I appreciate this offer. I will kill Zahed. How can he help me?"

Shilmani and Burki spoke again, then Shilmani said, "We will set up a meeting for you and Zahed. He will think you are one of the opium smugglers I told him about. You will come with us. And when the door closes, you will put a bullet in his head."

"Okay."

"Captain, I'm not sure this is such a good idea."

I looked at Treehorn. "Thanks. No other opinions needed." I faced Burki. "How soon can we meet with Zahed?"

"Soon."

I turned to Shilmani. "Ask him about our captured man. Does he know where our guy is being held?"

After a moment of conversation, Shilmani turned to

me and shook his head. "No idea. But Zahed would want to question him himself, so probably in Sangsar."

"Ask him what he thinks the best-protected place is in that town."

Shilmani did. Both men laughed. Shilmani turned to me. "He says the police station. The jail. But it is probably too obvious."

We had dozens of maps and intelligence on Sangsar, but sometimes that intel did not indicate the function of some buildings unless streaming satellite video of the comings and goings of the inhabitants made it obvious— or if there was, of course, a sign on the building.

I drew an imaginary rectangle across the carpet and said, "Can you tell me in what part of the town we would find that building?"

Shilmani already knew. He pointed directly in the middle of the rectangle. I sighed. Of course—as deep into the town as you could get.

"So if I kill Zahed, your boss gets to keep all of the profits."

"That's what he thinks, but you and I know better."

"We do?"

"There's always another man to take over for Zahed."

"Yes, there is. Do you know who that might be?"

"I have a cousin who works as a courier for Zahed."

"You do? Why did you wait to tell me?"

"To protect him. And my family."

"I see."

"I will get more information from him."

I finished my tea and smiled at Burki. "I really appreciate this help."

He raised a brow. "Okay, okay." He made a gun with his fingers. "You kill Zahed.

As we drove back through the town, we took a side street that ran parallel to the bazaar. A few kids on old bicycles were racing along the street and pointing as they passed the alleys. A huge crowd had gathered along the shops and stalls, and I could see people throwing things into the center square. Were those rocks? I couldn't quite tell.

"What's going on?" I asked Shilmani.

"Nothing. Never mind. We have to keep going."

"No way," I said. "Pull over."

"Please, Scott. You don't want to go there."

"Why not?"

"Because you won't understand."

"You heard me. Stop this car."

Shilmani took a deep breath. "You have to promise that if I stop, you will not interfere."

"What are you talking about?"

He pulled over, threw the car in park. "You'll see."

NINETEEN

Harruck had never mentioned this issue to me, and I later found out that he'd known all along and had simply been hiding it. The news was simply another of the burdens he'd carried on his shoulders, and it made me understand—at least a bit more—why his stress level was constantly in the red zone.

I ran down the alley and reached the back of the crowd. Treehorn and Shilmani were just behind me.

There, in the middle of the road, was a brown sack, but when I got closer, I realized that a person was covered in that sack and buried up to the shoulders. The person was struggling, so I had to assume the hands were tied behind the back.

"Boss, is that what I think it is?" cried Treehorn.

"Aw, jeez." I gasped.

A circle had been drawn in the road around the victim, and no one stepped inside that circle. From the periphery, they threw their stones, occasionally hitting the person in the head. Each time a stone made direct contact, the crowd roared.

"I did not want you to see this," said Shilmani. "And I did not realize it would happen so soon. We would have planned the meeting another day."

"Why is this happening?" I asked as the crowd chanted *God is great* and my mouth fell open.

"This is retribution for her sins."

"Her sins? What the hell did she do to deserve this?"

Shilmani didn't answer. A rock crashed into the woman's head, and the sack began to stain with blood. The crowd grew even louder, and a blood frenzy now widened the eyes of those nearest the circle's edge. The women hurtled their rocks even more fiercely than the men. I started forward, but Shilmani grabbed me—as did Treehorn.

"If you interfere, you will commit a crime," said Shilmani.

"Okay, okay," I said, fighting for breath and relaxing my arms so they could release me.

"Her hands are tied behind her back, but if she can escape the circle, she will be free," Shilmani explained. "She's only buried up to her shoulders to give her a fighting chance. Men are buried up to their heads."

"You didn't answer my question. What did she do?"

"She had sex outside marriage."

"I knew it," said Treehorn. "These women can't do anything without getting punished for it."

"We'd have to kill most American women if this were our rule," I said.

"I know. It seems you Americans engage in this behavior quite a bit."

"It just happens," I said.

Shilmani made a face. "I still don't understand how he convinced her to do it."

"You mean the guy?"

He hardened his voice. "Yes, the American soldier from your camp."

I considered going to Harruck's office and telling him what I'd seen, but I realized the men needed something from me. And I felt badly for them. They'd been lying around the billet all day, just wondering what the hell was happening.

Ramirez had come back from the hospital with some antacid to soothe his stomach. He was lying in his bunk with his arm draped over his eyes.

I called the group forward, and after a few seconds, he was the last to gather around.

"Got a couple things going on. We'll be back up in the mountains tonight. Engineering op. We're going to blow those tunnels."

"Hoo-ah," shouted Brown and Smith in unison.

"I want to do everything we can to avoid engaging

the enemy. They don't call us the Ghosts for nothing. We'll show them why."

Hume raised his hand. "Any word back on the HERF guns yet? Do we know if they've got more?"

"I know the spook is working on something, and we have to assume they have more. Nolan, we still got two spare Cross-Coms, right?"

"That's right."

"Good, I'll be taking one and Joey's got the other."

Ramirez frowned at me.

He was still in command of Bravo team. I wasn't going to change anything. I'd decided that my paranoia should have no effect on the way I ran my team. And in retrospect, I think that was a good decision.

Up to a point.

"Something else going on you should know about." I looked to Treehorn, who just sighed. "The water guy? Burki? He wants us to kill Zahed. Seems the fat bastard screwed him over on the deal with the new well, so that guy, the translator guy Shilmani, is going to help us set up a meeting with Zahed."

"Whoa, whoa, whoa," said Brown. "How's that going to work? You don't plan to go in there alone, do you?"

"Shilmani says he's got a cousin who's a courier for Zahed. I'll probably be going in with him."

"And when does this happen?" asked Nolan, wincing over the whole idea.

"Pretty soon, I'm guessing."

"Then we need to work something out. The HERF

guns don't affect the chips in our bodies, so we can still track you."

"You mean in case they take me prisoner."

"So let me get this straight," said Ramirez. "You're going to walk into a meeting, put a bullet in Zahed's head, and expect to walk out of there alive?"

"With a little help from you guys."

The group chuckled. Ramirez's expression remained deadpan. "Boss, I think it's crazy."

"Couple other things," I said. "Higher's planning a big offensive to sweep through Sangsar. They're using Warris's capture as an excuse. It'll take them a couple of weeks to work out the logistics, so we need to drag our boots on Freddy's rescue . . ."

"Hey," Treehorn began, throwing up his hands. "I got no problem with that, since that punk wants to burn us all."

"All right. Let's go over the maps, plan the detonation points, and be ready to roll for tonight."

The call came in while I was finishing up dinner in the mess hall. I remember stepping out there, looking at the mountains haloed by the setting sun, and thinking, *This is it. This is the death call.*

That was a very long walk to the comm center.

I was feeling numb by the time they guided me over to the cubicle, and my brother's voice sounded strangely absent.

"Hello, Scott, this is your brother Nicholas."

He was always so formal, so well educated and scholarly. He always talked about being articulate. I didn't want him articulate at that moment. I wanted him sobbing.

"Hey, Nick." My voice was already cracking.

"Dad passed away about an hour ago."

"Okay."

"Can you come home? We can delay the funeral for you, but I'll need to know as soon as possible."

Before I could answer him, a commotion behind me caught my attention. I told him to hang on.

A group of officers and NCOs was gathered around a flat screen, where a videotape was being played on the Al Jazeera network.

There was Fred Warris, dressed like a Taliban and sitting cross-legged with a group of Taliban fighters standing behind him. I couldn't hear what he was saying, but that didn't matter.

I told Nick I'd call him back. I drifted outside like a zombie and just stood near the door. I closed my eyes and thought of my father's workshop, filled with the heavenly scent of sawdust. And I pictured his handmade coffin propped up on those sawhorses. I was also certain he'd left detailed instructions about his funeral.

I could take the emergency leave. Just bail out on all the bullshit. Maybe not even come back. Maybe just go AWOL and let them arrest me. I was entertaining every crazy thought I could, thinking of ways to self-destruct to hold back the tears.

My father had taught me how to be a man. I owed him everything. He was gone.

I don't know how long I was standing there when Harruck and the XO rushed up and Harruck just looked at me. "Have you heard? They put Warris on TV!"

The terms for Warris's release, presented by the man himself in the video, were quite simple: Stop all construction in Senjaray. Pull the U.S. Army company out. Pay the equivalent of five hundred thousand American dollars. Release nearly a dozen captured Taliban fighters and leaders.

I was sitting in the comm center on a conference video call with General Keating, Lieutenant Colonel Gordon, and Harruck's battalion commander.

"We're not going to negotiate with these bastards," said Keating. "And I'm going to make sure we step up our timetable. I want a full-scale raid to happen within the next seven days. I want to make that happen. I don't care what it takes."

Gordon just shrugged.

Harruck's boss was a yes man.

I shook my head in disgust.

"Mitchell, you got a problem with all this?"

"Sir, you told me I wouldn't have any air support for this mission, and unless that's changed, we'll be moving in much too slowly with a large force. Zahed's got spies planted all over this district. He'll see our ground forces coming in, and he'll be out of there long before they arrive. You won't get him, and I doubt you'll get Warris. We need to be dropped by chopper. Shock and awe. That's the only way it'll work."

"I'd have to agree with Mitchell," said Harruck. "We can't afford to blow this. We can't afford any counterattacks down here. We're making great progress so far."

I sat there, debating whether I should tell them about Burki and my plan to have a face-to-face meeting with Zahed. Part of me considered the idea that if I managed to bring in the guy alive, I'd be a hero and they could call off the whole offensive and save the taxpayers a lot of money. The other part of me, the realist, said, no, that probably wouldn't happen; the offensive would go on because Keating was very upset now, and the old man would have his blood. So nabbing Zahed wouldn't affect that outcome.

But I was intrigued by the idea of talking to Zahed. Perhaps I was suicidal, but the fat man had caused so much trouble in the area, created so many headaches, that I just wouldn't be satisfied until I met him in the flesh.

And if I presented that cup of soup to "the committee," they'd all want to pee in it, thinking it'd taste better. A crude but accurate metaphor.

Perhaps, I quipped to myself, we should change our name to Rogue Recon.

Then I realized once again that if I didn't tell them what I had in mind, we'd be digging ourselves deeper graves. So I just took a breath and spilled the beans:

"Gentlemen, I'm in the process of setting up a meeting with Zahed."

"Are you serious, Mitchell?" asked Keating.

"Yes, General, I am. One of my contacts in the village works for the water man, who wants me to kill Zahed. My contact has a cousin who works for the fat man himself. Let me go in there and talk to them."

"No, not you, Mitchell," snapped Harruck. "We'll send in a professional negotiator."

I started laughing. "I've got the translator, and they're setting me up as an opium smuggler, so once I get in there, we'll spring the trap on Zahed. There won't be any negotiations."

"Now that sounds like a plan," said Keating. "We don't sit around and chat while they're about to chop the head off an American soldier. What do you need, Mitchell?"

I faced Harruck and the others on their screens. "I just need to be left alone so I can do my job, sir. And I need evac when the fireworks begin."

Harruck was shaking his head. "General, with all due respect, sir, don't you think an ambush operation like this can do more harm than good? If Mitchell fails, they'll behead Warris on TV, and they'll all be gone before we can launch our offensive. It's a lose-lose, if you ask me."

"We didn't ask you, Captain. And Mitchell will not fail."

Keating looked at me.

I gave him a curt nod. "My team is heading up into the mountains tonight. There's a small cave network they'll try to use to get down into the valley and attack the school and police station. We're going to blow it up."

"Maybe we should delay that operation until you meet with Zahed," said Gordon.

"Colonel, I'd prefer to take care of that first." I gave Gordon an emphatic look.

"All right, Captain, understood."

I wanted to blow the caves first in case I didn't make it back. Maybe I was growing a soft heart, but I kept imagining Anderson standing out there with those construction workers and those school kids and all of them dying under a hail of bullets. The cave network, like the bridge we'd blown, was an avenue of approach that needed to be eliminated.

After the meeting, Harruck pulled me aside and said, "I'll have a Bradley and rifle squad ready for you."

I softened my tone. "Thanks."

"I'm sorry, Scott, but this is, as far as I'm concerned, the beginning of the end for you."

"Why's that?"

"If you do get that meeting with Zahed, I don't think you'll come back. I think you're making a huge mistake. I don't know what this is about . . . your ego . . . you trying to prove something to higher. You should've been relieved."

"And that's the difference between you and me."

"Oh, yeah?"

"Yeah. I've got faith in that fat old bastard."

"Zahed?"

"Yeah."

"Why?"

"Because I've got something he wants—all that water from the new well. He's been cut off. He won't like it."

"So what you're saying is you *are* going to negotiate with him."

"Not exactly . . ."

I grinned because I couldn't believe I'd used those words, but I had.

TWENTY

About an hour before we were set to leave on the demo mission, Harruck came out to our billet, and the expression on his face didn't look promising. The guys groaned, figuring the mission was off and that higher had more politically correct plans in mind.

But it turned out that my sister had notified the Army of my father's passing. I wasn't going to say anything, not even to the team.

"Scott, I'm very sorry to hear about your father." He then explained how he'd heard.

"It's all right. Thanks."

"You should have told us. You need to go home. You need to pay your respects."

"Would that make it easier for you?"

He tensed, glanced away a moment, then faced me. "Forget all this bullshit. I'm talking to you as a friend."

"I thought our friendship was over."

"I'm trying to keep this professional. Not personal."

I couldn't repress my sigh of disgust. "Good luck with that. Well, thanks for coming out, then."

"So, you're not taking a leave?"

I snorted. "I e-mailed my brother. I've already told him I can't come."

"You're putting this in front of your father's funeral? Are you sure? Are you sure you won't regret this for the rest of your life?"

"Simon, I lost a guy here. I've got another guy who was captured. One of your men got killed while up there with me. I've got a young captain trying to help a village. I just can't walk away now. I won't regret it. My family understands. My dad would understand."

He took a deep breath, gave a curt nod. "All right. Good luck, then."

I'd missed more births, birthdays, anniversaries, holidays, and even funerals than I could remember. It didn't get any easier. In fact, it got harder, and every time I spoke to my brothers or my sister on the phone, I had to reassure myself that the life I'd chosen was the right one because the distance between me and "the real world" grew larger every year.

And yes, I'd lied to Harruck. My brothers and sister would not understand. They would never tell me, but I could see it in their eyes, quite clearly. My sister once told me that I never did anything for myself. That wasn't true. But as I stood there, watching Harruck go, I couldn't help but resent some of the sacrifices, and I surrendered to the guilt of not attending my father's funeral because yes, I'd put my job first. I'd given a lot to the Army, to the Ghosts, but missing Dad's funeral . . . maybe that was too much.

We hitched a ride aboard one of the supply Chinooks, and we had that pilot drop us off about a kilometer east of the mountains. We set down in a well-protected valley not far from our FARP (Forward Arming and Resupply Point), used by gunships, Blackhawks, and Chinooks alike, so our bird was not a curious sight in that zone. We would hike in with less chance of being detected by Taliban fighters posted along cliffs that overlooked the village. Their gazes would be trained on the more obvious lines of approach, and we'd be coming up on their flank.

Ramirez and I wore the two Cross-Coms so we could easily detect friend from foe, but the others were blind because of the last HERF gun blast, so our Alpha and Bravo teams would need to stick together. Treehorn, our one-man Charlie "team" and sniper, would be posted outside the main exit tunnel we'd chosen, ready to pick off anyone who pursued us. We chose not to wear body armor to move more swiftly through the tunnels. Again, my plan was to avoid all enemy contact.

Yes, that was the plan. Would it survive the first enemy contact? Of course not.

A remarkably cool breeze tugged at our turbans and *shemaghs*, and if you spotted us hiking along the ridges, you would swear we were drug smugglers or Taliban.

Ramirez was more quiet than usual, but I think he appreciated my business-as-usual attitude, even if it was a disguise. The mission took priority. We both knew that.

But I would still keep a sharp eye on him. He led Jenkins, Hume, and Brown, and I'd told Brown in private that because Joey wasn't feeling good I wanted him to look after the sergeant. He said he would.

I kept Smith and Nolan close, and as we approached the first cave entrance after about sixty minutes of rugged and slow climbing, I sent off Bravo team to the second entrance, about a quarter kilometer west of ours and located about two hundred meters higher up the mountain. The caves and adjoining tunnels were roughly shaped like two letter Ys attached at their bases, with pairs of entrances on either side of the mountain. When my team got into the first tunnel and reached the cave area where Warris had been cut off, our lights revealed a fresh passage dug through the debris.

"Ghost Lead, this is Treehorn. I'm in position, over."

"Roger that. What do you got out there?"

"Nothing. Not even any guards. Weird."

"All right, hang on."

I gestured for Smith and Nolan to start planting the first set of charges, while I crept off farther down the tunnel, toward the starlight at the end of the jagged seam in the rock. I paused at the edge and stole a look into the valley below. Sangsar lay in the distance, a few lights flickering, the majority of the homes blanketed in deep shadows.

Warris was down there, somewhere, perhaps in some dank basement, being questioned, having battery cables attached to his genitalia, having insects shoved in his ears. Was he man enough to keep his mouth shut? Was he willing to die for his country? Had I taught him enough?

I grinned over a strange thought. Maybe his hatred for me would help keep him alive. He'd tell himself, *I need to survive this so I can burn the bastard responsible.* I accepted that. And even wondered, were I to rescue him, if he would change his mind, keep quiet, tell me that was his thank-you for pulling him out of hell. But no, the world was hardly that simple, and Warris's moral high ground was pretty damned high. Rescue or not, he'd want to hang me.

"Ghost Lead, this is Blue Six, in position, over."

"Roger that, Blue Six, stand by," I told the Bradley commander. Harruck had come through and our ride home was waiting.

I slipped just outside the cave and pulled up the satellite imagery in my HUD. The monocle covering one of my eyes flashed as the data came through.

Glowing yellow lines that represented the series of caves and tunnels moved through a wireframe image of the mountain chain. The diamonds indicating Bravo team flickered on and off, and the signal grew weaker the deeper they moved. That I even got some signal was surprising. So far, no red diamonds within the mountain or outside.

Had Zahed just called back all of his guards? Were they all just tired? Why had they left the tunnels completely unprotected?

My hackles began to rise, and that smell I detected was not the dampness of the tunnel but an ambush.

"Ghost Team, this is Ghost Lead. I don't like this. No defenses here. Plant your charges and let's get the hell out as fast as we can."

"Roger that," said Ramirez.

I was beginning to lose my breath. Something was wrong, but I couldn't put my finger on it. I ran down the tunnel, back to where Smith and Nolan were working.

"Are we set?"

Nolan looked up at me. "Remotes good to go. Need to finish up at the entrance where you just were."

"All right, let's go," I said.

"Ghost Lead, this is Ramirez! I just got out of my tunnel. Scanning the village now. They got mortar teams setting up just outside the wall. They got tipped off again!"

Just as we reached our exit, a shell hit the mountain just above us, the roar deafening, a landslide of rock and dirt beginning to plummet. "Back inside! Ghost Team! Fall back! Fall back!"

Two more shells struck the mountainside, the ground quaking beneath our feet, the ceiling cracking here and there. The bastards would seal up the caves for us—but their plan was, of course, to bury us alive.

"Ghost Lead, this is Treehorn! The Bradley has come under attack. I don't know where they came from! They might've been buried in the sand the entire time! They got at least twenty guys down there! More in the mountains coming down. Should I engage?"

"Negative, negative! Don't give up your position yet!" I cried.

He'd said more were coming down from the mountains. Why hadn't the satellite picked them up and fed that data into my Cross-Com? Was it just interference from the terrain?

I gritted my teeth and led Nolan and Smith back to the main tunnel and exit. As we neared the intersection where the cave-in had occurred, shouting echoed, and I threw myself against the side wall, with the guys just behind me, then rolled to the left, my rifle at the ready, as two Taliban fighters came through the newly dug passage through the cave-in. I gunned both of them down before I could finish taking a breath.

They hit the ground—and so did a grenade tossed at us from their comrades on the other side.

As I turned back, I raised my palm, screaming for the guys to hit the deck. We all started toward the floor as the grenade exploded behind us, the concussion echoing, and what sounded like a million tiny rock fragments pelted my clothes—

Just as I crashed onto my belly.

The terrible and expected ringing in my ears came on suddenly, and when I looked up, I couldn't see anything. I lost my breath. I thought maybe I'd died, but then I realized my turban had fallen down across my face. I shoved it up, rose, and found hands pulling me to my feet.

"You okay?" Smith asked, his angular face creased deeply with worry. I couldn't hear him; I'd just read his lips.

I indicated that my ears were ringing. He nodded and mouthed the same thing. Nolan was next to him, waving us onward as he drew a grenade from the web gear hidden beneath his shirt. He tossed the grenade down the intersecting hall, and we all bolted ahead as the seconds ticked by and the grenade exploded, just as we neared the more narrow exit.

And two Taliban fighters rolled toward us, rushing in from outside.

Nolan was on point and opened up on them, but they'd started firing as well, their rounds ricocheting off the ceiling just past us. Smith and I, caught in the back, had no choice but to drop away. We couldn't fire with Nolan in our way.

The gunfire was strangely muffled but growing louder as my hearing began to return.

With arms flailing, the two fighters fell on top of each other.

Nolan turned back to me, his eyes wide.

Then he just collapsed himself.

"Cover us!" I shouted to Smith, then rose and rushed to Nolan. I slowly rolled him over onto his back. He looked okay. I began to pull back his shirt, and then I spotted them, one near his shoulder, and one much lower, near his heart. Nolan's trademark spectacles had been knocked to the side of his head, and he was blinking hard, trying to see.

The blood was gushing now as he struggled for breath, and I struggled to get past his web gear.

"In my pack, I got some big four-by-four gauze," he said between gasps.

I ripped off my *shemagh* and shoved it beneath the web gear and applied pressure. My first instinct was to get on the Cross-Com and shout, "Nolan, got a man down!"

"Captain, tell John not to feel bad. Tell 'em we're buddies forever. Okay?"

"I will, Alex," I said, applying more pressure as he began to shiver violently.

Nolan was referring to John Hume; they'd become best friends, fighting hard and playing hard. Guys would tease them about being "too close," but they were more like brothers. I knew losing Nolan would crush Hume. Crush him.

Smith, who was up near the exit, suddenly ducked back inside as gunfire ripped across the stone where he'd been standing. "We are so pinned down here."

I was about to answer when another mortar round struck far down the tunnel, and the ground shook. Somewhere back there, another cave-in was happening, the rocks and dirt streaming and hissing, and not five seconds later a wall of thick dust rolled through the tunnel toward us.

When I looked down again, Nolan was not moving. I checked his neck for a pulse. That round had, indeed, struck his heart, and when I checked the side of his shirt, it was soaked thick with blood.

Footfalls resounded up the tunnel, and suddenly through the dust came a figure. I snatched up my rifle, took aim, and held my breath.

"Hold fire!" came a familiar voice. The figure tugged down his *shemagh*. Ramirez. He glanced over his shoulder. "Come on! We've linked up with the Captain!"

As the others rushed up behind him, Hume spotted Nolan lying at my side and rushed to him.

"Alex!"

"He's gone," I said evenly.

"Aw, no," Hume cried. "No, no, no."

For just a moment—perhaps only three seconds—we all stood there, frozen, staring down at Hume and Nolan, no sound, no movement, just the burning image of our fallen brother, and then—

"Ghost Lead, this is Treehorn, they got RPGs moving in on the Bradley. Permission to open fire!"

I shuddered back to reality. "Negative, hold fire! Do not give up your position." I switched channels to speak to the Bradley commander. "Blue Six, this is Ghost Lead, over."

I waited, called again, nothing. Couldn't even warn the guy and his squad. The vehicle's big machine gun was already drumming as several more booms struck and silenced it.

"They got the gunner!" shouted Treehorn. "They got the gunner! They're swarming the Bradley. Swarming it now!"

Two more shells struck the mountain, and the ceiling began to crack right near my head.

"I'm taking him out of here," said Hume, his eyes already burning.

"You got it," I answered. "Treehorn? Get set! We're coming out!"

TWENTY-ONE

Alex Nolan was a smart-aleck kid from the streets of Boston who'd become a senior medical sergeant with the Ghosts. He often looked like a geek, but when he opened his mouth, wow, he was all attitude fueled by an insatiable curiosity and great intellect. He was even a Mensa member. Still, there were times when he could throw a switch and be the most caring and sympathetic operator on our team. The last time we were in Afghanistan, I'd seen him spend hours with sick villagers. He'd always ask the same question: "Are your animals sick, too?" When you operated in third-world countries and people became ill, you could sometimes trace the problem back to their livestock.

With the letter to Matt Beasley's family still fresh on

my mind, I couldn't believe I had to write another one. I wasn't used to losing operators, especially two on a single mission.

We'd been all over the world, working on operations far more taxing than this one. And while they kept telling me this situation was complicated, on the surface it seemed much safer when compared to the operation I'd run in China, penetrating deep into the heart of the country to take out a cabal of rogue generals. Hell, we'd had a hundred chances to be captured or killed and had slipped past every one of them.

Now we'd been charged with nabbing one fat-ass terrorist, and I'd already lost two good men, some of the most valuable personnel in the U.S. Army. I was already feeling burned out, like a has-been operator who'd gotten his men killed.

With my own eyes burning, we rushed outside the tunnel and I ordered the guys to set off the charges. Thumbs went down on wireless detonators, and the multiple booms echoed, as though someone were kicking over a massive drum set that clattered and crashed off a giant stage. I could only hope our charges had swallowed some of the insurgents inside.

I led Alpha team along a rocky path that descended sharply to our left. Ramirez and his team would take the path to the right. I didn't want us together in case the guys on this side of the mountains had mortars, too. And to be perfectly honest, it was convenient to have Ramirez away so I didn't need to watch my back.

RPG fire arced like fleeing fireflies, and two cone-shaped

denotations rose skyward as though the Taliban had ignited a massive bonfire to celebrate their victory over the infidels.

"All right, Treehorn, cut it loose!" I ordered.

The sniper's gun boomed, and his rounds came down like God's hammer, decisive, deadly, dismembering all in their path.

But the Taliban were quick to answer.

Gunfire cut a line so close to Hume that he tripped and fell forward with Nolan's body draped over his back.

We rushed to help him back to his feet, and that was when muzzles flashed from the ridgeline about fifty meters above.

I raised my rifle as the red diamonds appeared in my HUD to help me lock onto the four targets.

The camera automatically zoomed in on one fighter raising a HERF gun toward me—and that was when my HUD went dead.

I might've cursed. Either way, the HERF blast was my cue to open fire, and Smith joined me. We drilled those bastards back toward the wall, while Hume got Nolan down onto the lower portion of the path. I wasn't sure if we'd hit any of them, but we'd bought some time.

Smith ceased fire, tugged free a smoke grenade, then tossed it up there a second before we both double-timed after Hume.

Treehorn's gun spoke again. And then again. He was the reaper. His words were thunder.

About twenty meters east of the now-burning Brad-ley, an insurgent lay on his belly, directing machine gun fire up near Treehorn, who returned fire, hitting the guy. The gun went silent—but only for a few seconds as that fighter was replaced by another, who quickly resumed showering Treehorn.

"Cover Hume. Get down the rocks and hold there," I ordered Smith. He nodded and hustled off.

I jogged back up the path toward Treehorn's perch much higher along the ridge.

He took one last shot, then bolted up and joined me. I waved him back along the path, and then . . . off to my left, about twenty meters up . . . a curious sight: another tunnel entrance. It must've been covered up by the Taliban because the rocks nearby appeared freshly shaken free by the mortars and our C-4 charges.

As we came under a vicious wave of gunfire that seemed certain to hit us, I rushed up toward the tunnel and practically threw myself inside.

Treehorn was a second behind me, breathless, cursing, literally foaming at the mouth with exertion.

AK-47 and machine gun fire stitched along the entrance, daring us to sneak back out and return fire. That was one dare I would not take. The machine gunner seemed to be chiseling his initials on the rock face.

I got on the regular radio, found it dead, and realized that maybe this time the HERF gun had managed to fry it, too. But then I also noticed the microphone had taken a hit. I was one lucky man—very close call. That bullet would've caught my side, perhaps even penetrated my spine.

Treehorn directed his light to the tunnel behind us. "Whoa . . ."

His surprise was not unwarranted.

The uneven intestine of rock swept outward and curved slowly down. It appeared to go much longer and deeper than any of the others we'd seen, and I was suddenly torn between venturing down to see where it went and making a break back outside to link up with the others. The machine gun fire had just died off. The second rally point would be just past the Bradley's position, along an old dried-up riverbed. Everyone knew it. I assumed Ramirez would be taking Bravo team there.

But I'd left Smith to look after Hume, who was carrying Nolan on his back, and those guys would need help.

"What do you want to do, Captain?"

I pulled out a brick of C-4 from my pack. "Man, we need to see where this goes, but we can't do it right now. Let's seal it up behind us and get back outside."

"Wait a second. Listen," he said.

Faint cries echoed up toward us.

I pricked up my ears again. "Sounds like . . . a kid . . ."

"I know. What the hell?"

I remembered the girl we'd found during our first night raid. And though I couldn't bear the thought of more children being tortured, we had to leave.

Something flashed behind us, and as I turned, my arm went up reflexively against the blast. The air whooshed past us, and only then did I realize I was being catapulted back into the tunnel. The entrance had been struck dead-on by an RPG. The starlight shining beyond went black, and I slammed into the floor, shielding my face from the rocks and dirt dropping all around me.

Then, a strange silence, the sifting of sand, my breathing, the dull echo in my head—

Suddenly the cave roof a few meters ahead came down, as though a massive boot had stomped on us. I scrambled backward like a crab and bumped into Treehorn, who had just turned on his penlight, the beam struggling to penetrate the thick cloud of dust. I winced and blinked.

"You okay, boss?" cried Treehorn.

"I'm good."

"They blew the goddamned exit!"

"Plan B," I finally gasped out. "Back on our feet. Come on, buddy . . ." I began choking and coughing on the dust.

We got to our feet, his light shining down the tunnel, mine joining his a few seconds later.

I stole a look back. The tunnel behind us had completely collapsed. It would take a half a day or more for us to dig ourselves out.

I tried to stifle my coughing and gestured for Treehorn to keep his light low and to move slowly, quietly.

Our shadows shifted across the cool brown stone, and a faint glimmer seemed to join our light, the flickering of candles or a lantern, not a flashlight, I knew.

Treehorn paused, looked back, put a finger to his lips.

We killed our lights and listened.

For a moment, I think I held my breath.

The cries we'd heard earlier were gone, replaced now by footsteps, barely discernible but there. I cocked a thumb, motioning for Treehorn to get behind me. I gingerly slipped free the bowie knife from my calf sheath.

Seeing that, he did likewise, his own blade coated black so as not to reflect any light. We held our position, unmoving, but our curious tunnel guest still seemed drawn to us.

As he rounded the corner, I slid behind him, grabbed his mouth with one hand and, with a reverse grip, plunged my blade deep into his heart. I felt his grimace beneath my fingers, the hair of his thick beard scratching like a steel wool pad. The forefinger and thumb on my knife hand grew damp, and after a moment more he struggled, then finally grew limp. I lowered him to the floor. The guy had been holding a penlight, and Tree-horn picked it up, shined it into the guy's face.

He was no one. Just another Taliban guy, wrong place, wrong time. We took his rifle, ammo, and light, then moved on, the tunnel growing slightly wider, the floor heavily trafficked by boot prints. Voices grew louder ahead, and I froze.

The language was not Pashto but Chinese.

We hunkered down, edged forward toward where the tunnel opened up into a wider cave illuminated by at least one lantern I could see sitting on the floor near the wall. Behind the lantern was a waist-high stack of opium bricks, with presumably many more behind it.

A depression in the wall gave us a little cover, and we watched as ahead, Chinese men dressed like Taliban hurriedly loaded the bricks into packs they threw over their shoulders. So Bronco's Chinese connection was a fact, and I wasn't very surprised by that; however, to find the Chinese themselves taking part in the grunt work of smuggling was interesting.

There were three of them, their backpacks bulging as they left the cave, their flashlights dancing across the floor until the exit tunnel darkened.

We waited a moment more, then followed, shifting past stacks of empty wooden crates within which the bricks had been stored.

Treehorn was right at my shoulder, panting, and once we started farther into the adjoining tunnel, I flicked on my flashlight because it'd grown so dark my eyes could no longer adjust.

Somewhere in the distance came the continued rattle of gunfire, but the heavy mortars had ceased. We reached a T-shaped intersection. To the left another long tunnel. To the right a shorter one with a wooden ladder leaning against the wall. I raised my chin to Treehorn, pointed.

He shifted in front of me, rifle at the ready. I pushed the penlight close to my hip, darkening most of the beam.

We neared the ladder. I was holding my breath again. Treehorn took another step farther, looked up—

And then he whirled back, his face creased tightly in alarm as a salvo of gunfire rained straight down and he pushed me backward, knocking me onto my rump. We both went down as yet another volley dug deeply into the earth.

I imagined a grenade dropping to the foot of the ladder, and my imagination drove me onto my feet, and Treehorn clambered up behind me. I stole a look back and saw the ladder being hoisted up and away. We raced back to the intersection and moved into the other tunnel.

I kept hearing an explosion in my head, that imaginary grenade going off over and over.

The beam of my penlight was jittering across the walls and the floor until I slowed and aimed it directly ahead.

Still darkness. No end to the tunnel in sight.

I stopped, held up my palm to Treehorn. "This could be one of the biggest tunnel networks in the entire country," I whispered.

"Yeah," he said. "Goes all the way to China."

I grinned crookedly at his quip, then started on once more, turning a slight bend, then eating my words.

The tunnel abruptly dead-ended. Unfinished. In fact, the Taliban still had excavation tools lining the walls: shovels, pickaxes, wheelbarrows . . .

I looked at Treehorn.

"Well, *I* ain't digging us out of here," he groaned.

I put my finger to my lips. Footsteps. Growing closer.

TWENTY-TWO

Working as a team leader in an ever-changing environment with ever-changing rules and restrictions becomes, as my father once put it, "an abrasive on the soul." Having toiled many years in the GM plant and enjoyed as many years out in his woodshop, Dad was a man who celebrated predictability. He did repetitive work at the plant, and when he created his custom pieces of furniture, he most often worked from a blueprint and followed it to the letter. He felt at peace with a plan he could follow. He always taught me that practice makes perfect, that repetition is not boring and can make you an expert, and that people who say they just "wing it" are hardly as successful as those who plan their work and work their plan. He told me he could never do what I did, though, because he would never find satisfaction in it. He needed something tangible to hold on to, sit on, photograph, admire . . . and he needed a plan that would not change. My father was a curmudgeon to be sure.

We'd argue about this a lot. But when I slipped off into my own little woodshop to produce projects for my friends and fellow operators, I understood what Dad was trying to tell me. You cannot replace the satisfaction of working alone, of listening to that voice in your head as it guides you through a piece of furniture. There was great beauty in solitude, and I sometimes wondered whether I should've become a sniper instead of a team leader. The exquisite artistry of making a perfect shot from a mile out deeply intrigued me.

Oddly enough, I was pondering that idea while Treehorn and I stood in that tunnel, completely cut off. I wished I'd had the luxury of only worrying about myself instead of feeling wholly responsible for him. When I was a sergeant, my CO would tell me that I'd get used to leadership but it would never get any easier. I doubted him. I assumed I'd find a comfort zone. But there isn't one. Not for me. There's a happy place of denial that I go to when things go south, but I can only visit there for short periods before they kick me out.

Thus, the big sniper was at my shoulder, in my charge, and I swore to myself I would not get him killed.

A figure materialized from the darkness.

I shifted reflexively in front of Treehorn as the figure's

light came up and a second person shifted up behind the first. I was blinded for a second, about to pull the trigger, when the shout came:

"Captain! Hold fire!"

I recognized the voice. Ramirez. His light came down.

I sighed. My beating heart threatened to crack a rib. "Joey, how the hell did you get in here?"

"We saw you get pinned down. So we came back up, pushed through a couple of rocks. It looks a lot worse than it is. It caved in, but up near the top of the pile we found a way in."

"You all right?" Brown asked, moving up behind Ramirez.

"We're good. I want C-4 at the intersection. What's going on outside?"

"Rest of the team's at the rally point," Ramirez said. "A couple more Bradleys came up. They put some serious fire on the mountains, so those bastards have fallen back. I think we're clear to exit."

I looked hard at Ramirez. "Thanks for coming back."

He averted his gaze.

That reaction made me wonder if he'd come back only because Brown had spotted us and left him no choice. Or maybe he was trying to get past what had happened and show me he still had my back; I just didn't know.

I shook off the thought, and we got to work. Within two minutes we had the charges ready.

"You sure about this?" Treehorn asked. "Still got that

other tunnel down there where they had the ladder . . . who knows what's up there . . ."

"We can't leave this open. We need to make it harder for them to cross over without being seen."

"You're the boss," he said. "Bet there's another exit we haven't found, anyway. If we get back up here, we can search for that one, too."

I nodded. "I bet we'll get our chance."

We left the intersection and reached the towering wall of dirt and rock, noting the fresh exit created by Ramirez and Brown, just a narrow, two-meter-long tunnel near the ceiling. We'd crawl on our hands and knees to exit. I was concerned about all the rock and dirt between us and the charges, so I gave Brown the order to detonate before we left. He clicked his remote. Nothing. I knew it. We'd gone too far off for the signal to reach through the rock.

But then I wondered if maybe his remote detonator had been damaged by the HERF guns. I'd forgotten about that. We all had.

"I'll do it," said Ramirez, removing the detonator from Brown's hand.

"And I'll come with you," said Brown, hardening his tone. "Could go with a regular fuse."

"I'll be right back." Ramirez took off running.

"Go after him," I ordered Brown. I had visions of Ramirez blowing himself up. "The detonator might not work."

"Like I said, I've got some old-school fuses. We'll light it up."

Treehorn began pushing his way through the exit hole. It was just wide enough for the big guy, and he moaned and groaned till he reached the other side.

Then he called back to me, "Hey, boss, why don't you come out? We'll wait for them on the other side."

"You watch the entrance," I told him. "We'll all be out in a minute. You scared to be alone?"

He snorted. "Not me . . ."

From far off down the tunnel came the shuffling of boots, a shout of "Hey!" from Brown. Aw, hell, I needed to know what was happening. "Treehorn, if we're not back in five, you go! You hear me?"

"Roger that, sir! What's going on?"

I let his question hang and charged back down the tunnel. When I reached the intersection, I found Ramirez shoving one of the Chinese guys toward me. The guy's wrists were zipper-cuffed behind his back, and Brown was shouldering the guy's backpack while he lit the fuse on the C-4.

"Look what we found," Ramirez quipped. "They dropped a ladder over there, and he came down here for something."

The Chinese guy suddenly tore free from Ramirez and bolted past us, back into the dead-end tunnel.

Ramirez started after him.

"Fuse is lit," shouted Brown.

"It's a dead end, Joey!" I told him.

"Good! He's a valuable prisoner," Ramirez screamed back.

Brown cursed, removed his knife, and hacked off the

sparking fuse. "I want to blow something up," he said. "I haven't got all night."

I made a face. No kidding.

The unexpected report of Treehorn's rifle stole my attention. He screamed from the other side of the cave-in: "Got a few stragglers coming up! Let's go! Let's go!"

I ran after Ramirez, and I found him at the dead end. The Chinese guy was lying on his back, straddled by Ramirez, and my colleague was pummeling the prisoner relentlessly in the face.

Although the image was shocking, I understood very well where Ramirez was coming from. He needed a punching bag, and unfortunately he'd found one. I wondered if he'd kill the guy if I didn't intervene. I gasped, grabbed Ramirez's wrist, and held back his next blow. The prisoner's face was already swollen hamburger, his nose bleeding.

"What're you doing?" I yelled.

Ramirez just looked at me, eyes ablaze, drool spilling from his lips. "He wouldn't come. Now he will."

I cursed under my breath. "Let's get out of here."

We dragged the prisoner to his feet and shifted him forward, and then suddenly the Chinese guy spat blood, looked at me, and said, "I'm an American, you assholes!"

The left hand doesn't know what the right hand is doing. My father used to say that all the time when referring to middle and upper management and to Washington and politicians. I was no stranger to decentralization, to being on a mission and realizing only after the fact that hey, someone else has the same mission. That my commanders were often not made privy to CIA and NSA operations in the area was a given; that spook operations would interfere with our ability to complete our mission was also a given.

That a Chinese guy we captured in the tunnel would give up his identity was damned surprising.

"I'm CIA!" he added, spitting out more blood. "I needed to bail on my mission."

"Why didn't you tell us?"

"Because I know who you are. I can smell you a mile away. Special Forces meatheads. I'm not at liberty to speak to you monkeys."

I snickered. "Then why are you talking now?"

"Look at my face, asshole!"

"Why'd you run?"

"Wouldn't you?"

"What the hell are you doing here?"

He smirked. "What're *you* doing here?"

I looked at Ramirez. "Cut him loose and help him get outside, then cuff him again."

"Hey, spooky," I said, breathing in the guy's ear. "If you resist, we monkeys will do some more surgery on your face. Got it?"

He turned back and glared.

Ramirez shoved him away. I regarded Brown. "You ready to blow this mother?"

He grinned. "I think this mother is ready to be blown."

"Indeed."

The glowing fuse was, for just a few seconds, hypnotic,

holding me there, a deer in the headlights. I thought back to those moments when I was the last kid on the playground, swinging as high as I could, hitting that place in the sky between pure joy and pure terror. The teacher would be shouting my name and I'd swing just a few more seconds, flirting with the combined danger of falling off and getting in trouble.

With a slight hiss and even brighter glow, the fuse burned down even more. I wondered, how long could we remain in the tunnel without blowing ourselves up?

"Okay, boss, let's go!" cried Brown.

I blinked hard and looked at him.

"Scott, you okay?"

I stared through him. Then . . . "Yeah, yeah, come on, let's go!"

Brown and I had just cleared the other side of the passage when the explosion reverberated through the ground like a freight train beneath our boots.

Treehorn was still near the tunnel's edge, the stars beyond him. He was crouched down, his rifle raised high. "Still out there," he said. "Just waiting to take some potshots at us."

"We need to get those Bradley gunners to help suppress that fire so we can make a break," I said.

"How?" asked Treehorn. "No comm."

"What're you talking about?" I said. "We're the Ghosts. If we were slaves to technology we'd never get anything done. Watch this, buddy . . ."

I fished out my penlight and began flashing SOS.

"Are you serious?" he asked me.

"As a heart attack, bro."

Whether the Taliban to our flank and above us could see the tiny light, I wasn't sure, but I continued for a full minute, then turned back to the guys.

And then it came: a flashing from one of the Bradleys.

"What're they saying?" asked Treehorn.

"I have no clue. I don't remember my Morse code. But we are good to go. So listen up. I'm going to make a break. I'll draw the first few rounds. You guys hold off a second or two, then get in behind me and we'll take the path to the east. Those Bradley gunners are ready, I'm sure. Got it?"

"Why don't we send out the spook to make a break?" asked Brown. "He wants to run away so badly."

"Hey, that's a good idea," I said. "You want to go, spooky?"

"I like your plan better," he said, licking the blood from his lips.

"I figured you would. Hey, you don't happen to know a guy named Bronco?" I wriggled my brows.

"Yeah, he's my daddy."

"Well, let's get you home to Papa." With that, I bolted from the cave, drawing immediate fire from the Taliban behind our right flank. I had no intention of getting hit and practically dove for the next section of boulders that would screen me.

Once the Taliban had revealed themselves by firing at me, the Bradley gunners drilled them with so many

salvos and tracers that the valley looked like a space combat scene from a science fiction movie, flickering red tracers arcing between the valley and the mountainside.

Brown hollered to go. Treehorn, Ramirez, and the
prisoner came charging down toward my position.
Brown brought up the rear.

Once they linked up with me, I led them farther
down while the Bradley gunners continued to cover us.
We were clearly identified as friendlies now.

My mouth had gone dry by the time we reached the
rally point five minutes later, and I asked if anyone had a
canteen. Ramirez pushed one into my hands and said,
"Our boy's got some explaining, eh?" He cocked a
thumb at the prisoner.

"Should be interesting . . ."

The Bradley gunners broke fire, and for a few long
moments, an utter silence fell over the mountains . . .

I glanced back at Hume, who was still sitting near
Nolan's body. A sobering moment to be sure. If I stared
any longer, I feared my lungs would collapse.

Out of the silence, in an almost surreal cry, a lone
Taliban fighter cut loose a combination of curse words
he'd probably memorized from a hip-hop song. Once his
shout had echoed away, roars of laughter came from the
crews and dismounted troops around the Bradleys.

We'd never heard anything like that. The Taliban were
usually yelling how great God was—not swearing at us
in our own language. And I didn't want them polluted

by America. I wanted them maniacal and religious and steadfast. They seemed a more worthy adversary that way. To believe they could be influenced by us was, in a word, disconcerting.

Harruck had a small planning room, and we all filed in, unfolded the metal chairs, and took seats around a rickety card table. The spook's face had been cleaned up by one of Harruck's medics, and he was demanding to make a phone call.

"What do you think this is?" I asked him. "County lockup?"

"We'll get to your phone call," Harruck told the spook in a softer tone than I'd used. He faced me. "What the hell is going on? Did you destroy the caves?"

"Most of them."

"And him?"

I took a deep breath and exhaled loudly for effect. "He's CIA and posing as a Chinese opium buyer or smuggler. His cover got blown. He ran into us before he could skip town."

"I demand to be released."

"Those are good demands," said Harruck. "We like them. Just give me a couple of minutes."

"No, right now."

Harruck's expression darkened. "What the hell are you people doing on my mountain? Why is your backpack full of opium? What the hell is your mission here?"

"Aren't you going to ask me about my face?"

Harruck looked at me. "No, I'm not."

The door suddenly opened and in walked Bronco, escorted by one of Harruck's lieutenants.

Bronco spoke rapidly. "Captain, we appreciate your help and assistance here, and if there's nothing else, I'd like to escort my colleague off the base."

Harruck eyed an empty chair. "Sit down, Bronco."

"Whoa, take it easy there, Joe. You got no idea what you're dealing with here."

I smote a fist on the card table, and it nearly collapsed. "I just lost another man. And I'm not walking out of here until you tell us what's going on, what your mission is here, and how it might affect what we're trying to do. As a matter of fact, XO, do us a favor and lock that door. Armed guard outside. No one's leaving until you two spooks cough up the truth."

"You can't do that, buddy. We have the right to walk out of here."

"Yes, you do. But we're way out here in the middle of nowhere," I said. "And we're all going to get along nicely, otherwise bad things will happen. Bad things."

Bronco shifted up to me. "Don't threaten me, soldier boy. I've been at this a lot longer than you. And as far as we're concerned, you know all you need to."

"Do you know the location of our captured soldier?" Harruck asked the prisoner point-blank.

"No."

"What's your name?"

He thought a moment. "Mike."

"Okay, Mikey," I began. "You guys are working on

some Chinese connection with HERF guns and opium. I get that. I'm just a jarhead, a monkey, but I get that. Does your operation tie directly to Zahed? I just need a yes or a no."

Bronco, sighed, frowned, then sighed again. "Does our operation link to Zahed? Well . . . not exactly."

I closed my eyes and thought of murder.

TWENTY-THREE

The "opium palaces," as they were called by the media, were mansions constructed by rich drug lords on the outskirts of Kabul, and a few were beginning to sprout up in Kandahar. One I'd visited in Kabul was on Street 6 in a neighborhood called Sherpur. That place was a four-story monstrosity with eleven bedrooms and had been constructed with the heavy use of pink granite and lime marble. The media referred to these mansions as "narcotecture" in reference to Afghanistan's corrupt government. There were massage showers, a rooftop fountain, and even an Asian-themed nightclub in the basement. The pig that owned it was finally busted by the police, but his brother-in-law was allowed to buy it from him and was renting it out for twelve thousand bucks a week. What a bargain.

Ironically, it was that very house, a somewhat infamous landmark now, that Bronco began to talk about.

"So basically what we'd like to do is move Zahed over there and dismantle his operation here. He's got a nice smuggling operation going on with the Chinese and the Pakistanis, so it's been difficult."

"We just want to kill or capture him. You want to play *Let's Make a Deal*," I said. "No go. We've got a ticking clock, and no time for this."

"Besides," added Harruck, "we're not authorized at this level to negotiate a joint operation with you. This has all got to go through higher."

"That's where you're wrong, Joe," said Bronco. "We all want to get Zahed out of here. That's the truth."

"You want to put him up in a mansion and turn him into an informant. He's got one of our guys, and he's parading him around on TV, threatening to kill him, making insane demands, and you want to do business with this clown."

"Exactly," said Mike, gently touching his swollen cheek. "He's worth a lot more if we keep him operating. Just not here . . ."

"So you guys supplied Zahed's men with the HERF guns because you knew Special Forces would be sent in here."

"Not true," said Bronco. "Zahed's got his own connections, and he's smart enough to know that you SF guys are after him. He's heard all about some of your *Star Trek* toys, and he loves the idea that he can knock you out with a twenty-dollar gun made in a tent in some shithole alley in China."

"Oh, he hasn't knocked us out. Not yet. I don't need toys to bring him down."

"Okay, Mr. Bravado. You're a badass, we get that," said Mike. "But when it comes to this place, that doesn't mean jack."

I turned to Harruck. "I think at this point, we should lock these guys up until we get higher down here and figure out what the plan is. As far as I'm concerned, they've both been interfering with our mission."

"Aw, that's bullshit, and you know it," said Bronco. "I took you to see the old men. I told you what you're up against here. And you still don't even know the half of it. The entire U.S. Army depends on the balance . . . like I told you."

"Yeah, you told me. Thanks." I stood. "Do the right thing, Simon. Hold these guys as long as you can. I'm going to see Zahed in the morning."

"You're what?" asked Bronco.

I grinned darkly at both spooks. "Have a good night."

Nolan's body would be flown out before noon. We'd have the small prayer service, as we'd had for Beasley, and we'd all look at each other and think, *We've lost one of our brothers and any one of us could be next.* When I got back to the billet, I chatted with the guys for a few minutes, and then we all turned in, emotionally and physically exhausted.

But I couldn't sleep, so I just lay in my rack, staring at the curved ceiling.

Brown was listening to his iPod, the tinny rhythm buzzing from his earbuds. I'd figured him for a hip-hop guy, but he loved his classic rock. I listened for a while, letting the tunes carry me back to moments past: my childhood, a stickball game in the middle of the street, a bully who'd beaten me up at the bus stop, a meeting with the principal when I cheated on a high school trigonometry exam and my father had come and persuaded the principal not to punish me too greatly.

I started crying. My lips tightened, and the deep grimace finally took hold. I fought to remain quiet. But I couldn't hold back the tears. My father was dead. I wasn't going to his funeral. And I'd just lost another teammate. I began to tremble, then clutched the sheets and finally took a deep breath. Then I began laughing at myself. I was a deadly combatant, member of a most elite gun club of highly trained killers. We were unfeeling instruments of death, not whiners and bed wetters.

I lifted my head and stared through the darkness, across the billet to Ramirez's bunk.

He was sitting up, watching me.

Every time we attacked the Taliban, they would regroup, re-arm, and counterattack.

What were we expecting? That our attacks would so

demoralize them that they would convert to Christianity and pledge to become loyal Wal-Mart customers?

I didn't know what time I finally fell asleep, but my watch read seven forty-one A.M. local time when the first explosions had me snapping open my eyes.

Ironically, the guys weren't springing out of their bunks but slowly rising, cursing, and Treehorn yawned and said, "And that's the morning alarm clock, Taliban style."

We ran outside, bare-chested, wearing only our boxers and brandishing our rifles.

I took in the situation all at once—front gate blown to smithereens, guard house on fire, gate falling inward. Machine gunners in the nests were focusing their fire on two small sedans, taxis from Kandahar, I guessed, one of which had probably carried the gate bomber.

An RPG screamed across the base and struck one of the barracks, tearing a gaping hole in one side and exploding within.

Sergeants were screaming for all the gunners to cease fire, and within thirty more seconds, it was over.

No gunfire, just more shouting, the hiss and pop of fires, personnel running in multiple directions like ants fleeing a sprinkler's flood. We all stood outside the billet, and after another moment I reasoned there wasn't anything else we could do, so I motioned for the guys to get back inside and get dressed and we'd head over to the barracks that'd been hit. Ramirez was last to go back in. He hesitated, then turned back to me. "Scott, I, uh . . . thanks for keeping all this between us."

I pursed my lips and forced a nod.

"I'm sorry."

My breath shortened. "Okay."

By the time we reached the barracks, all the fires had been put out and we were asked to remain along a piece of tape cordoning off the area. Harruck was there and told me the attack was against Gul. "We got a warning yesterday that if we didn't turn over the governor, we'd be attacked."

"Why didn't you give me a heads-up?"

"Because I've been getting those warnings all the time. Most of them are fake or they don't act on them. They order us to leave, say they'll attack the next day, and they don't."

"Anyone hurt?"

"Lost two more at the gate. Damn it. Barracks was empty, thank God. They were already up for chow, and the governor is staying on the other side, up near the gunner's nest."

"Good idea. How'd they get so close to the gate again?"

"Gul's got people coming and going all day. I'm setting up a new roadblock. They'll need to get past there first before they get near the gate."

"Could've done that in the first place."

"Didn't see the need till now."

I sighed. "Live and learn. And Simon, in a little while I'm going over to see Shilmani. All they told me was that they'd set up the meeting with Zahed 'soon.' I'm going to tell them they've got twenty-four hours."

The XO came dashing over and faced me. "Captain? There's a call for you in the comm center."

The call was from General Keating. I wasn't surprised. Harruck had been forced to release Bronco and his buddy, Mike, after a couple of big shots from the agency flew in from Kandahar and raised hell. Keating, for his part, was ducking from the piles of dung being hurtled at him from our competing agencies. He just wanted to get me in on the fun.

"I don't care what they're telling me, Mitchell. If you can get in there, get our boy out, and drop the fat man at the same time, then we've done our job. They're trying to persuade me to think about this big picture while they cut deals with terrorists and drug runners, but that's not the way we operate, is it?"

"No, sir."

"Very well, then. Where are we now?"

"Other than what I put in my report?"

"Frankly, Mitchell, I haven't had time to read your report. I've had the CIA barking in my ear for two hours."

"We took out the cave network. I lost a guy doing it. We intercepted an agent."

"Yeah, yeah, I know all about that."

"And now I'm working on a meeting with the fat man himself."

"How the hell will you pull that off?"

"Just leave it to me, sir."

"And just what do you plan to talk about?"

"I don't plan to talk about anything, sir, if you hear me clearly."

"Loud and clear, son. Loud and clear."

Treehorn and I went back out to see Burki and Shilmani. More tea. More idle conversation, until a very tall, very lean man with a wispy beard arrived and sat with us.

"This is my cousin. He does not wish you to know his name."

"So what do we call him?" asked Treehorn.

Shilmani posed that question to the man, who answered rapidly in Pashto. Shilmani glanced up and said, "You can just call him Muji."

"Tell him that's kind of a slang phrase for Mujaha-deen fighters."

Shilmani did, then faced us. "He knows. His grand-father was one."

"Okay. Tell him I need to see Zahed right away."

Shilmani spoke with Muji at length, and all Treehorn and I could do was sit there, sipping tea. The conversation sounded like a debate, and finally Shilmani regarded me with a frustrated look. "Maybe tomorrow."

"I have to see him by tomorrow. No later. Tell him that there is no time to waste. I mean it."

After a brief exchange, Muji rose, nodded, and hurried out of the shack.

"I want you to come to my house for dinner," said Shilmani. "Your friend can come, too."

"Why's that?" asked Treehorn. "You think that this will be our last meal?"

"It could be, and I must tell you now that your plan to put a bullet in Zahed's head will not work. You need something better. My cousin tells me that no one sees Zahed now without being strip-searched first. Perhaps your weapon could be poison, or something as easily concealed."

"We'll think about it. What time tonight?"

"Sundown."

"Okay, we'll be there."

We drove about a quarter mile down the road, made our right turn to head through the bazaar area, and found the road blockaded by two pickup trucks.

Suddenly two more sedans roared up behind us, and Treehorn started cursing and shouted, "Ambush!"

He was about to grab his rifle and jump out of the Hummer. I was at the wheel and told him to hang on. "They're not firing. Let's see what's up."

I raised my palms as the men, who for all the world appeared to be Taliban with turbans and *shemaghs* across their faces, pulled us out of the Hummer.

My words in Pashto were ignored. I kept asking them what they wanted, what was going on, we weren't here to hurt them. One guy came up and suddenly pulled a black sack over my head. I started screaming as others dragged my hands behind my back and zipper-cuffed them.

And then I really panicked. How the hell could I have been so stupid? Shilmani was probably in bed with Zahed and had arranged this entire pack of lies so that they could kidnap us. Now they'd have *three* American prisoners . . .

Treehorn was screaming and struggling to get free. I yelled for him to calm down, we'd be okay.

"We should've killed them all!" he said, his voice muffled by the sack presumably over his head. "We should've!"

They shoved me into the backseat of one of the cars, driving my head down and forcing me to sit.

I was a Ghost officer. Neither seen nor heard.

And never once had I been taken prisoner.

TWENTY-FOUR

As someone used to being in control, I could hardly believe that I was helpless and at the mercy of my captors.

I kept telling myself, *You're Captain Scott Mitchell, D Company, First Battalion, Fifth Special Forces Group. This does not happen to you.*

My emotions flew in chaotic orbits. One second I was furious, wanting to curse and scream and shove my way out of the car. The next moment I was scared out of my mind, picturing myself hanging inverted from a rope and being tortured in ways both medieval and merciless.

We drove, with Treehorn in the seat next to me. He kept trying to talk, but our captors shouted for him to be quiet. They knew a little English. I assumed they wouldn't answer our questions, so there was no reason to talk until we arrived at wherever we were going.

I took only small comfort in the fact that Gordon could still locate Treehorn and me via the signals from our Green Force Tracker Chips (unless, of course, we were taken to a cave or the chips were removed from our bodies). And yes, I had assumed we were being captured by the Taliban—initially, at least. As the car ride continued, I began counting off the seconds and trying to estimate how far they were taking us from the village.

I tried to make myself feel better by concocting some elaborate scheme that involved Bronco and his CIA buddies capturing us for some reason—maybe to threaten us or force a conversation, something. Bronco did wield some power in the village, having longstanding relationships with all the players, so I wouldn't have put it past him to engage in a little payback and some threats. He could have paid off some local guys to pick us up and deliver us to him.

The road grew very rough, jostling us in the seats, and the driver directly in front of me began arguing with the passenger. I focused on the conversation, tried my best to ferret out the words, but they always spoke so rapidly that my hearing turned into a skipping CD, just . . . getting . . . a word . . . here . . . there . . .

"Boss, I'm a little worried," said Treehorn.

"I know. Don't talk," I snapped.

The men hollered back at us.

At that point I began to feel sorry for myself. I'll admit it. I'd grown a little too comfortable in the village, believing that since Burki wanted me to kill Zahed, I could move a bit more freely and not be threatened. Sure, we dressed like the locals and were beginning to grow out our beards, but I'm sure it wasn't difficult to ID us as foreigners.

I heard my father telling me, *Son, you really screwed up. You watched a guy murder another soldier and lied about it. You basically got two of your men killed. And now you've gone and gotten yourself captured. Are you having a bad day or what? What the hell happened to you? Don't you remember what your mom told you? You're destined for some great things . . . so I have to ask you, son, what the hell happened?*

My eyes were brimming with tears. I kept calling myself a fool and wanted to apologize to Treehorn. He was going to die because I'd made poor decisions. All of the axioms of leadership didn't mean a goddamned thing to me anymore. The Special Forces creed was a joke. I had a sack over my head and was being driven to hell, where a fat man lounged near a pool of lava, sipping on tea.

I started reflecting on everything: my pathetic relationships with women, how I'd tortured poor Kristen for so many years, how she kept lying to me and saying this was the exact relationship she wanted, long-distance and infrequent, when I could see the ache in her eyes. What kind of life had I made for myself? Was I truly happy? Were all the missions and the sacrifices really worth it?

Like I said, I was really feeling sorry for myself.

Any operator who tells you he has no doubts, that he

is fully committed to the choices he's made and the sacrifices to come, is, in my humble opinion, lying. There
will always be the doubts, and they were, at that
moment, all I had left.

I'd estimated the car's speed at about thirty miles per
hour and had counted off about thirty minutes, give or
take, so I figured we'd gone about fifteen miles when the
car came to an abrupt halt, the dirt hissing beneath the
tires.

More chatter from the driver and passenger. The zipper cuffs were digging into my wrists and my shoulders
were on fire by the time they opened the door and
yanked us from the car. We were guided about twenty
steps away, and then one man said, "Stay."

"Boss, I say we make a break for it. I'd rather get shot
trying to escape."

"Relax, brother. We're going to be okay."

"Dude! We're not okay!" he shouted.

That drew the reaction of the men. I heard a thump,
Treehorn groaned, and I hollered, "Treehorn, you okay?
You okay?"

"Yeah." He gasped. "They just whacked me!"

The wind was tugging at my loose shirt and driving
the sack deeper into my face.

We weren't in the village, and we hadn't crossed the
mountains. I was sure of that. We would've felt the
mountain road, heard the engine groaning. The road
had been relatively flat.

Suddenly, the sack was ripped off my head, and I was blinded by the glare. It took a few seconds of squinting for my eyes to fully adjust.

Treehorn stood next to me, squinting as well.

They'd taken us west down A01, the main road, to a little truck stop area where several tractor-trailers were lined up. I wasn't sure if the place was a gas station or what, but I definitely knew we'd headed west because off to the east I could see Kandahar in the far distance and a plane taking off from the airport.

Without a word, the two men got back in the car, threw it in gear, and left us standing there on the side of the road, our hands still cuffed.

"What the hell?" Treehorn gasped.

I whirled, faced the truck stop. A small, blue booth stood near several large trees whose limbs were being thrashed in the wind. I wondered if that was a phone booth, so I gestured with my head and Treehorn and I started walking over there, the wind kicking sand in our faces.

From behind several of the parked trailers came a half dozen more gunmen, AK-47s swinging to come to bear on us.

"Oh, great," I said. "And I just thought they were playing a prank on us."

"Remind me to laugh later," said Treehorn. "Or at least before they kill us."

From behind the gunmen came a familiar face that left me with a deep frown.

Shilmani.

And then, from behind him, came Kundi, the village headman and land owner, shaking his head at us.

I called to Shilmani and quickened my step toward them. "What the hell is this?" I added.

"Please, Scott, it is very unexpected." Shilmani's eyes were bloodshot, and blood was dripping from one of his nostrils.

"You guys better release us right now," said Treehorn.

"That's right," I said.

"No," said Kundi, shaking his finger at us. "We talk first. Right here."

"Shilmani, tell this asshole if he wanted a meeting, he could have asked for it."

Shilmani glanced away, and, his voice cracking, said, "Burki is dead."

My mouth fell open. "Say again?"

"Burki was just shot and killed. Right after you left. My cousin betrayed us. He told Kundi everything— about us hiring you to kill Zahed."

I remembered the conversation I'd had with the old man that Bronco had taken me to see:

"Kundi is your son, and your son negotiates with the Taliban."

"Of course. I fought with Zahed's father many years ago. We are both Mujahadeen. The guns we used were given to us by you Americans."

Of course Kundi was loyal to Zahed. Like father, like son.

I widened my eyes on Kundi and started toward him.

The half dozen guards he'd brought along cut me off—
but what was I going to do with my hands still cuffed?
"You killed Burki?" I asked the old man. "Wasn't he
your friend?"

Shilmani translated. Kundi threw up his hands and
rattled off something about betrayal. I thought I caught
a word of that.

"He says Burki was altering the deal on the water. It was
not Zahed who had changed the terms of the agreement."

"Do you believe that?" I asked Shilmani.

"No, I do not. I was there when Zahed's man came
and told us about the new terms."

"Tell him to let us go. Tell him if doesn't let us go,
I'm going to make a few phone calls, and there's going
to be a lot of trouble. And we'll cut off access to the well,
that's for sure . . ."

Shilmani took a deep breath and reluctantly translated.

Kundi's eyes grew wide and maniacal. He marched
up to me, got in my face, his crooked yellow teeth bared.
"You . . . go home . . ."

I felt like saying, *Let me go and I'll catch the next flight
out. To hell with the politics, this place, the mission. To hell
with it all.*

But the bastard challenged me, managed to capture
me, even, and I wasn't going to take any more of his
bullshit. So what I did say was, "I'm not going home
until I either capture or kill your good buddy Zahed."

Shilmani translated.

Kundi stepped back. The gunmen lined up.

"What the hell, boss?" groaned Treehorn. "Are they getting ready to shoot us?"

Kundi heard the whomping first. He whirled around, lifted a hand to his brow.

Then I heard it. We all did. Two choppers: a Blackhawk and an Apache screaming in from the east, from Kandahar.

"We're late getting back," I told Treehorn.

"Good deal," he said.

Suddenly, Kundi waved for his men to retreat behind the trailers. They ran off, as did the old man, who was shouting back at Shilmani.

"I'm sorry, Scott. Really. I am," cried Shilmani. "And Scott, maybe you can help me! They took my daughter! They took my daughter!"

With that Shilmani bolted off.

It was interesting trying to explain to the Blackhawk crew how we'd managed to get our sorry asses kidnapped, and I called ahead to Harruck to have someone pick up our Hummer—that was, providing the villagers hadn't set it on fire. Turned out they hadn't.

During the chopper ride back to the FOB, Gordon contacted me to say that while they'd been scanning for Green Force Tracker Chips they'd picked up a brief signal from Warris's GFTC. Intel indicated that he was being moved, and Gordon had pinpointed the entrance to yet another tunnel complex.

It was time to make our move for a rescue.

* * *

"So you got yourself taken prisoner," said Harruck, producing two glasses for us. It was going to be straight whiskey this time and it was barely past noon.

We sat in his office, me still rubbing my wrists, him intent on filling our drinks to the brim.

I took mine and sucked it down like a man who'd found an oasis. The burn nearly made my eyes roll back. After a long exhale, I said, "I'm so over this."

"You and me both."

"It's tearing us up. All of us."

"It is. You ever think it'd be like this? I mean when you first joined up?"

"Oh, yeah, of course. I was totally stoked about the futility of war."

He snorted. "Me, too."

"But maybe now we've caught a break."

That drew his frown. "Really? You know they've gone back on the TV. They're going to kill Warris if we don't meet their demands in twenty-four hours. Keating has stepped up plans for the offensive."

"And you know what's going to happen," I said. "If I don't get out there, they're going to kill Warris, they'll launch that offensive, and the media will report on all the innocents who were killed. We'll be the bad guys all over again."

The XO knocked, then entered. "Sir, the governor's back. He's screaming again."

"Tell him to fuck off," snapped Harruck.

I laughed under my breath.

"Tell him I'm in a meeting," Harruck corrected.

"Okay, and Dr. Anderson is outside, too. She says all the workers just walked off the job. They just . . . left . . ."

"What?"

"I don't know what's going on, sir, but I'm willing to bet it all goes back to Kundi."

"That's a safe bet," I told the XO. I stood. "I'm gearing up. I'm taking the team out tonight. We've got actionable intel on Warris's location. We'll find him. And maybe we'll find Zahed."

Harruck was already shaking his head. "There's nothing to talk about here. Like you said, they'll kill Warris, the offensive will happen, and all my work here was for nothing. Actionable intel is just an excuse for C-4 and gunfire."

I raised my brows. "I'm taking one more shot, and all I need is a little evac if it all hits the fan."

"You're dreaming, Scott."

"I'm not. If I can find Warris—if I can do that, they won't have to launch the offensive. If I can take out Zahed, that's icing on the cake."

"We've got more enemies than the Taliban here. Bronco wants Zahed rich and alive and feeding the agency information. Kundi wants the status quo. Even the people here would rather deal with Zahed. We're the only idiots that want him dead. If you kill him, the Taliban will retaliate."

"We'll dismantle and demoralize them. By the time I'm done, they won't know what hit them."

"I don't believe you anymore, Scott. And I can't support you."

"I know when it comes down to it, you'll do the right thing. You won't leave me hanging out there."

He took a deep breath. "Just get out."

I returned a lopsided grin. "Thanks for the drink."

TWENTY-FIVE

The satellite images that Gordon had provided were both excellent and disconcerting. The tunnel entrance where Warris's signal had last been detected overlooked the northeast side of Sangsar, so we'd need to hike through one of the mountain passes off the main road, then hike another half kilometer to reach the top and descend down to the tunnel, all the while making sure we were not spotted.

With the men gathered inside our billet, I went over the hardcopy images, indicated our route, and asked for suggestions about our evac.

"Any word on CAS?" asked Brown.

I gave him the usual look.

"Not even a Predator?" asked Hume. "I mean, Jesus God, we've lost men up there. Not even a friggin' drone?"

"I'm working on it," I said. I had sent Gordon the request. Even if we couldn't get fire support, the Predator guys could pick up the thermal images of guards positioned near and around the tunnel entrance. I'd said we were willing to take any kind of intel via sensor because anything that's a sensor has to talk to everybody else.

"Before we leave, I want to put something on the table," said Ramirez, his voice growing uneven.

My heart might have skipped a beat. I cautioned him with my gaze, which he met for only a second.

"What's up?" asked Brown.

"Look, nobody's said anything about it, but we need to talk."

"Joey, I know where this is going," said Treehorn. "We're all in this together. We don't need to do that."

"I think we do," Ramirez said, raising his voice. "Because if we rescue Warris, then he'll start squealing like a freaking pig—and we're all going to pay for that." He looked at me. "Warris is not loyal to the Ghosts. Not the way we are. Isn't that right, Captain?"

I just shook my head. Was he threatening me now?

"I am not having this conversation," said Brown, raising a palm. "I am not going there."

"YOU HAVE TO GO THERE!" Ramirez shouted at the top of his lungs—

We all froze, shocked by the outburst.

Brown whirled back, leaned over, and got squarely in Ramirez's face. "No, I do not. So you'd best shut up now, Joey. Just shut up."

Ramirez began to lose his breath. "He tried to relieve the

captain of his command. The captain refused. We refused to acknowledge him. We're all going down if Warris talks. All of us! It's like we're going out to save the guy who's going to chop off your heads! What's wrong with that picture?"

"Why are you so worried?" asked Treehorn. "I don't give a rat's ass what that punk says. It's his word against ours. Screw him."

"Harruck will back him up," said Ramirez. "I'm telling you, if we rescue his ass, we're done, busted down to regular Army, maybe even discharged."

"I'll take all the heat for that," I said, my tone in sharp juxtaposition to his. "No worries, guys."

"You can try to take the heat, but that won't matter," said Ramirez. "He'll try to hang us all. And I'm not going to let that happen. Not for a second."

"Then what're you saying, Joey?" asked Brown.

"You *know* what I'm saying."

Treehorn threw up his hands. "Aw, no way. I'm not listening to this."

"Look, we do everything in our power to rescue him, but unfortunately, he doesn't make it back—"

"Oh my God," said Hume with a gasp. "Joey, are you insane? Do you know what the hell you're saying?"

"THIS AIN'T A GODDAMNED WAR! IT'S NOT!" he shouted.

I looked at Ramirez. "Maybe you're going to stay behind."

"No, *sir*."

"Then you're done talking. You're just going to shut

up and do your job—and our job is to rescue one of our brothers and bring him back. And that's what we're going to do. Do you all read me—loud and clear?"

They boomed their acknowledgment.

I pointed a finger at the door and glowered at Ramirez. "Outside."

We shifted out together, with the heat of the team's gazes on our shoulders.

He paced and shuddered like a rabid dog.

"I need you tonight. You're one of the best guys I've got," I began.

"We can't rescue Warris."

"You're getting all bent out of shape for nothing. Who knows if we'll even find him? Worry about him barking later. Not now."

"We can't trust anybody, can we?"

"What're you talking about?"

He shrugged, then squinted toward the setting sun. "This place . . . it's driving me crazy."

I nodded. "It's the sand. Just gets everywhere. Shower doesn't even help . . ."

He sighed. "No way to get clean. Not here."

"Look, bro, I can't do this without you. I need my Bravo team leader sharp and ready. We're good. You should know that. We're good."

"Okay. But Warris . . . I just don't know."

"Don't do anything stupid."

"That sounds like a threat."

"No. It's an order."

He took a long breath, cursed, then started back toward the billet.

I echoed his curse.

At about two A.M. local time, we borrowed a civilian pickup truck and drove out past the bridge we'd blown, working our way parallel along the riverbank till I found the shallowest-looking spot. We parked there and waited.

What I didn't tell the guys was that after I'd had my talk with Harruck and he'd been reluctant to promise any help, I'd gone outside and met with the XO, who was more than happy to take a break from the screaming governor and irate humanitarian lady (although we both once more agreed that she was a looker). I'd called the XO Marty, which made him wince, but I was trying to gain his trust.

"I'm wondering if you guys could move up a couple of Bradleys, put them way into the defile. Do it about oh two hundred."

"Why?"

"I want the Taliban in the mountains to focus on you guys to the west and not us."

"Did you ask the CO?"

"I'm asking you."

He thought a moment. "I see. And what do I get in return?"

I ticked them off with my fingers: "Money, power, fame, hookers, and booze."

He grinned. "You prima donnas in SF are clever bastards. But I'm serious—what's in it for me?"

"What do you want?"

"How about a healthy dose of respect?"

"Marty, you got to earn that on your own, but two Bradleys would make one hell of a down payment in my eyes."

"Okay, but I can swallow this much easier with a lot of beer."

"You got it."

"Two Bradleys," he said.

"Yeah, and can you have them put up a flare when they're in place?"

"Wow, you really want a party."

"You know it."

"Well, Harruck's been hitting the bottle a lot. I'm sure he'll be drunk and asleep by then . . ."

Wouldn't you know it, lo and behold, the flare arced high in the sky.

I whispered a thank-you to the XO.

The guys freaked out. "Relax, that's our cue," I told them. "Let's move."

We waded through the hip-high water, holding our AKs above our heads. The water felt thick and warm, like motor oil, and I imagined snakes and piranhas and other assorted demons coiling around my legs as we made the crossing.

For the hell of it, we brought along our last two

Cross-Coms that hadn't been fried. Again, I wore one, Ramirez the other. The mountain pass looked clear as we neared the bottom. In fact, several combatants had shifted over to where the flare had gone up. I counted at least fifteen enemy fighters on that side of the mountain, keeping a close watch on the Bradleys, the red diamonds floating over each of their positions in my HUD.

We began our ascent, the path rock-strewn and as rugged as I'd expected. Though we'd dressed like Taliban, the one exception was our boots. We wouldn't give up our combat boots for a pair of sandals, not in those mountains. And when it came time to boogie, we sure as hell shouldn't worry about stubbing our toes.

But our heavy boots, now filled with water, squished and slogged as we climbed, and I grew annoyed that we couldn't move more quietly.

A data bar opened in my HUD, showing an image of a Predator drone flying high above the mountain range. The image switched to an officer in his cockpit, which was—quite remarkably—on the other side of the world inside a trailer at Nellis Air Force Base in Las Vegas.

"Ghost Lead, this is Predator Control, over."

"Go ahead, Predator."

"We have visual confirmation of your target tunnel. Count two tangos outside the entrance, two more approximately ten meters above. We also see a heavy gun emplacement approximately twenty meters east of the entrance with two tangos manning that position, over."

"Roger that, Predator, can you send me the stream?"

"En route. Recording looks clean."

"Can I call on you for fires?"

"Standby, Ghost Lead."

I signaled for a halt and crouched down behind two long rafts of stone, like fallen pillars from an ancient palace. "Got a Predator up there," I told the team in a whisper, widening my eyes on Hume, who nodded and shook a fist. "Waiting to hear if he can drop some Hellfires if we need 'em."

"Ghost Lead, this is Predator Control. We are not authorized to provide fire support. However, I've personally sent your request up the pipe to see if we can't get authorization. Do call again, over."

"Roger that," I told him, understanding his meaning. The controller wanted nothing more than to drop his bombs and help us out. His finger was poised over the trigger. All he needed was an officer with the guts to give the word.

"They might help us," I told the guys after a long breath. I signaled once more to move out.

We were coming in from the east side of the tunnel entrance, so I told Treehorn to move ahead. His job would be to take out the gunners in the machine gun nest. He'd do that with the silenced sniper rifle he'd brought along. Ramirez and his team would focus on the two guys up top, bringing them down with knives or with their silenced pistols. I'd take Smith and Jenkins to a southerly approach of the main entrance.

We spent another thirty minutes moving into position, the night growing more cool and calm, the wind dying. In the distance, across the vast stretch of sand, a

Bedouin caravan trekked slowly toward Senjaray, the group traveling in the more tolerable temperatures of the night. A long line of camels laden with heavy bundles wound off into the shadows.

And for a moment, I just watched them, rapt by the image, as though we were living in a different century.

"In position," said Ramirez.

"Got the gunners in sight," reported Treehorn, relying on our conventional radio.

I replied to each, then gave the hand signals for Smith and Jenkins to move ahead of me as we made our approach toward the entrance. A crescent moon gave us enough light to see the footprints in the path ahead. We were taking a well-worn path that, despite the risks, would keep us silent. Every rock, smaller stone, and pebble was an enemy as we drew closer.

The path turned sharply to the right, hugging the mountainside, with a sheer dropoff to our left. And there it was, down below: Sangsar, as quiet as ever. A spattering of lights. The slight flap of laundry on the lines. I lifted my binoculars and scanned the walls, spotted a cat milling about, and a man, knees pulled into his chest, sleeping near one gate, his rifle propped at his side.

Smith held up his fist. We stopped, got lower. He had two, just ahead. He slipped back, as did Jenkins.

They looked at me: *Okay, Captain, you're up.*

I took a deep breath and started forward, testing every footfall, turning myself through sheer willpower into a swift and silent ghost.

TWENTY-SIX

For me anyway, there's a delayed emotional reaction after killing a man. Like most combatants, I've trained myself to go numb during the act and let muscle memory take over. I think only of the moment, of removing the obstacle while reminding myself that this man I'm about to kill wants to kill me just as badly. So, I reason, I'm only defending myself. They are targets, a means to an end, and the fragility of the human body helps expedite the process.

That all sounds very clinical, and it should. It helps to think about it in terms of cold hard numbers.

I once had a guy at the JFK School ask me how many people I'd killed. I lied to him. I told him if you kept count you'd go insane. But I had a pretty good approximation of the number. I once got on a city bus, glanced at all the people, and thought, *I've killed all of you. And all the rest who are going to get on and get off . . . all day . . .*

Strangely enough, months after a mission, without any obvious trigger, the moment would return to me in a dream or at the most bizarre or mundane time, and I would suddenly hate myself for killing a father, a husband, a brother, an uncle . . . I think about all the families who've suffered because of me. And then I just force myself to go on, to forget about that, to just say I was doing my job and that the guys I'd killed had made their choices and had paid for them with their lives.

I would be just fine.

Until the next kill. The next nightmare. The next guilt trip. And the cycle would repeat.

The all-American hero has dirt under his nails and blood splattered across his face . . .

And so it was with that thought—the thought that I would suffer the guilt later—that I raised my silenced pistol and shot the first guard in the head.

A perfect shot, as assisted by my Cross-Com.

I had but another second to take out the other guy, who, of course reacted to his buddy falling to the ground and to the blood now spraying over his face.

He swung his rifle toward me, opened his mouth, and I put two bullets in his forehead before he could scream. His head snapped back and he dropped heavily to his rump, then rolled onto his side, twitching involuntarily.

A slight thumping resounded behind us. One. Two.

Treehorn reported in. Guards at the heavy gun were dead. "Roger that. You man that gun now, got it?"

"I'm on it," he answered. "Big bad bullets at your command!"

I waited outside the entrance while Smith and Jenkins dragged the bodies back up the path and tucked them into a depression in the mountainside.

By the time they returned, Ramirez and his group were coming down to join us. I held up an index finger: *Wait.*

"Predator Control, this is Ghost Lead, over."

"Ghost Lead, this is Predator Control, go ahead."

"Do you see any other tangos near our position, over?"

"We do see some, Ghost Lead, but they're on the other side of the mountain, moving toward the Bradleys. You look clear right now, over."

"Roger that. Ghost Lead, out."

Now I would piss off Ramirez. I looked at him. "You, Jenkins, and Smith head back up. Man the same positions as the guards you killed."

"What? That wasn't part of the plan," Ramirez said, drawing his brows together.

"It is now. Let 'em think nothing's wrong. Brown? Hume? You guys are with me. Let's go."

I left Ramirez standing there, dumbfounded. No, he wouldn't get his chance to get near Warris, and I'd just told him in so many words, *No, I don't trust you.*

Brown took point with a penlight fixed to the end of his silenced rifle. I forgot to mention earlier that none of us liked the limited peripheral vision offered by night-vision goggles—especially in closed quarters—so we'd long since abandoned them during tunnel and cave ops. Moreover, if we were spotted, the bad guys wouldn't think twice about shooting a guy wearing NVGs because he was obviously not one of them. It was pretty rare for the Taliban to get their hands on a pair of expensive goggles, though not completely unheard of. As it was, we'd offer them at least a moment's pause—a moment we'd use to kill them.

The tunnel was similar to all the others we'd encountered, about a meter wide and two meters tall, part of it naturally formed, but as we ventured deeper we saw it'd been dug or blasted out in various sections, the walls clearly scarred by shovels and pickaxes. Soon, we shifted along a curving wall to the left, and Brown called for a halt. He placed a small beacon about the size of a quarter on the floor near his boot. My Cross-Com immediately picked up the signal, but even if we lost our Cross-Coms, dropping bread crumbs was a good idea in this particular network. We all had a sense that these tunnels were some of the most extensive and vast in the entire country, and finding our way back out would pose a serious challenge.

Brown looked back at me, gave a hand signal. We started up again.

In less than thirty seconds we reached a fork in the tunnel, with a broader one branching off to our right. Brown placed another beacon on the floor. I took a deep breath, the air cooler and damper.

"Man, I got the willies," whispered Hume.

"You and me both," Brown said.

After aiming his penlight down the more narrow tunnel, Brown studied the footprints in the sand and rock. Both paths were well-worn. No clues there.

I pointed to the right.

Brown looked at me, as if to say, *Are you sure?*

I wasn't. But I was emphatic. I wouldn't split us up, not three guys.

Dark stains appeared on the floor as we crossed deeper into the broader tunnel. Brown slowed and aimed his penlight at one wider stain. Dried blood.

And then, just a little farther down the hall, shell casings that'd been booted off to the sides of the path gleamed in Brown's light.

We shifted another twenty meters or so, when Brown called for another halt and switched off his light. If you want to experience utter darkness, then go spelunking. There is nothing darker. I'd lost the satellite signal for the Cross-Com, so I just blinked hard and let my eyes adjust. Brown moved a few steps farther and then a pale yellow glow appeared on the ceiling about five meters ahead, the light flickering slightly. My eyes further adjusted, and Brown led us another ten or so steps and stopped. He pointed.

A huge section of the floor looked as though it'd collapsed, and the rough-hewn top of a homemade ladder jutted from the hole. The light came from kerosene lanterns, I guessed, and suddenly the ladder shifted and creaked.

My pulse raced.

We crouched tight to the wall as the Taliban fighter

reached the top. He was wearing only a loose shirt and pants, his hair closely cropped, his beard short. He was eighteen, if that. Tall. Gangly. Big Adam's apple.

Brown signaled that he had this guy. I wouldn't argue. Brown was in fact our resident knife guy and had saved his own ass more than once with his trusted Nightwing blade.

I winced over the crunch and crack, the scream muffled by Brown's gloved hand, and the slight frump and final exhale as the kid spread across the tunnel floor and began to bleed out. The diamond black knife now dripped with blood, which Brown wiped off on his hip.

We examined the kid for any clues, but all he had was a rifle and the clothes on his back. Brown edged forward toward the ladder and glowing lanterns below. Then we all got down on our hands and knees and crawled forward. Once we neared the lip of the hole and the ladder, we lowered ourselves onto our bellies, and I chanced a look down.

The chamber was circular and about five meters in diameter, with piles of rock and dirt along one wall where, indeed, the collapse had occurred. The opposite wall was stacked from floor to ceiling with more opium bricks wrapped in brown paper, and beside those stacks were cardboard boxes whose labels read MEAL, READY-TO-EAT, INDIVIDUAL. DO NOT ROUGH HANDLE WHEN FROZEN. U.S. GOVERNMENT PROPERTY. COMMERCIAL RESALE IS UNLAWFUL. There had to be fifty or more boxes. We'd seen MRE trash littering the tunnels earlier, but I'd had no idea they were smuggling in so much of the high-carb

GI food. I wondered if Bronco was helping these guys get their hands on this "government" property.

Before we could shift any closer and even descend the ladder, someone rushed up behind us. We all rolled to the tunnel walls. Then, just as I was bringing my rifle around and Brown was switching on his penlight, a Taliban fighter rounded the corner and held up his palm. "Hold fire!" he stage-whispered.

He pulled down his *shemagh*. Ramirez.

Brown cursed.

Hume swore.

I'm not sure how many curses I used through my whisper, but more than four.

We spoke in whispers:

"You didn't answer my calls," Ramirez said.

"We're cut off down here," I answered, slowly sitting up as he crossed to me. I put a finger to my lips. "What?"

"The two Bradleys are pulling out of the defile."

"Why?"

"I don't know. They wouldn't answer my calls, either."

"Aw, Simon must've woke up," I said. "Damn it."

"I contacted the Predator. He's still got a way better sat image than we do. He said the guys are moving back over here. I left Treehorn on the machine gun, but I figured I'd come down to warn you."

"Where are Smith and Jenkins?"

"Still outside the entrance."

"All right, get back out there."

"Any luck here?"

"Joey, go . . ."

He hesitated, pursed his lips. "Yes, sir."

Brown looked at me and shook his head. Was this some kind of lame excuse to get himself back in the action? We didn't know. But if he was telling the truth and the Taliban were shifting back across the mountain, then the clock was ticking more loudly now.

Hume edged up to me. "I'll take the ladder."

I gave him a nod. He descended, then gave us the signal: *All clear for now.*

We followed him down to find another tunnel heading straight off then turning sharply to the right.

"Damn, this place is huge," whispered Hume.

Several small wheelbarrows were lined up near the stacks of opium, and I got an idea. We piled a few stacks into one barrow, and then Brown led the way, pushing the wheelbarrow with Hume and me at his shoulders. We were happy drug smugglers now, and we'd shout that we had orders to move the opium.

We reached the turn and nearly ran straight into a guy heading our way. He started shouting at Brown in Pashto: "What are you guys doing?"

Well, I thought we'd have time to explain. But I just shot him in the head. He fell, and Brown got the wheelbarrow around him while Hume grabbed the guy's arms and I took the legs. We carried him quickly back to the chamber and left him there. Then we hustled back after Brown and found the tunnel sweeping downward at about a twenty-degree angle. Brown nearly lost control of the wheelbarrow until we finally reached the bottom and began to hear voices. Faint. Pashto.

Maybe it was the adrenaline or the thought that outside our guys would soon be confronted, but I shifted around Brown and ran forward, farther down the tunnel, rushing right into another chamber with about ten sleeping areas arranged on the floor: carpets and heavy blankets all lined up like a barracks.

I took it all in.

A single lantern burned atop a small wooden crate, and two Taliban were sitting up in bed and talking while six or seven others were sleeping.

I shot the first two guys almost immediately, with Hume and Brown rushing in behind me and opening fire, the rounds silenced, the killing point-blank, brutal, and instantaneous.

Killing men while they slept was ugly business, and I tried not to look too closely. They'd return in my nightmares anyway, so I focused my attention on a curious sight near the crate holding the lantern—a pair of military boots, the same ones we wore. I picked them up, placed them near mine to judge the size.

"Warris's?" Brown whispered to me.

I shrugged. We checked our magazines, then headed on, still pushing the wheelbarrow.

The next tunnel grew much more narrow, and we had to turn sideways to pass through one section. As the rock wall dragged against my shirt, I imagined the tunnel tightening like a fist, the air forced from my collapsing lungs, and I began to panic. A quick look to the right said relief was just ahead.

Brown had to abandon the wheelbarrow, of course,

and once we made it onto the other side, the passage grew much wider, as revealed by Brown's light.

My nose crinkled as a nasty odor began clinging to the air, like a broken sewer pipe, and the others cringed as well. Our *shemaghs* did nothing to help. I didn't want to believe that the Taliban had created an "outhouse" inside the cave, but judging from the smell, they might have resorted to that.

I stifled a cough as we shuffled farther, almost reluctantly now. The odor grew worse. We reached a T-shaped intersection, where the real stench came from the right, and I thought my eyes were tearing.

Brown shoved down his *shemagh*, held his nose, and indicated that he did not want to go down the right tunnel.

And that's exactly where I signaled for him to go.

He shook his head vigorously.

I widened my eyes. *Do it.*

And then I began to gag, caught myself, and we pressed on. I held the *shemagh* tighter to my nose and mouth without much relief.

A voice came from behind us, the words in Pashto: "What's going on now?"

Hume turned back and Brown raised his light.

It was a young Taliban fighter, his AK hanging from his shoulder as he raised his palms in confusion.

He squinted at us more deeply until Brown directed the light into his eyes.

I couldn't see, but I think Hume shot him. Thump. Down. The body count was racking up too swiftly for my taste, but the presence of those boots gave me hope.

We left that guy where he fell and forged on toward the terrible stink.

"I can barely breathe," said Hume.

"Just keep going," I told him.

The ground grew more damp, and up ahead, about twenty meters, were a pair of broad wooden planks traversing another hole in the ground, the result of yet a second cave-in, I guessed. Just before the hole another tunnel jogged off to the left, with faint light shifting at its far end. At the intersection, I saw that the other tunnel to our right curved upward and the night sky shone beyond—a way out, but on which side of the mountain range? I was disoriented.

And then from the other side of the hole and the planks came two Taliban, rifles lowered but still ready to snap up. They were talking to each other when they spotted me and Brown, and one looked up, shouted something.

I shot the guy who screamed.

Brown fired at the other one . . . and missed! That bastard took off running and hollering like a maniac.

And from behind us, down in the hole, where the stench of human feces and urine rose to an ungodly level, a muffled cry rose and echoed up across the rock.

TWENTY-SEVEN

I charged after the guy who'd sprinted away, my heart drumming in my ears. The tunnel curved abruptly to the left and then made an abrupt right turn. The guy reached a ladder at the tunnel's dead end and started up it. I shot him before he made it halfway, and he came down with a heavy thud, shaking and raising his hands in surrender. Under different circumstances, I might have taken him prisoner. Instead, I shot him again, then swung around, saw the lantern lighting the path in one corner and more stacks of opium, along with crates and boxes of ammunition.

Someone shouted a name, then asked, "Where are you?" in Pashto.

I stole a quick breath, glanced up.

There, framed by the hole in the ceiling, was a man leaning down, his bearded face glowing in the lantern. I gritted my teeth and shot him, too, in the face. He came tumbling down and crashed onto the first guy. He was older, gray beard, his body trembling, nerves misfiring.

Still riding the massive wave of adrenaline, I mounted the ladder, which I guessed led into another chamber. I was about to reach the top and turn around when someone rushed into the tunnel below, startling the hell out of me.

"Boss!" Brown whispered.

I came down two rungs, my heart palpitating. Brown was waving at me to come back, his teeth bared.

"What?"

He mouthed the words: *We found him!*

During my first tour in country, my team captured an Afghan policeman who'd been working secretly as an interrogator for the Taliban. He shared with us the orders from his boss: "I want you to torture them with methods so horrible that their cries of agony will scare even the birds from their nests, and if any one of them survives, he will never again have a night's sleep."

This guy described in vivid detail the creative methods he and his comrades employed to slowly and systematically kill their prisoners. The generous use of electricity, insects, water, and clubs would've made even the most iron-stomached soldier grimace as he listened to the tales.

Consequently, when we found Warris, my imagination had already run wild . . .

But I'd forgotten they wanted him in good condition. They still wanted to negotiate, and I'm sure Zahed was heavily influenced by the company he kept, otherwise Warris would have been much closer to death. I took one look past the planks, and in the tiny shaft of light created by Brown, I grimaced tightly.

Warris was sitting naked in a foot-high pool of water, urine, and feces. He'd been gagged, his hands cuffed behind his back, and when he saw us, saw me remove my *shemagh*, his eyes lit with recognition. He struggled to his feet and began crying. His face was bruised and battered, but otherwise he had all his appendages and could still move.

I'd never seen a soldier, especially one from my own unit, look as helpless and pathetic, and I suddenly didn't care what he said about me—politics and bullshit be damned. We were going to get him out of there, out of tunnels, out of that godforsaken country.

We'd brought about fifty feet of paracord in one of the packs, but we didn't need it. Hume rushed back to fetch the ladder. The hole was about nine feet deep, the ladder about seven feet long, so we'd get him out the easier way. With Hume standing guard, Brown and I lowered ourselves down the ladder, and I descended to the bottom rung, just above the cesspool. I could barely look at Warris. "It's all right, buddy. We're getting you out of here."

I removed his gag, and he swallowed and said, "Thank you." He began crying again. "I won't forget this."

"Don't worry about it."

"But Scott, I can't lie about it . . . about what happened. I can't live with myself if I do that . . ."

My tone hardened. "You know what I think? I think that if I save your ass right now, and you still turn me in, that'll be harder to live with than just lying. And really, all you have to do is keep your mouth shut. That's it. You think about that . . ."

He bit his lip, then suddenly nodded.

"Can you climb?"

"I think so."

"Then let's move."

They'd used a pair of our plastic zipper cuffs, and, with a penlight in my mouth, I carefully sawed through them. With that done, I started up the ladder, and he ascended behind me. I ordered Hume to go fetch some clothes from one of the guys we'd killed, along with an extra shirt to use as rag. God, we needed to wipe him off. He reeked. Hume hurried away, and once we pulled Warris out, he backhanded the tears from his eyes and said, "I've been down there most of the time. They cleaned me up to make the videos. I've barely had anything to eat or drink. I'm dying."

"Easy, we'll get you something," whispered Brown. "They got MREs down here."

Within two minutes, Hume came dashing back with the clothes and a concerned look. "I heard some crying up there," he began, cocking a thumb over his shoulder. "You know what I'm thinking . . ."

"Give me that goddamned ladder," I barked.

"Captain, do we really have time for this?" asked Brown.

"Indulge me for three minutes," I said. "While you clean him up and get him dressed."

I dragged the ladder back up to the next hole in the ceiling, ascended, and stepped into another chamber with more boxes of MREs. A narrow tunnel led to a second, even wider area where a few lanterns burned brightly.

My mouth must've fallen open.

Girls ranging in age from perhaps twelve or thirteen up to seventeen or eighteen were dressed in tattered clothes, bound and gagged, and sitting along the wall, a few sleeping, others staring blankly at me, and a few more crying through their gags.

At the far end of the room was a sleeping area piled high with pillows and blankets, and I shuddered as I imagined what went on there. Zahed would, of course, deny any wrongdoing; he could blame it all on his men, argue that in some respects he did not have control over them. And, of course, he'd be lying. He allowed this to go on, and in doing so, created a nightmare for the parents of these poor girls.

I caught a blur of movement from the corner of my eye, and then from a tunnel exit near the back came another fighter. I raised my silenced pistol and put two rounds in his heart. I wanted to put fifty.

I whirled back, lowered my *shemagh*, and in Pashto said to the girls, "I will help you."

One girl in particular fought more violently against her binding and gag. As I crossed to her, she began to look familiar, and then, with a start, I knew she was

Shilmani's daughter, Hila. I heard him screaming again, *"They took my daughter!"*

They'd tied up the girls with cheap nylon rope and gagged them with scarves. I untied Hila's gag, and she moved her mouth, licked her lips, and began to speak in a rapid fire that I didn't understand.

"It's okay . . ." I said in a soothing tone.

She surprised me. "Thank you. I . . . what they did . . . I cannot see my family again . . ."

"You speak English?"

"My father taught me."

I grinned weakly in understanding. "Okay. That helps. All I know is, we're going to get you out of here. All of you. Do you understand?"

"Yes."

"Can you tell them for me?"

She nodded. I finished cutting her arms and legs free. She stood and spoke rapidly to the girls, who all began nodding. Brown came rushing into the chamber, took one look at the girls, at me, and said, "Jesus Christ."

"We're getting them out."

"Are you kidding me?"

"Nope."

"Aw, this has really gone to hell! We came here for Zahed, and we're going home with them!"

Hila turned back to face me. "You came here for Zahed?"

I leaned over and nodded slowly.

She glanced away, a pained look coming over her face. "He is very bad man."

"Yes, he is."

She pursed her lips, glanced back at the girls, as if thinking it over, then said, "I know where he is . . ."

All the intelligence assets of the U.S. government had been unable to locate the fat man, in part because the intelligence they gathered was being corrupted by Bronco and his associates. Nevertheless, I would never, for the life of me, bet that the location of my target would be spoon-fed to me by a teenaged girl who'd been taken prisoner.

When I reflect and calculate the odds of what had happened, how I'd met Shilmani, how Hila had come to recognize me, what had happened to her and how she'd come to learn where Zahed was located, I could only blame fate.

Or the merciless universe.

Because if I hadn't listened to her, if I'd just dragged them out of the cave and gotten out of there, I would've only had to deal with keeping Warris quiet—

And not the rest of it.

"Help me cut 'em free," I told Brown. "Come on, come on."

The words escaped my lips, and not two seconds later, the chamber quaked and dust fell from the ceiling.

"What the hell?" Brown gasped.

"Captain!" cried Hume. "I hear gunfire coming from somewhere outside! And mortars!"

"We have to move now, Scott!" added Warris.

"We're coming! We've got some girls up here. They're coming down. We're getting them out!"

As Brown freed the girls, Hila told them where to go, and one by one they took off running.

"They made us drink wine," she told me as I cut another girl free. "They made us do things."

"I know. It's okay."

"No, it's not okay. I am filthy. I am not a woman anymore. I am a dog."

I looked at her, grabbed her hand. "You're not a dog."

"But I can never go home."

She started removing the gags from the remaining girls and reassuring them, while the guys kept screaming for me to come. The final two girls dashed off.

"All right, get them and Warris out of here. Ramirez and the rest of Bravo should be waiting for you," I told Brown.

"What about you?"

I lifted my chin to Hila. "She knows where Zahed is."

"Boss, what if she's wrong?"

I widened my gaze on Hila. "Are you sure?"

She gave an exaggerated nod. "I hate him. He was the first one to have me. I know where he is."

"Oh my God," Brown muttered under his breath.

"I'm going with her."

"Not alone," said Brown. "You fight with your buddy."

I shoved my silenced pistol into Hila's hand. "That's right. She's my buddy."

She looked at me, scared, the weight of the pistol causing her shoulder to droop.

"You're crazy," said Brown. "This is crazy!"

"Just listen to me, Marcus. I need you to protect

Warris. I need you to get him out. I'm worried about Joey, you know that."

"I know, boss. I won't let Joey do anything stupid."

"Good. 'Cause I'm betting Warris won't talk."

"Me, too. He owes us. Big-time."

"All right, so when you get out, contact Gordon. Tell them to track my chip. You'll know where I am."

"Will do." He thrust out his hand. "See you soon, you crazy mofo."

I gave him a firm handshake. "Thank you, Marcus."

Then I turned to Hila. "Which way?"

My father raised three sons and a daughter, and my sister Jenn was unquestionably Daddy's little girl. The old man was a hardcore disciplinarian with us boys, but my sister could get away with bloody murder. As a kid I could never understand his leniency toward her and was entirely jealous of it. As I got older, I didn't begrudge my sister anymore. In fact, it took my entire life for me to realize that Dad was a cynic who simply needed my sister to remind him of all the beauty still left in the world.

I wondered if Shilmani had felt likewise about Hila. As she led me through the next tunnel, I wondered if he'd be able to look Hila in the eye after what had happened to her. I knew the culture. I knew what happened to girls like her. But I didn't want to believe that.

She held up my pistol, and I had my rifle at the ready now, with the penlight attached. She led me down two more tunnels, and we descended yet another ladder into a small room with crates piled to the ceiling.

"Guns," was all she said.

"So you came through here?" I asked.

She frowned a moment, then realized what I was asking. "Yes, yes."

"Zahed is here? In the mountain?"

She stopped and shook her head.

"No?"

"No."

"Then where is he?"

"He is in Sangsar."

My mouth fell open. "Aw, no. That's no good. What do you think we're going to do? Walk right down this mountain and into the village?"

I guess I had spoken too fast. She frowned in thought, then finally said, "No, no. We don't walk. We'll run." She tugged my arm, but I stopped dead.

"We can't go to Sangsar."

"Yes, we'll go!"

"How?"

She made a gesture with her hand. "Under . . ."

"You mean there's a tunnel that leads all the way there?"

She beamed at me.

While I was heading off to Sangsar, Brown, Hume, and Warris, along with the group of girls, were rushing back through the tunnels, following the beacons we'd left.

The guys were not happy with my decision to free the girls and attempt to save them, but they obeyed orders and later told me they would've done the same thing. It was sickening to realize what'd been happening in there.

Warris had told them that my decision to search for Zahed alone was foolish and indicative of my poor judgment. Brown had told him that saving his sorry ass was also indicative of my poor judgment. I liked that.

As Hila and I kept moving, I reminded myself that no, you could not generalize and say that all Taliban liked to rape young girls, but we could definitively state that Zahed's men had taken it upon themselves to establish a terrible prison for them. The acts were inexcusable and when I looked at Hila, even for just a second, I wanted to kill Zahed more than anything. He was, in my mind, the symbol for all that was wrong with the country, all that was wrong with the war. And my hatred burned hotter as she dragged me by the wrist and led me down the next tunnel.

The emotions were all over the place at that moment. I felt as though I'd been chasing the fat man all my life, and soon there'd finally be closure, but then I worried for Hila and imagined my own death, the gunshot to my heart, the throbbing pain, the blood seeping into my lungs.

The passageways grew shorter, each ending abruptly with another ladder that we took down, always down, and it was clear we were descending the mountain from the inside. A lantern lit the passage at each ladder, and we encountered no resistance. I grew more at ease—

Until at the end of the next passage we spotted a man coming up a ladder.

Hila fired at him first, the kickback of the pistol startling her. She hit him in the shoulder with the first round, but the second went over his head and ricocheted off the wall.

I put two rounds in his chest, and he fell backward off the ladder. I ran over there, checked below. No other movement. Thankfully, he'd been alone.

It wasn't until I started back that I felt the pain in my arm and stopped, directed a second light down, and saw that I'd been hit, probably from that ricocheting round.

She saw it, too, and started crying and pointing to herself, as if to say, *It's my fault.*

"It's okay," I said. "Just caught me a little. See? In and out?"

I reached into my back pocket, where I kept a small plastic bag filled with antiseptic wipes and bandages. I handed the kit to her. "Fix me up. Quick," I said.

She nodded and got to work, applying the antiseptic and the bandage. The wound looked worse than it was, but it still hurt like a mother. When she was finished, I thanked her and she grabbed me by the other arm. "This way."

We climbed down the next ladder and found ourselves in a concrete drainage pipe that left me hunched over. The pipe ran straight away for as far as I could see, and I guessed that it led all the way under the village wall and into Sangsar proper. I still couldn't receive any satellite signals on the Cross-Com, so I just took it off and shoved it in my hip pocket.

The pipe was littered with rocks and lined with a fine layer of sand, but there was certainly no water, so although I'd described it as a drainage pipe, its primary use was clear: smuggling. There were both boot and tire tracks in the sand. They'd brought wheelbarrows into the pipe or other wheeled carts to move their opium back and forth.

I had to get word of this passage back to higher, in the event I didn't make it back. I'd thought bombing the tunnels we'd found would help stop the attacks on Senjaray, but we'd barely put a dent in Zahed's clandestine highway. But this pipe, this could be the main artery, I thought.

We were losing our breath, and as we picked up the pace and continued on for meter after meter, I repeatedly glanced over my shoulder to watch the light drift away and the darkness consume the rest of the shaft.

"Are we getting closer?" I asked her.

She looked at me. "Close?"

"Zahed is here?" I asked.

"Soon," she said.

TWENTY-EIGHT

While we had been considering a major offensive against the Taliban, they had, unsurprisingly, been thinking about the same thing. And unbeknownst to us, they had planned to launch their attack only a few hours after I'd taken my team into the mountains. Call that ironic and interesting timing.

What gave them pause, however, was our placement of the Bradleys in the defile and the firing of that flare. My simple diversion had changed the enemy's entire battle plan. We later learned that they thought we'd been tipped off, and that had sent Zahed into a state of panic. From what we could gather, he launched a half-hearted offensive, committing only about half of his troops to the fight, while pulling the rest back to Sang-sar to help ensure his escape.

But I was unaware of those facts as Hila took me through the concrete pipe. Had I known that Sangsar would be swarming with at least two, maybe three hundred of Zahed's best trained fighters, I might've given the decision more thought.

But I was blithely unaware.

And Hila had assured me that the fat man kept only two or three guards around him at all times.

Not three hundred.

Far ahead, my light finally picked out the edge of the pipe, which led directly into another tunnel, one only about three meters long.

The air was filled by other scents I couldn't quite discern: incense, cooked meat, burning candles, something. And then I paused, glanced back at Hila. "Here?"

She raised an index finger, and her gaze turned up.

I nodded. The concrete pipe had led to a tunnel that I believed emptied into a basement.

With a gesture for her to remain behind me, I shifted farther into the tunnel, reached the edge, then hunkered down and slowly lifted my penlight.

"Whoa . . ." The word escaped my lips before I could stop it.

We were in a basement all right, a huge one. Fifteen-foot-high concrete walls rose around the perimeter, and I estimated the depth at more than one hundred feet. The place had been converted into a subterranean warehouse, with long rows of opium bricks, crates of ammunition and guns, and more MREs, along with dozens and dozens of wooden boxes whose contents were a mystery.

I shifted to one box and opened it to find a bag labeled in English: ammonium nitrate fertilizer. I snorted. Fertilizer for making bombs.

At the back of the basement rose a wooden staircase leading up to a door half open, flickering light wedging through the crack. When I looked back, Hila was right behind me. She hadn't held back like I'd asked.

I glanced up at the wooden planks and ceiling, listened as people shifted and creaked overhead. Hila's breathing grew louder. I leaned down, grabbed her wrist, and led her along a row of opium bricks, then crouched down at the back.

"Zahed is up there?"

She nodded.

I thought of the Predator, of somehow getting a signal off to that controller, getting him to bomb the whole place while we escaped back through the drainage pipe. Simple. Clean. The only problem was I couldn't confirm that the fat man was up there. I wanted to see him for myself.

"Is it a house up there?"

"Yes. He stays in a big room."

"All right." I didn't think I could get more out of her, and she wanted to come with me.

"No," I told her. "You stay here, be quiet, and wait for me . . . okay?"

She looked about to cry.

"Please . . ."

"Okay."

As I stole away, shifting quickly from row to row of crates and opium bricks, I asked myself, *What the hell am I doing?*

The door at the top of the staircase creaked open, and two Taliban fighters came charging down the stairs with a purpose. I tucked myself deeper into the crates and just watched them jog through the basement and head straight into the tunnel. I looked far down the row at Hila, hidden between two crates now. She'd heard them but she didn't move. Perfect. That kid had a lot of courage, all right.

I gave myself a once-over and tightened the *shemagh* around my face. I was about to step forward and mount the staircase when I thought better of it and shifted back to my spot. I was panting. What the hell had just happened? Had I just chickened out? I wasn't sure. I dug into my pocket, ripped down the *shemagh* again, then donned the Cross-Com and gave the verbal command to activate the device.

The monocle flickered, came to life, but the HUD showed no satellite signal. I was still too deep. I removed and pocketed the unit, then took several long breaths. I checked my magazine, my second pistol with silencer, was ready to rip open my shirt to expose the web gear beneath and the half dozen grenades I carried.

Once more, the door above opened, and three more Taliban fighters came running down and dashed across the basement, on their way toward the tunnel.

I kept telling myself that if I waited any longer, the fat man would be gone. Either he was up there right now packing his bags, or maybe it was all for naught. Maybe he'd already left.

Well, there was only one way to find out.

My arm was stinging again as I hustled up the stairs— a reminder that getting killed was going to hurt. Oh, yeah. I shivered and passed through the door.

A long hallway stretched out in both directions. A living room lay to the left, with tables, chairs, even a very Western-looking leather sofa and flat-screen TV mounted to the wall, all very posh despite the mud-brick walls. Candles burning from wall sconces lit the pathway to my right, where a large kitchen with bar and stools, again very Western, was set up beside another eating area.

Someone shouted behind me. I turned to him, a guy about my age with a salt-and-pepper beard.

He asked me something, then asked me again.

I shook my head. He shoved me out of the way and jogged down the hall. I ran after him. "Wait!" I cried in Pashto. "I need to see Zahed!"

But he kept running. I slowed, reached the edge of the kitchen as something or someone moved behind me. I whirled.

Hila stood there, pistol in one hand.

"I told you to stay down there!" I cried through a whisper.

"Come on," she said. "Let's go see Zahed! I know where!"

She grabbed my wrist and tugged me toward the hall-way ahead.

I grabbed her by the mouth, pulled her into the kitchen, then ducked down beneath the bar and stools. I rolled her over, my hand still wrapped around her mouth, and said, "If they see you, they'll kill you."

She didn't move.

I slowly removed my hand.

"You have to go back," I told her, pointing down toward the basement.

She shook her head.

I gestured to my eyes. "If they see you, they will kill you."

"I know what you said. I don't care. I am dead already. To my family. To everyone who knows me. Let me help you. Let me get revenge against Zahed."

The decision pained me. If I dragged her along, the second we were spotted we'd be accosted, maybe even shot. I could concoct some story, but I didn't like that. I didn't want her around. I couldn't bear to see her get killed, not after what had already happened to her.

I told myself that if I could save her, maybe it all meant something. Maybe I wasn't just a puppet whose strings were being pulled by asinine politicians.

But she could save me time, get me to Zahed more quickly. I would have to comb through the entire house. She seemed to know exactly where he'd be.

She made the decision for me. I released my grip on her at the sound of approaching men, and she bolted around the bar before I could grab her.

The men passed, heading toward the basement door, and she ran out into the hall, waving to me.

So it was the middle of the night in a small town deep in the desert of southern Afghanistan, and I was chasing a teenaged girl carrying a pistol through a terrorist's house. If I started a conversation like that, would you believe me? I wouldn't believe me.

Hila ran all the way down the hall, made an abrupt right-hand turn, and when I followed, I found her stopped dead, raising her pistol at another man coming toward us.

She shot him right in the heart. As he fell, she ran past him, down another hall with doors lining both sides. I was indeed crazy. I'd turned the girl into a cold-blooded killer; then again, maybe Zahed was responsible for that.

As we ran I couldn't help but realize this wasn't a house but a mansion, perhaps the biggest place in the entire town, although you wouldn't know it when looking on Sangsar from above. The buildings were so closely situated that it was hard to tell where one ended and the other began. The doors here were ornate as well, heavy oak, deeply carved. The fat man had spared no expense.

Hila reached a door at the end, pushed through it, and ran inside.

I called after her, reached the doorway, turned into the room, and found her at the far end, running toward a window, a real window, which was rare to find.

We were in a massive bedroom with a four-poster bed, heavy furniture, and yet another flat-screen TV.

It was like a room in a five-star hotel that had been built in a neighborhood of utter squalor. Very surreal. I'm sure parts of the village didn't have electricity, but Zahed sure did; either that or he ran his TV off a generator.

I rushed to the window to find Hila pointing. "There!" she cried. "There!"

Across a long, tree-lined courtyard, past fig trees and a wall covered in rose bushes, were the silhouettes of three men standing near a wrought-iron gate.

One of them had to be the fat man. He was tall, six feet five at least, and huge, more than four hundred pounds, I guessed.

Stacks of luggage were lined on the walkway beside them. They were waiting to be picked up.

Damn it. I tried the window. Locked. I couldn't find a way to open it! I turned back—

And when I did, a man was standing in the door with his AK pointed at us. "What're you doing?" he asked in Pashto.

I shifted in front of Hila but didn't raise my rifle. "The infidels come from the basement," I tried to say.

The man took a step forward and frowned. Aw, no. I must've made a mistake. Maybe I'd told him his mother was a whore, I wasn't sure.

Before I could react, another man jogged up beside the first and began screaming and tugging at his buddy.

I stole a look out the window.

A car had rolled up outside.

The first guy shouted at me again. I threw myself to one side, raised my rifle, and fired a salvo into him and his buddy, no silencer, just me and the AK dishing out lead loud and clear. Both went down, but the first guy had started firing—

And Hila let out a scream.

As both men fell, I clambered up, shouldered my rifle, and rushed to Hila, who'd fallen onto her back and was clutching her side. I immediately pulled away her shirt and saw that a round had pierced the right side of her abdomen, no exit wound.

I chanced another look out the window. The wrought-iron gate was open. The three men were fighting over something, their voices raised as they rushed to get in the car while two others hurried to load the luggage.

"This hurts," said Hila. "Please. Can you help?"

"It's not that bad. You'll be okay."

She clutched my hand. "Please. I need help."

"But I need to go," I told her. "He's outside. He's going to get away . . ."

She grabbed my hand even tighter as tears welled in her eyes.

TWENTY-NINE

I'd thought Hila would beg me to stay with her, but she narrowed her gaze and said, "Okay. Get him. Then come back to help me."

"I will."

"Okay."

I understood now. She had wanted to die, but ironically the gunshot now gave her the will to live. I dragged her behind the bed, out of view from the doorway, and then I grabbed the pistol I'd given her, tucked it into my waistband, and bolted to my feet. I seized a pillow from the four-poster bed, then braced the pillow in front of my face. With a running start, I launched into the air and let out a string of curses as I crashed through the window and landed in a shower of glass on the dirt below.

The three figures ran toward the car now, a black Mercedes, probably fitted with bulletproof glass. I came rolling up with the pistol in my hand and shot the two guys loading luggage.

The driver opened his door and raised a pistol. I shot him, and then, as I sprinted toward the gate, I got my first clear look at the men:

Bronco.

His Asian buddy "Mike."

And the fat man himself, decked out in silk robes and clean turban and with a beard that splayed across his chest. He wore big gold and diamond rings, and when he faced me, he frowned for a second as both Bronco and Mike reached down to draw weapons.

"Unh-uh," I said, tugging down my *shemagh*.

"Aw, Joe, I can't believe you're this stupid," said Bronco, slowly raising his palms now. "Didn't you get your new OPORDER? We got you pulled off this job. Finally . . ."

"You're bluffing. I got nothing."

Zahed eyes narrowed in fury, and he turned to Bronco and began screaming. I didn't catch very much, but he'd said something about Bronco being the fool.

All three of them backed toward the car.

"Don't move," I warned them.

"We have to leave," said Mike. "You have no idea how important this is or the extent of this operation."

I craned my head at the sound of multiple helicopter engines echoing off the mountains. We couldn't see them yet, but they were coming . . . and more gunfire echoed from the hills. Harruck had committed some forces all right, and I wondered if the Predator controller had finally been granted permission to unleash his bombs.

"Tell Zahed I'm taking him into custody," I told Bronco.

The old spook shook his head. "Joe, you're wasting your time. If you take him in, I'll get him released—all because your people haven't even contacted you yet. What a joke."

I raised my pistol even higher and began to lose my breath. Bronco was right. It *was* all just a game. I could bring in Zahed, and yes, they probably would get him released. Nothing would change.

The satellite phone tucked into my back pocket began to ring.

"So I guess you know the rest," I tell Blaisdell, as she scrutinizes me with those lawyer eyes flashing above the rim of her glasses.

She glances down at my report. "Yes, it's all here." She sighs. "I don't want you to have any unreasonable hope. You admitted what you did right here. In addition to the obvious charge, they're going for dereliction of duty . . . failure to keep yourself fully apprised of a fluid tactical situation . . . conduct unbecoming an officer."

"What was I supposed to do? Lie? I've done enough of that already. And there were witnesses."

"Let me ask you. Do you think what you did solved anything?"

I take a deep breath and look away. "I don't know. I just don't know."

"The report tells me what you did. It doesn't say how you feel about it."

"How do you think I feel? Ready for a party? Why does that even matter?"

"Because I'm trying to see what kind of an emotional appeal I can make. Unless somebody decides to take a huge risk, to go out on a limb for you, then like I said, I don't want you to have any unreasonable hope at this point."

"Unreasonable hope? Jesus Christ, what do you people expect from me?"

"Captain. Calm down. I'm still recording, and I'd like you to go back and finish the story. If there's anything you might've left out of the report, anything else you can remember that you think might help, you have to tell me right now . . ."

I served with a guy named Foyte, a good captain who wound up getting killed in the Philippines. I was his team sergeant, and he used to give me all kinds of advice about leadership. He was a really smart guy, best-read guy I'd ever met. He could rattle off quotes he'd memorized about war and politics. He always had something good to say. When he talked, we listened. One thing he told me stuck: If you live by your decisions, then you have decided to really live.

So as I stood there, staring into the smug faces of the

two Central Intelligence Assholes, and looking at Mullah Mohammed Zahed, a bloated bastard who figured that in a few seconds I'd surrender to the futility of war, I thought of Beasley and Nolan; of my father's funeral; and of all the little girls we'd just freed in the tunnel. I thought of Hila, lying there, bleeding, waiting for me, the only person she had left in the world. And I imagined all the other people who would be infected by Zahed's touch, by the poison he would continue to spread throughout the country, even as one of our own agencies supported him because they couldn't see that the cure was worse than the poison.

How did I *feel* about that?

I desperately loved my country and my job. If I just turned my back on the situation because I was "little people," then I was no better than them.

Lights from the first helicopter panned across the village wall behind us, the whomping now louder, the reactionary gunfire lifting up from the ground.

My satellite phone kept ringing. I figured it was Brown or Ramirez, so I ignored it.

A roar came from the troops somewhere out there, and a half dozen RPGs screamed up toward the chopper, whose pilot banked suddenly away from the incoming.

Zahed began to smile. Even his teeth had been whitened. The CIA had pampered his ass, all right.

Bronco was about to say something. Mike had his gaze on the helicopter.

The trigger came down more easily than I had anticipated, and my round struck Zahed in the forehead, slightly off center. His head snapped back and he crashed back into the Mercedes and slid down to the ground, the blood spray glistening across the car's roof.

Bronco and Mike reacted instantly, drawing their weapons.

I shot Bronco first, then Mike.

But I didn't kill them. I shot them in the legs, knocking them off their feet as I whirled and sprinted back toward the shattered window. My phone had stopped ringing.

"You're going down for this, Joe! You have no idea what you've done! No idea!"

There was a lot of cursing involved—by both of us—but suffice it to say I ignored them and climbed back into the bedroom, where Hila lay motionless.

I was panting, shaking her hands, gently moving her head. I panicked, checked her neck for a carotid pulse. Thank God. She was alive but unconscious. I dug the Cross-Com out of my pocket, activated it, changed the magazine on my pistol. I gently scooped up Hila, slid her over my shoulder, then started out of the room, my gun hand trembling.

"Predator Control, this is Ghost Lead, over."

A box opened in my HUD. "Where you been, Ghost Lead?"

"Busy."

"CAS units moving into your area, over."

"Got 'em. Can you lock onto my location?

"I've got it."

"Good. I need Hellfires right on my head. Every-thing you got. There are no civilians here. I repeat, no civilians. We got a weapons and opium cache in the basement. I want it taken out, over."

"Roger that, Ghost Lead. I still have no authoriza-tion for fires at this time, over."

"I understand, buddy. Tell you what. Give me ten min-utes, and then you make your decision—and live by it . . ."

"Roger that, Ghost Lead."

With a few hundred Taliban fighters to defend the village, I had a bad feeling that they'd manage to either move or simply secure all those weapons and opium. Better to take the cache out of the picture—blow it all back to Allah. I wasn't sure how committed Harruck's Close Air Support was, either.

I had considered for the better part of two seconds taking Hila straight outside and trying to link up with one of the choppers, but the place still swarmed with Taliban. I'd rather take them out one or two at a time in the tunnels. So I carried her back to the basement and descended the stairs.

"Ghost Lead, this is Predator Control. I've just received an override order. I have clearance to fire. But I will lose the target in four minutes, fifteen seconds, over."

"Let the clock tick," I told him. "But don't miss your shot. I'm getting the hell out of here."

"Roger that, Ghost Lead. Godspeed."

I nearly fell down the staircase near the bottom, caught my balance, then turned toward the tunnel at the far end. Judging from the sounds above, most of the Taliban were engaging the choppers or putting fire on the mountainside. I didn't expect to encounter much resistance in the tunnel, so when I cleared the rock section and ducked a bit lower to enter the drainage pipe, I froze at the sound of voices.

I doused the penlight in my other hand.

Flashlights shone ahead. I set Hila down. I flicked the penlight back on.

Oh, no. There was a long line of guys, maybe twenty, maybe more, coming right at us.

I saw them.

They saw me.

They screamed.

I reached into my web gear and produced a grenade.

They screamed again.

I pulled the pin and pitched the grenade far down the pipe, then threw myself over Hila as three, two—

My satellite phone started ringing again.

One.

I cupped my ears as the grenade went off with a blinding flash and rush of air, as the men shrieked now, and I suddenly rose, damning my ringing phone to hell, and unleashed salvo after salvo through the smoke and gleaming debris.

Then I screamed ahead, told them to run away or die, I think. Something pretty close.

The pipe grew very quiet, save for my ringing phone. I cursed, pulled it from my pocket, and realized it'd been General Keating on the line.

Aw, damn. I'd get with the old man later. I switched off the phone, picked up Hila, and eased my way forward as far ahead, footfalls sounded, though no flashlights lifted my way. I neared the area of the explosion, saw how the concrete had been blasted apart, then realized the earth above had nothing to support it. Below were a half dozen men shredded into bloody heaps.

I reached up with my finger to check the stability of the ceiling, and that was when the entire section of earth came down on top of me. It all happened so fast that I didn't realize how much dirt had fallen until I tried to move my legs. Trapped. I managed to bring up one arm and brush it from my face. I spit dirt, then glanced up . . . and there it was about a meter above, an open hole and the stars beyond. The gunfire popped and cracked, and two mortars exploded somewhere beyond.

I started writhing back and forth, trying to free myself, when I heard more voices. I wasn't sure which side of the tunnel they were coming from. I began to panic, shoving my arm more violently and trying to kick. The earth to my right began to give away, and suddenly I fell sideways and out of the pile, sliding down a hill of dirt that was spreading to Hila.

"Ghost Lead, this is Predator Control. Thirty seconds, and you are still too close to the drop zone, over."

"Roger that," I said, then coughed. "I'm moving out. You just do your job!"

"Mitchell, this is Keating," called the general as another video box opened in my HUD. "I've been trying to get a hold of you, son! Your orders have changed!"

So I ripped the Cross-com off my head and turned it off. It was a little late for that shit.

The passage through the pipe was completely blocked. I thought if I could get us up on top of the pile, I might be able to push Hila through the hole and up top.

But I had no idea what we'd find up there. I needed to chance a look for myself. I climbed back up, pushing back into the dirt, and up through the hole until my head jutted out. I was facing the mountainside, muzzle flashes dancing across the ridgelines. I turned around to face the village and saw at least forty Taliban fighters racing directly toward me running behind a pair of pickup trucks with fifty-calibers mounted on the back, the guns spewing rounds.

But then, from somewhere behind me came the hiss of rockets, and just as I turned my head, I saw an Apache roar overhead and the pickup trucks explode in great fireballs not thirty meters from my head.

I ducked back into the hole. The Predator controller was about to drop his bombs. I hustled down and grabbed Hila. I moved her higher across the dirt mound and toward our escape hole. I shifted around to try to shield her from the blast, then took two long breaths and listened for the first impact.

THIRTY

I tucked in as tightly as I could, and the next few seconds felt like a lifetime.

For a moment, I thought the controller had changed his mind or been ordered to abort.

But then, just as my doubts were beginning to take root, twin detonations, somewhat muffled at first, originated from behind us, well off into the basement. Not three heartbeats later came a roar unlike anything I'd ever heard, followed by a massive tremor ripping through the ground.

As the earthquake continued, a wave of intense heat pushed through the tunnel behind me, and I gasped and started dragging Hila higher toward the hole, fearing that all the air would be consumed before we escaped.

That I moved farther up was the only thing that saved us from a wave of fire that rushed through the pipe. I kept groaning and dragging her higher, my boots slipping on the dirt, as dozens of smaller explosions began to boom, and I knew that was all the ammunition beginning to cook off. Then came a horrible stench as the opium began to burn. My eyes filled with tears, and for a few seconds I thought I'd pass out before someone grabbed my arm and began pulling me up.

There was screaming, but I couldn't identify anyone above the cracking and booming from below, as well as more booming from the village as I was suddenly hoisted out of the hole and plopped down in the sand.

I blinked hard, saw Brown and Smith there, with Brown digging back into the hole and pulling out Hila. He was wearing the Cross-Com I'd given to Ramirez.

Behind us, the helicopters were still engaging the Taliban fighters on the ground, but most of them were retreating back toward the walls.

However, at least one machine gunner set up behind a jingle truck opened fire, and we all hit the deck a moment before the Apache gunship whirled around and directed a massive barrage of fire that not only tore through the gunner but began to shred the truck itself.

"I've got her," yelled Smith, scooping up Hila and gesturing toward the mountainside. "The tunnel's up there! Let's go!"

Brown pulled me back up. "We locked onto your chip as soon as you got close to the top. You okay?"

"More than okay. I got Zahed."

Brown was all pearly whites. "Hoo-ah! Mission complete, baby. Let's roll!"

The three of us ran back toward the hills, with the choppers covering our exit. Brown was in direct contact with them, and he said that he'd sent the others off toward two rifle squads that had come up through the defile. They were bringing back one Bradley to pick up the girls. We took a tunnel I hadn't seen before, which Brown said led up to one of the mountain passes.

As we neared the exit and emerged onto the dirt road, we looked down toward Senjaray and saw the Bradley pulling away. The girls we'd rescued were, I later learned, safely onboard.

We were almost home.

"Hold up," I said, as we crossed around some boulders. We squatted down. "We need to get her out of here faster than this." I looked to Brown. "Can we get a Blackhawk to pick her up?"

"I'm on it. But we'll still have to get down to the valley over there."

"All right." I dug into my pocket, switched on my satellite phone, and saw there was a message from General Keating. I took a deep breath, dialed, and listened.

And my heart sank.

"I repeat, son, we need to pull you off this mission. Abort. Abort. Stand down . . ."

He'd said a lot more than that, but those were the only words that meant anything. Bronco hadn't been bluffing.

At that moment, though, I was glad I hadn't heard the message, but I wondered whether I would've shot Zahed anyway, despite the order to stand down.

I wondered.

I'd like to think that my experience and honor would've led me to make the right decision. But the politics and grim reality were far too powerful to ignore.

"Captain, you don't look so good," said Smith.

"The order to stand down came in, but I, uh, I guess I missed it. Zahed's dead anyway."

"Good work," said Brown.

"Ghost Lead, this is Hume, over."

"Go ahead, John."

"Jenkins and I got on the Bradley, but we got cut off from Warris and Ramirez in the tunnels. We figured they'd link up with us down here, but they didn't show up, over."

"Roger that, we'll find them."

"Paul, you get her down there to link up with the chopper?" Brown asked Smith.

"I'm on it."

"Then I'm with you, Captain, let's go!"

We rose and jogged off, back into the tunnel, while Smith carried Hila toward the valley.

"I'm afraid of what we'll find," said Brown.

We linked up with another section of tunnels, ones we'd already marked with beacons, and we stepped over four or five bodies of Taliban fighters.

Brown and I spent nearly an hour combing the tunnels.

No tracker chips were detected during those moments when I'd slip outside to search for a signal, so we had to assume both men were still underground.

Sighing in disgust, I told Brown we needed to get back and see if we couldn't get a search team in the tunnels by morning.

"You think they got captured?"

"I don't know what to think," I told him. "But we can't stay up here all night."

We hiked down from the mountains and toward the village. The firing had all but stopped, and the gunships had already pulled out and were heading toward Kandahar.

As Brown and I reached the defile, we were met by a horrible sight:

Anderson and Harruck were standing in the smoking ruins of the school, shattered by Taliban mortar fire. The once tall walls of the police station, whose roof was about to be constructed, looked like jagged teeth now, with more smoke coiling up into the night sky.

Anderson was crying. Harruck glared and cried, "Thanks a lot for all your help!"

Fifteen minutes later I was getting my gunshot wound treated. All the girls had been taken back to the hospital as well, and they were all staring at me, as if to say thank you. Hila had been rushed into surgery.

I was patting my fresh bandage when Brown came running into the hut and cried, "Captain! Get out here! You're not going to believe this!"

I rushed away from the nurse and made it outside, where Warris was being helped out of a Hummer. He was ragged and filthy and still reeked. His eyes were bloodshot and he just looked at me vaguely as I rushed up to him.

"Fred, where the hell were you?"

It took a few seconds for him to focus on me. "They found me down in the valley."

"Where's Ramirez?"

He swallowed. "I, uh, I don't know."

I raised my voice. "What do you mean?"

"I MEAN, I DON'T KNOW! NOW GET OUT OF MY GODDAMNED FACE!" He shoved me aside and headed toward the hospital.

I grabbed him by the shoulder and spun him around. "You're going to talk right now."

"I'll talk, all right. No worries about that!"

"Where's Ramirez?"

"We got separated. I don't know what happened. I looked for him, and he was gone. That's all I know."

"Where is he?"

He glared at me, then turned and walked away. I started after him, but Brown grabbed my shoulder. "Don't . . ."

I talked to one of the doctors, who told me Hila would pull through just fine. They'd removed the bullet. The doc did take me aside and tell me she'd found evidence of rape on all the girls. I explained the situation, and she said, as I already knew, that none of the families would want these girls back, and if we revealed what had happened to them, their fates could take an even sharper turn for the worse.

"We'll see if we can get them to an orphanage," I said. "The woman who's in charge of the school project, Anderson? We'll see if we can get help from her."

I still vowed to find Shilmani and tell him I had gotten his daughter out of there. I wanted to tell the man how bravely she'd fought and how she'd literally saved my life. I wasn't sure if that would change anything, but I wanted him to know.

However, the fan was dialed up to ten, and the camel dung was about to hit it and fly for miles.

I was ordered to Harruck's office before I even returned to my billet.

When he was finished cursing his head off and sucking down his drink, he looked at me and said, "I hope to God you think this was worth it. At least give me that much. At least let me know that you still believe in what you did, because if you don't . . ."

"Zahed needed to die. I'm sorry about the consequences. He's dead. Maybe things will change here. Maybe not."

"Well, I'm done here. I'm out. That's a change. You win. I lose. We did nothing here. Nothing."

I might've stolen two hours of sleep before I dragged myself back up and fought with the guards at the gate, who wouldn't let me and Brown leave the base.

"I have direct orders from the CO. Your team is

confined to the base. You'll have to take that up with the CO, sir."

I did. Harruck was sleeping, but the XO spoke to us. "Word came down. There are some boys from Kandahar flying in to talk to you guys."

"Army Intel?"

He shook his head. "Spooks."

"Do you realize what you've done?" Bronco screamed, and that was the edited version of his question, which in truth had contained curses and combinations of curses I hadn't heard before.

He and his sidekick had escaped from Sangsar, gotten treated for their gunshot wounds, and linked up with their superiors. The group of four decided they would interrogate the hell out of me all morning. I'd grinned at the crutches both Bronco and Mikey had used to get into the room.

With arms folded over my chest and a bored look on my face, I repeated, "I don't have to talk to you, and I won't. So piss off."

Bronco attempted to describe the length and breadth of their operation, and he leaned forward and told me that I'd ruined years' worth of work, murdered an unarmed man, and that the agency would see me hang. Blah. Blah. Blah.

I told them all where to go, then stormed out. They couldn't hold me. They couldn't do jack. I went back to Harruck and told him I was going to see Shilmani and that if he tried to stop me, I'd have him brought up on charges.

He started laughing and just waved me off. His laughter sounded more unbalanced than cynical.

Brown and I caught up with Shilmani at the shacks on the outskirts of town. He was loading water and would not look at me as we approached.

"Listen to me, please," I began. "We got Hila. She's in the hospital. She's okay."

He froze at the back of his truck and just stood there a moment, his breathing ragged before he began to cry.

I looked at Brown and turned away. I was choked up myself. I could barely imagine what Shilmani was going through. He had to convince himself that his daughter was dirt now because his culture dictated how he should think. In fact, if we didn't get the girls to an orphanage and simply call them "war orphans," they would all be arrested and sentenced to prison. That's right. The system did not distinguish between victims of rape and those who willingly had relations outside marriage.

"Do you want to see her?" I asked.

"I can't."

"You would have been so proud. She fought at my side. And she saved my life."

"Scott, don't tell me any more. Please . . ."

"Why don't you take your family and get the hell out of here? There's got to be a way out."

He finally looked at me, backhanded away the tears, and said, "This is my life."

By late in the day I got called to the comm center and learned that General Keating was waiting to speak to me.

"Mitchell, you make it damn near impossible for me to get your back when you play it this close to the vest. If the president weren't distracted by twenty other problems, I'd be pulling KP in the White House mess."

"I understand, sir. And I've been running an obstacle course here myself."

Okay, I was speaking through my teeth, and though I highly respected the man, I wanted to unload on him, too. He'd had no idea what I'd just gone through, but I wasn't about to cry on his shoulder.

"I'm pulling you back to Fort Bragg. I'd advise you to lay low but I know you don't work that way, so once you're back home you'll be confined to quarters. We'll put on a show until JAG takes its best shot or you're last month's news."

"Sir, Joey Ramirez is still MIA."

"I know that, son, and the search will continue. But we've got Warris running off at the mouth and trying to ruin your career. I want you out of there."

"Warris is an asshole. Sir. He'd bitch if you hanged him with a new rope. It's my word against his."

"For now, he doesn't need witnesses, Mitchell. Because I believe him."

"Sir?"

"Easy, son. I agree. He's a fool. But I know he's telling the truth—because I know you. And your men. But between him and the CIA, they're not going to back off. I've got to deal with it."

"Where does all this leave me, sir?"

"From where I'm sitting, this operation has become a perfect storm of botched communications. And because of the political ramifications in Kabul, as well as here, higher's out for blood. It's why they have officers, son. Someone's got to fall on his sword. Someone will take the fall for this mess."

"And blood flows downhill . . ."

"It's Newton's law, Scott. Simple as that."

I closed my eyes and massaged them. "I understand, sir. For the good of the service . . ."

"That bastard Zahed needed killing, and you gave it to him. You did a fine job, soldier, no matter what you hear, no matter what they say."

"But you still don't have my back, do you, sir?"

He took a deep breath, looked torn—

And broke the connection.

By dinnertime the team had packed up the billet. We were being driven to Kandahar, where we'd catch the first of many flights back home.

They'd refused to allow us to participate in the tunnel search, but before we left, Harruck sent a man out to fetch me. The guy led me to a small tent behind the hospital, the makeshift morgue, where Ramirez lay across a folding table.

He'd been shot in the head. Point-blank.

"Oh, dear God," I said aloud.

"Any other wounds?" I asked one of the other soldiers there.

"Nope. Must've caught him by surprise."

I cursed and rushed out of there.

And all I could see was Warris raising a rifle to Ramirez's head and pulling the trigger.

I found the punk lying in his bunk, staring at the ceiling. He had no time to get up. I leaned over him and screamed, "YOU KILLED HIM, YOU RAT BASTARD, DIDN'T YOU? YOU KILLED HIM! YOU KILLED HIM!"

I guess Brown had seen me running toward Warris's quarters and had come after me because he burst through the door and rushed over, believing I was going to strike Warris. He grabbed my wrist and hung on.

Warris started cursing and told me I'd lost my mind and why the hell would he kill Ramirez?

"Because he knew you were going to blow the whistle on all of us. And he probably threatened you, didn't he? He told you if you talked, he'd kill you, right?"

A guilty expression came over Warris, and he tried to hide it by tightening his lips.

"You killed him!" I repeated.

"Your career is over, Mitchell. It's all over now. You're old news. Even the Ghosts are a waste. Every other agency, State, DoD—the entire alphabet tribe—undermines what we do. We're history."

"No, you're history. Count on it!"

I shoved Brown aside and hustled out of the room. I stormed back to the billet, wrenched up my duffel, and lifted my voice to the men. "Let's get the hell out of here!"

But we didn't leave right away. The guys wanted to pay their last respects to Ramirez, and they all went over to the hospital and did that. I waited by the Hummer and found myself in an awkward conversation with Dr. Anderson.

"So now you go home, and the next Zahed takes over? We have to start from scratch."

"I don't know what to tell you."

"Don't you even care?"

"I care too much. That's what's killing me. That's what's killing us all."

EPILOGUE

We weren't ghosts who returned home. We were zombies. War-torn. Down three men. Feeling little joy in our "mission completed." I spoke briefly with each of the men, and they shared my sentiments.

Colonel Gordon told me that Warris had friends and relatives in high places, which was why his loyalties tended to lean toward regular Army operations, even though he'd chosen a career in Special Forces. In fact, Gordon said that Warris had even written an article published in *Soldiers* magazine detailing his thoughts about a dramatic shift in Special Forces operations and mentality, an argument against elitism and what he deemed as special privileges granted to our operators.

Well, the punk really got a taste of our "special privileges" by spending some time in a hole full of crap. That's how we prima donnas in SF live the high life.

During one layover, I got a call from Harruck, who told me Anderson had placed the girls in a good orphanage, but then the facility had been raided by Taliban who said the girls had been raped and that they were all going to face charges. Hila was, of course, among that group. Would she spend twenty or more years in jail? I didn't know, but Harruck said he had a few ideas. He then surprised me: "You were wrong about me, Scott. I'm not a politician. And I'll prove it to you."

And then, as we were boarding our final flight back to Fort Bragg, Gordon called again to tell me the spooks were going for a charge of murder.

Apparently, Mullah Mohammed Zahed wasn't just the Taliban commander in the Zhari district. He was the warlord leader of a network of men—warlords, Taliban leaders, and corrupt public officials—who were part of a massive protection racket in the country. It seemed the United States was paying tens of millions of dollars to these men to ensure safe passage of supply convoys throughout the country.

We imported virtually everything we needed: food, water, fuel, and ammo, and we did most of it by road through Pakistan or Central Asia to hubs at Bagram air base north of Kabul and the air base at Kandahar. From there, local Afghan contractors took over, and the powers that be thought hiring local security was a brilliant idea so we could promote entrepreneurship. Indeed, it had struck me as curious when local Afghan trucks showed up at the FOB loaded with our military supplies. I'd assumed the Chinooks had brought in everything, but I was wrong.

So . . . Zahed was indirectly being paid by the United States to provide protection to the trucks delivering supplies to our base, even though we were his mortal enemies. What an opportunist. He had to profit in every way imaginable: from our supply lines to each and every improvement we'd made in the village. If he could, he would've been the one to sell us the guns we'd use to kill him!

Gordon said the network was making more than a million a week by supplying protection. There was a symbiotic relationship between the network and the Taliban, who were being paid not to cause trouble and were also being employed as guards. Many of the firefights, Gordon said, were the result of protection fees being docked or paid late. The gunfire had nothing to do with purging the "foreign invaders" from their country. Hell, the invaders were paying their salaries.

So this was the lovely oasis that Zahed had nurtured. And there wasn't a single piece of high-tech weaponry— no laser-guided bullet, radar, super bomb, nothing— that would change that. One Ghost unit had taken out a man. We couldn't reinvent an entire country.

And then, the final kicker: Gordon had learned that the CIA was already negotiating with Zahed's number two man, Sayid Ulla, who had taken up residence in that opium palace in Kabul. Pretty much everything Bronco had told me about the agency's intentions and desires had been a lie. And I felt certain that they had supplied the HERF guns to Zahed's men and attempted to use the Chinese as fall guys.

So nothing would change. I'd taken out a thug, but in a country with very little, thugs were not in short supply.

As I wrote a letter to Joey's parents, I once again tried to convince myself that my life, my job, everything . . . was still worth it, even as murder charges loomed.

I'm sorry to inform you that your son died for nothing and that this war messed him up so much that he killed an innocent American solider in order to protect our unit.

I typed that twice before I got so mad I slammed shut the laptop.

If the plane seat could have swallowed me, I would've allowed it. All I could do was throw my head back and think about how badly they were going to burn me. And when my mind wasn't fixated on that, I'd see Shilmani crying . . . and think about Hila being thrown in a rank cell . . . and see some yellow-toothed scumbag count cash handed to him by Bronco.

I reached down under my seat, dug into my carry-on bag, and produced a letter that had been part of a care package sent to me by the volunteers of Operation Shoe-box, a remarkable organization that sent personal care items, snacks, books, and dozens of other items we all needed so desperately. The folks even included toys we could hand out to children during our missions. I'd never met a soldier who wasn't smiling as he opened up one of those packages.

The handwritten letter I'd received was from a thirteen-year-old boy from Huntsville, Alabama.

Dear Soldier:

My name is James McNurty, Jr., and I want to thank you very much for serving our country. I know it must be hard out there for you, but if you take good care of yourself and eat good, you will have a good day of fighting.

I want to tell you about my dad, who was also a soldier. He died in Iraq while trying to protect us. He was a very great man and he told me that whenever I see a soldier I should thank him or her. So while I cannot see you, I still want to thank you for helping us and for believing in our country. My dad always said that no matter what happens, he loved us and the United States of America. My dad said being a soldier is a great honor, so maybe I will be one someday, too. I hope you can stay happy. I know it is hard.

Thanks very much.
Your friend, James McNurty, Jr.

"See this?" I tell Blaisdell, pulling the letter from my breast pocket. "This is the only thing keeping me sane right now. Some kid in Huntsville actually believes in what we're doing."

She sighs. "That's nice. But they're going to argue

that you should have answered your phone, that you ignored incoming communication and killed Zahed, an unarmed man."

"My mission was to kill him. I carried out my orders. The abort came too late. I was the commander on the ground, I saw the opportunity, I made the decision, and I completed the mission. That's what you're going to argue. If higher can't make up their minds about what to do, then it's my job to make that decision."

"They're not going to see it like that. You're asking them to take responsibility for their broken system, and as you've implied, even General Keating can't save you now."

I snort. "Is there anything else you need? Did you get it all? Because I'm going to be very busy for the rest of the day, trying to get drunk."

She rises and pushes her glasses farther up her nose. "Off the record, Captain, I'm very sorry about what's happened to you. In some respects you're a victim of the system, but you had a choice. You could have at least tried to take Zahed into custody. And they're going to argue that, too. You simply shot him. They'll argue that you wanted to kill him."

"You're damned right I did."

She starts to say something, thinks better of it. "I'm going to review all of this with my colleagues, and I'll contact you tomorrow."

I shrug and lead her to the door. She looks back at me, a deep sadness filling her eyes, as though she's glimpsing a man at the gallows.

Then she just leaves. I get another drink, plop into

the recliner, and turn on ESPN, where I learn that even the Reds lost their game, 9–4, damn it.

I must've dozed off and the knocking at my door continues for a while until I suddenly rush up and answer it.

"Holy shit." The curse escapes my mouth before I can censor it.

It's General Keating himself, out of uniform, wearing a golf shirt and Dockers. He pushes past me, slams shut the door, then lifts his voice. "What the hell are you doing here? Feeling sorry for yourself?"

"I'm confined to quarters."

He goes over to my window and snaps open the blinds, letting in the late-afternoon sun. "I flew in this morning. Then I spent the whole day in a videoconference with those assholes in Langley."

"Well, I'm sorry I upset your day."

"Don't flatter yourself, son. Some of your tactics might give me heartburn, but you ain't got enough horsepower to put a dent in my day. I think you underestimated Harruck. That boy went to bat for you big-time."

"What do you mean?"

"He used his friend, the humanitarian worker, to do some digging. Turns out that little girl you saved witnessed Bronco and Mike on the scene of Warris's torture, and they failed to report any of it."

I frown. "Then Warris can burn them, maybe get me off?"

He shakes his head. "We called in Warris. He made a

deal with the CIA to keep his mouth shut, so long as they helped him burn you."

"He admitted that?"

"No, Bronco and Mike did. I can't get to those two, but I'm kicking Warris out of the Army for conduct unbecoming."

"So Warris wanted to bring me down with the CIA's help. His plan backfires, and he gets burned himself."

"Enough justice for today."

"Ramirez might disagree. Doesn't he count?"

"An Article 118 murder charge is out of the question. However, integrity's what you do when nobody's looking. You won't find *that* in the UCMJ. That's why Warris is history."

"What about me? Am I free?"

"You're going on temporary duty to Walter Reed for evaluation."

"What? You think I'm crazy?"

"Nah. I might if you'd answered that phone. Scott, you bivouacked a long time in that fucking valley of woe. Let's placate them for now, okay?"

I sigh deeply.

"Look, son, this has been tough for all of us."

"Tough? A hangover is tough. This has been a god-damned nightmare, and yeah, maybe I should sit my ass in a psych ward so I can decide whether I want to do this anymore . . ."

"Are you kidding me? When you get out of the hospital, I'm promoting you to major. You'll be general by the time I get through with you. I told you the Army's changing, and we old-school boys need to adapt."

I couldn't hide my twisted grin. "One minute I'm going to Leavenworth, the next I'm being promoted. I'm crazy. The system's crazy . . ."

Keating crosses to the kitchen, lifts my empty scotch bottle. "You're crazy drinking this crap. We only drink Glenfiddich single malt. Didn't I teach you that?"

"You did, sir."

"All right, then, pack your bags, soldier."

"I will. But first I want you to read something."

I hand him the note written by James McNurty, Jr.

He reads it, then looks up, a sheen now in his eyes.

"Being a soldier is a great honor," I remind him. "But are we honoring the profession? Or maybe, just maybe, they're asking too much of us. Just a little too much."

He takes a deep breath, returns the letter, then says, "Hurry up and pack. Then we'll get some real scotch."

Readers thought they knew the whole story in
Tom Clancy's Splinter Cell®: Conviction...

They were wrong.

TOM CLANCY'S
SPLINTER CELL®
ENDGAME

WRITTEN BY DAVID MICHAELS

Third Echelon operative Sam Fisher knows that several disastrous missions have depleted the ranks of
the Splinter Cells. What he doesn't know is that a
stunning piece of evidence has been uncovered—
pointing to a traitor within their ranks...

Convicted without a trial, hunted without mercy . . .
Sam is that man.

penguin.com